I DON'T BLAME YOU

By Frances Badalamenti

For information contact:
Unsolicited Press
Portland, Oregon
www.unsolicitedpress.com
orders@unsolicitedpress.com

Cover design: John Phemister
Editor: S.R. Stewart
Editor: Victoria Storm
ISBN: 978-1-947021-88-4

For Remy Blue

I DON'T BLAME YOU

PROLOGUE

While she is dying and while the baby is growing inside of me, my mother and I sit together, a warm spot of sun coming through the window, shining down onto the antique dark wooden table. Two cycles of life gazing toward each other, both so alive in the streaming light.

"I need you to help me with a project," my mother says to me. It's early evening, and the sky has turned muted cobalt blue. I am about to leave the assisted living facility in central New Jersey where she has been living in a small studio apartment for the past few months, after the previous months of cancer treatments had her in the hospital and then rehab. I'm feeling restless from being indoors for many hours on a beautiful summer day, anxious from being among the sick and the fragile. I want nothing more than to go back to my hotel room a few miles up the highway, so I can stand under a hot shower and then catch up with my husband, who is across the country in our home in Oregon. His life still in motion, mine on temporary hold.

My mother has a project, I think to myself, as I drive under the facility's covered entryway and out of the circular parking lot. Maybe this is something the hospice social worker recommended, a way for my mother and me to connect on an intimate level, something we have not done since I was a child. That would have been before my mother left my father. Before she began taking refuge in bed. When

I still trusted her. When I still felt safe enough to get close.

As I drive down the highway, I remember back to her last stay in the hospital. My mother must have been having a lucid moment in between painkiller nods. I was sitting on a chair next to her bed reading an article in that Buddhist magazine, *Tricycle*. She turned her head to the side to look at me, her dark brown eyes soft and rheumy with age and fatigue. "You used to brush my hair," she said to me in a silly, juvenile voice, one that has always made me bristle with disgust.

It took a moment, but then came a vivid memory from my childhood. I did remember brushing my mother's hair.

"Ana, you wanna brush my hair?" my mother would ask as I watched sitcoms after dinner.

"Okay," I would say.

Her eyes closed, but I could tell she was still alert. The magazine was splayed open on my lap. I didn't say, I remember, Mom. Instead, I laughed uncomfortably, mostly out of shame, because my sister still brushed her hair, often tending to her personal needs. And I was not comfortable being that physically close to my mother anymore, that intimate. While my mother drifted into an opiate-infused sleep, I gazed out of the hospital window onto a covered parking area. I hadn't been close to my mother since brushing her hair as a ten-year-old child

As my mother fell in and out of consciousness, I also thought back to a night over the past winter when she'd had to be hauled away in an ambulance.

My mother had been struggling desperately to breathe for many hours. She had finally awoken my sister to say that she needed to go to the hospital. My mother had moved in with my sister and her two children seven years prior. When I arrived at my sister's apartment, I could see that the back of my mother's head was matted from hours of restlessness and panic. Her skin was clammy and sallow. I was ashamed of her appearance, even though she was in such a desperate state. I turned to my sister.

"Can you brush her hair?" I said.

My sister didn't hear me. I ran into the bathroom to get a brush, but when I returned, two thick-framed men had come through the door and were talking to my mother and my sister.

One of the paramedics was a kind, empathic man in his late twenties. As his partner took her vitals, he looked at my mother.

"Are you having a hard time breathing again, Tessa?" he said in a soft, comforting tone.

"Yes," my mother said between choking breaths.

This same young paramedic had come on a stress call a few weeks earlier and obviously remembered my mother. It seemed as if my mother reminded him of someone close to him. A grandmother. His own mother. "You're gonna be okay. We're gonna help you," he said. And there I was standing in the middle of the living room in some kind of sick shock, concerned about the state of my mother's hair as they administered oxygen and lifted her onto an archaic-looking wheelchair. I watched from the doorway as the two men wheeled my mother through the cold night and then hoisted her heft into the ambulance, that sad nest of matted brown hair bobbing up and down until the two doors were shut.

As I sat remembering this by my mother's hospital bed, a nurse came in to check on my mother, who had fallen asleep. When the nurse left, I remembered perching on the top part of our couch in the one-bedroom apartment that my mother and I had moved into after my parents' divorce. This was when the apartment still smelled of fresh paint. It was that brief window of time when everything was brand new, hopeful, secure. We had money from my parents' recent divorce settlement. My mother seemed temporarily content, not unraveled and unstable as she had been over the previous year.

My small legs dangled over my mother's soft, doughy shoulders, my socked feet reaching the top of her large saggy breasts. She sat upright as I ran a wide round brush through her straight black chin-length hair, the same brush she would secure under the bottom of her hair and leave there while she put on her makeup, using it like a big curler. The musky smell of her white scalp reminded me of dirt. I could see that there were little red bumps in her side part. She asked me to brush over them for relief, saying they were itchy.

"Ahhhhhh! That feels good, honey," she said.

This was years before I would run into my room and slam the door, avoiding my mother. By that point, the two of us had been sharing a one-bedroom apartment for too long, my mother sequestered to a pullout couch in the living room, so I could have my own space. My father had already married my stepmother and was living a mile up the road in the big four-bedroom house with the huge yard where our family of six had moved after we left Queens for New Jersey, a supposed Garden State of suburban hopefulness.

***

It is the morning after my mother asked me to help her with a project. I leave my nondescript corporate chain hotel room that I got for a hundred dollars a night on a discount travel website. I pull into a small strip mall and park in front of an old-school deli, too-familiar giant signs for Thumann's and Boar's Head meats taking up the entire front window. Turkey and Havarti for me, liverwurst for my mother, both on hard rolls, lettuce, tomato, mustard, pickles on the side. Two coffees.

By this point I have been living in Oregon for six years, so these Jersey delis have become nostalgic, novelties, not unlike ornate Greek diners and Dunkin' Donuts. When I order the liverwurst sandwich, the middle-aged dark-haired deli guy with an enormous belly under his white apron looks at me funny, like he had me pegged as a picky vegetarian NYC train commuter. Trendy-looking designer jeans, fitted heather-gray American Apparel T, with an equally large baby belly, and green-and-white Saucony running shoes.

"It's for my mother," I say with a big smile.

What I don't say is that she has adopted bizarre food cravings since having multiple rounds of cancer treatment. It is not unlike the strange food cravings that I had during my first trimester of pregnancy, which seems like years ago even though it was only a few months ago. I craved foods from my childhood. Frozen ravioli with a thin red sauce. Plain cheese pizza, not too much cheese. Elbow macaroni with just a little butter and salt. My mother grew up poor in the Bronx, and liver and liverwurst were foods she ate as a kid when there was some extra money around. Sometimes on payday when I was growing up, she would come home from work, change out of her skirt and blouse and into housedress, rinse her nylons in the bathroom sink, hang them to dry in the bathroom, and then stand at the stove in our small kitchen frying up liver and onions in a pan, the odors causing me to dry heave and run out the front door as if the place were on fire.

I pull into the mostly empty guest parking lot at the assisted living facility, the white paper bag from the deli on the passenger seat of my car. The facility is a collection of newly built, cream-colored structures that sit on an expansive grassy area on the outskirts of Princeton, New Jersey. The place looks as if it was built in three days, four tops. I have recently started calling it "the assisted living palace" because the exterior and interior design is so overly garish. Big sculpted columns. Flowery wallpaper. Victorian-inspired furniture. Bright red carpeting. A splash of gold. I can see through the fancy facade to the truth that lurks beneath the surface. And although there are various levels of care at the facility, most of the people living here are quite elderly, many are quite sick, and some, like my mother, are in the last months of their lives.

When I walk into my mother's unlocked apartment, I find her sitting in the comfortable dark brown lounge chair that my older brother Mike bought for her recently. A pair of smudged drugstore reading glasses are perched at the tip of her prominent Roman nose. And on a tray table to her side is a wooden box that I recognize immediately. I know that it contains family photographs. She looks good today, my mother. Better than she's looked in months. Her skin no longer sallow and gray—she now has a rosy pallor. On her head is a recent growth of short black and gray hairs. And her body is almost the exact size and shape it was when I was a child, before she stopped caring for herself physically.

She was always a bigger-bodied woman, busty and curvy, what she referred to as "the Italian curse." Like my father, my mother is full Italian American, and many of the women in our family, both sides, tend toward the more full-bodied type. A lot of the men are pretty big-bodied too. I somehow got skipped over and have always been petite, lean, and sinewy. I often tell people that I am Sicilian farm stock. One time, a number of years ago, I was in the city looking for a dress to wear to a friend's wedding. My mother called and when I told her that I couldn't find anything that fit properly, that most dresses were too big for me, she said, "Oh, what a problem you have, my Ana!"

In the last years of her life, beginning around the time when she stopped working and especially after she moved in with my sister, my mother went sedentary and fell into a habit of comforting herself with rich foods. After the appearance of the cancer, a late-stage tumor in her lung, and once the treatment had commenced and then ended, she lost her appetite, and with that went a lot of that depression weight. To me, she has come full circle, as this is how I knew her body when I was a child, so in a sense, I see her as I did when I was a little girl. Before the sight of her upset me.

"Hi, Ma," I say, placing the bag from the deli on a small wooden table next to the galley kitchen area.

"Hi, my sweetheart. Did you sleep okay?" she asks.

"Fine," I say.

"And how's Drew? He must miss you."

"He's good. Just busy with work."

"Here, honey, put these on the table," she says.

My mother hands me a few photographs. I set them out on the table and put out the sandwiches and coffee.

"Oh, yum!" my mother says, ripping the white paper off half of the liverwurst sandwich.

She tears off a small chunk of the sandwich and pops it into her mouth. My mother has always had awful teeth and sickly gums. Over the past few decades, as she slowly let herself go to shit, she lost all of her teeth. I believe that a majority of them got pulled because of infection. Even though she had dental insurance for the years that she worked, she never got herself implants or dentures. I never asked why. The condition of her teeth was something that was never discussed in her presence. My sister thinks it was because our mother feared the pain and discomfort of dental work. I always thought she just didn't give enough of a shit. So when she eats, she gnashes the food between her gums, causing me to cringe with disgust every time her jaw moves up and down.

I pull back the plastic tab from the lid of my coffee cup, take a long sip, and look down at the photos that my mother has handed me. There is my mother and her younger sister, my aunt Joanie, as small children, maybe five and six, my mother only slightly older. Both girls with their black hair neatly pinned and bowed. My mother's hair is stick straight and thick, tucked behind her prominent ears, while her sister's hair is a pile of dramatic wide curls that sit on top of her head. Both girls are clad in flouncy white dresses that were made by their mother, my grandmother, a seamstress by trade. The two girls stand upright in front of a Bronx tenement building. Most likely it is Easter Sunday, as it looks like it could be springtime and my grandmother raised the girls as Catholic. They were sent to Catholic school and spent a lot of time with the nuns because my grandmother, a single mother, had to work long hours to pay rent, to buy food. "They practically raised us," my mother used to say, referring to the nuns. "They loved us, but they were also very strict," she would say.

This photo must have been taken after my grandfather, a man I never met, left my grandmother to raise their two young girls alone. I don't bring up my grandfather to my mother, not wanting to turn the sweet, sunny calm that swirls around the room into a heavy darkness. But I do think about the fact that my mother has siblings other than my aunt Joanie. My grandfather had five other children after he left, but he never married the woman.

My mother tells me to pin the rigid sepia-toned photograph to a corkboard, next to an image of my grandmother, a classically attractive Italian woman with soft porcelain-white skin, dark hair coiffed and pinned, thick bright red lips. In the photo, my grandmother is wearing a bright yellow dress and holding me as a newborn baby. She is looking down at me adoringly. I am swaddled in a cream-colored knit blanket, my eyes closed, my tiny face rosy. I wonder if my grandmother came after my mother gave birth to each of her four children, but decide not to ask my mother, as that topic is so loaded with emotion for me.

The bright summer sunlight casts a warm glow on the room. I take a few bites of my sandwich and sit quietly for a moment as my mother picks through more photographs. She eats only a quarter of her sandwich before putting it away. "I'll eat the rest later," she says. She must not be feeling well, I figure. My thoughts turn despairing at the idea of another episode. The emergency room. The crippling fear. The air conditioner hums, and the television prattles away on low in the background, creating benign white noise.

"Hey, Ma," I say.

"Yeah, honey, what is it?" she asks.

My stomach twitches.

"Drew's mom will come after the baby is born,"

I blurt out.

I do not look at my mother, who is sitting across from me. Instead I peer down at the pile of photographs strewn over the small table.

"No, no, no, I will be there!"

She insists that she will make the trip from New Jersey to Oregon. Even though she often relies on oxygen tanks to breathe. Even though she is no longer able to walk more than a few steps on her own. Even though her six months to live has already expired.

Her stubbornness slaps me in the face. Again, I am a ten-year-old child. How many times in my life have I tried to challenge my mother? It often had to do with how she felt about certain people.

"She's just in it for the money," my mother would say about a new friend's wife.

"But she's a good person," I would argue.

"No, she's not," my mother would respond, with no supporting information to back her stance.

"There's a hair in my food," I would say at the dinner table.

"There is not!" she would snap.

"But it's right here," I would say, pulling the long black hair from my bowl of pasta.

"It's your own hair," she would say.

"But it's long like yours, Ma!"

***

I have come to understand that the period after a baby is born can be a sweet, sacred time. I know it is often customary for the woman's mother to come and serve as an interim baby nurse. To wash and fold laundry. To cook familiar foods. To sooth the crying baby. To comfort the frightened new mother. But I could not have my mother there even if she weren't sick and close to dying. The anger and frustration from many years of unpaid bills, unwashed laundry, an empty refrigerator, run way too deep. There was always love, yes, so much love. But when you're a kid, going without lunch on a field trip overrides the love.

In the palm of my hand is a portrait of my three older siblings and myself sitting on a plastic-covered red-and-black couch in our house in Queens. They are in their teens. I am about four, the baby of the family by a long stretch of ten years. We are all dressed in full-on seventies garb, my two brothers with flared collars, polyester suits, and winged hair, my sister in a knee-length striped dress and platform shoes, me sitting on the lap of my brother, who is ten years older than me, in black patent leather shoes, white tights, and a blue cotton dress.

"You were such a nightmare that day," my brother Mike has told me.

"What do you mean?" I asked.

"You wouldn't sit still for the photographer, and Dad wanted to kill you."

Whenever the portrait of me and my siblings surfaced over the years, and the behind-the-scenes story emerged, I would always try to envision my parents in the background. They had split up after twenty-five years of marriage, about four years after that photo was taken. They had four children, three already grown into adults by that point. And yet I was still just a kid, only eight years old when they divorced. So the memories that I have of my parents being together are blurry, sifted through a long-forgotten filter.

When I think about my father getting frustrated because I wouldn't sit still for the photographer that day, I see a lean middle-aged man with a dark mustache wearing a white V neck and thick black-framed glasses, ignoring the pleas of a very anxious full-bodied woman in a knee-length skirt and a button-down blouse who is smoking incessantly. "It's okay, Mike. Just have her sit on her brother's knee," she must have said. "Will you just sit still for one minute, Ana!" my father most likely pleaded with me.

As the afternoon light fades, I hang a small corkboard that now contains a cluster of family photographs on a wall next to my mother's bed. For the last months of her life, my mother will be able to look at all the people whom she loves most. Her four children. Her own mother and her sister. Her six grandchildren.

"Do you think it will be a boy or a girl?" I ask as I tidy up the kitchen area before leaving to go back to my hotel.

She looks down at my swollen belly.

"A boy," she says, firm.

HARDSCRABBLE

ONE

A month has passed since my last visit to New Jersey. My mother no longer gets out of bed. She relies on nurse's aides to feed her small bites of food, to keep her body clean, to administer medication. She asks for a sleeping pill. She asks for an antianxiety pill. She needs a drink of water. She needs to be shifted to a more comfortable position. There never seems to be a comfortable position. And now my mother is no longer able to talk on the phone. The telephone has always been an extension of my mother, an appendage.

When I think about my mother, the first thing that comes into my mind is cigarettes. All those years of sitting and smoking and staring. And then I think about the telephone.

Not long after my parents divorced, my mother had to find a way to supplement the alimony and child support payments that she got from my father. So she began working fulltime as a secretary at a large Japanese camera company about ten miles away from where we lived. Before she met my father, my mother had taken coursework in shorthand and typing—so she had acquired basic secretarial skills, even though they sat dormant for the twenty-five years that she was homemaking. My mother remained at that camera company for many years, up until she could no longer take care of herself and was let go. She had begun calling in sick a lot, and her pay had started getting docked, so bills and rent had often been left in arrears.

When my mother lost her job, she also lost her apartment. That was when she moved in with my older sister, by that point a divorcee and single mother raising two young kids in Central Jersey.

Even after she stopped working, my mother continued to operate through a secretarial lens. In a lot of ways, she was always a secretary, always yacking on the phone, always jotting down notes and making extensive shopping lists and coordinating things. I am a lot like this myself, very detail oriented and organized. Everything has a place. But our mother took it a step further, often making and changing doctor's appointments for all of her kids even when we could manage just fine ourselves. It seemed to give her purpose.

"Ma, could you call Dr. Spencer and see if I could go in next Thursday instead of this week?" I would ask her.

"Sure, honey," she would say.

And then you'd get a call back from her later confirming the appointment change. One time she even quit one of my jobs for me. She had a great phone presence—very professional and clear—and we would abuse the shit out of her skills.

When I was a kid, she worked nine to five Monday through Friday, so after school, I would let myself into our apartment. Unless I was hanging out with a friend, I would watch shitty television until she got home. There is one cold winter evening that really sticks out in my mind. The sky had turned a deep, dark blue. The tree branches were barren, the wheat-colored ground frozen and hard; a crystallized coating of ice blanketed everything. I had just run from my friend Janine's apartment around the corner in nothing but a sweatshirt and jeans and tube socks, no jacket, no shoes, my ears burning from the sharp cold air. We had been in Janine's room since after school, me sitting on her pink canopy bed as she practiced lacing up her silken pink ballet toe shoes.

"Can I try those on?" I had asked Janine.

Her father, a balding man whose wife had just left him to raise their two kids on his own, was in the kitchen cooking dinner, and the smell of roast beef was making me hungry.

"No, they are my toe shoes! They were made special for me!" Janine barked.

"Okay, fine," I said and stormed out of her room.

"Ana, are you staying for dinner?" her father asked me on my way out.

"No thanks!" I said, even though I wanted nothing more than to stay for dinner.

When I got home, my mother was in the kitchen boiling pasta. I sat on the couch with a pit of pain in my stomach. At some point before I went back to school the next morning, I needed to have her sign a form, so I could watch a special film in my fifth-grade health class. I wanted nothing to do with this film—I especially didn't like the idea of the boys being separated from the girls, and the nurse who showed the film, a round old lady with white hair who ran those Popsicle sticks through our hair looking for lice, creeped me out. And I knew the film had something to do with the things that make me feel uncomfortable and scared.

So I sat on the couch as the television ran through commercial after commercial after commercial. I was waiting for *The Brady Bunch* to end, so I could approach my mother with the form. I did not want her to know that I was going to watch this film, because then she might want to talk to me about the things that I had read about the year before in that Judy Bloom book, *Are You There God? It's Me, Margaret.* When a friend had shown me a passage about blood and pads and belts, we were hovering in the stacks of our town library. I wet my pants, and she gave me her jacket, so I could tie it around my waist while we walked home.

I worked my way through a bowl of plain spaghetti and then took to the couch. The dinner dishes were swimming in a pool of suds, a layer of murky water spilling from the rubber dish drain onto the counter. The apartment smelled of my mother's musky body odor and rotting garbage and cigarette smoke. The air was thick with dry heat, as the windows had not been opened for months. The shiny plastic handset of a brown phone was stuck to my mother's ear as she leaned into the side of our tattered, flowery couch, the cushion where she sat popping up, exposing crumbs and hair and pennies. One thick bare leg was tucked under the other, my mother's long hard toenails and calloused feet exposed. Every once in a while, she let out a loud cackle, indicating that she was speaking with her sister, my aunt Joanie. I tuned out her conversation and focused on my show, the kitchen clock ticking away in misery. Another pain ripped through my belly as I palmed the form that needed to be signed, hidden away under a couch cushion.

On the glass-top coffee table, there was a soft pack of Benson & Hedges 100s, torn at the top. Next to the pack of cigarettes, there was an ashtray with a thousand lipstick-stained butts cascading from it. My mother was now in the middle of her third cigarette of the evening, each one making me more and more angry while the pain inside my stomach rose. I wanted to smash the cigarettes. I wanted to yank the phone cord out of the wall. I wanted to tear up the form. I did not want the show to end. And more than anything, I did not want to see a film about the things that involved women and blood.

I knew that on the other side of town my best friend, Elise, was having the form signed by her mother. I wanted a mother like Elise's—her mother kept their house clean, and she made her lunch in brown paper bags that she folded neatly at the top. And even though Elise was not allowed to watch television, I would have rather had her mother, because her mother sat at the dining room table and helped Elise with her homework. Her mother knew when she had a test, and they went over questions together. And Elise was able to talk to her mother about the things in the film, and they didn't even make her stomach hurt.

The show had ended, and my mother was sitting in the kitchen by the window, flicking her fingers at her eyelashes. When my mother flicked her eyelashes, it meant she was worried about money, my brother Mike always told me. I wanted to cry as I shoved my fist into my stomach to stop it from hurting. I yanked the form out from under the couch cushion and brought it to my mother with a crusty pen from the junk drawer.

"We have to watch a film in school," I said and stared at her. "Can you sign this?"

"Okay, honey," she said.

I watched as she signed the form in her wide loopy script, not asking any questions, returning to the flicking of the eyelashes, to the smoking of the cigarettes, and to the staring out of the window. And then I went into my room and I lay down on my bed, curling my knees into my stomach because sometimes that made all of the hurt go away.

***

There are no more cigarettes, and now there is no more phone. My mother no longer has the energy to lift her head to speak. And since I am across the country, we are unable to communicate. Even though we were never known to have long, drawn-out phone conversations like she always did with my aunt and my sister, as an adult, I felt a sense of comfort in just checking in with her, and I could tell that she felt a sense of relief at just checking in with me.

"What are you making for dinner tonight?" my mother would ask as I puttered around my kitchen in Portland.

"Just some salmon and rice," I would say.

"Oh, that sounds yummy," she would say. "Tell my Drew I said hello, okay, honey?"

"Yeah, Ma."

I kept my conversations with my mother short and on the surface, never disclosing anything too personal. There were too many years of bullshit about my mother never having enough money, about the bills and rent not getting paid, how she needed to borrow money, how she needed to pay somebody back but couldn't. It's like all the things that frustrated me about my mother—the way she would stare vacantly into the air; the picking at her eyelashes while smoking at the kitchen table; the borrowing of money from the neighbor downstairs; the phone calls to my friends' houses just to make sure I was there, which made me flinch every time the phone rang; the constant disarray and filth and unkempt nature of everything around her—all of it just disappeared when she couldn't talk on the phone anymore. Now all I want to say is: I don't blame you. I can't blame her for where she came from. I didn't know this as a kid who was in desperate need of a haircut, but I know this now as a thirtysomething adult about to become a mother myself.

***

Before she met my father, my mother's life was filled with grief and poverty. She and her younger sister, my aunt Joanie, were raised by a struggling single mother in a run-down cold-water flat in the Bronx. They lived in the Belmont neighborhood off of Arthur Avenue, a predominately Italian neighborhood. My mother was born in 1935, my aunt Joanie in 1937, smack in the middle of the Great Depression and just before World War II.

One evening, my grandmother, a full-figured woman, who at the time was in her late twenties, answered the door and found an obviously pregnant and much-younger light-haired woman standing in their dingy, darkened hallway.

"Who the hell are you?" my grandmother asked this woman.

"I am carrying your husband's child."

My grandmother didn't say anything back to that woman. She just slammed the door in her face.

"Who was that lady?" the little girls asked.

"Nobody important," my grandmother answered.

After that incident, my grandfather never came back home. He left my grandmother to raise the girls on her own and never gave them any money. My mother was five, and my aunt was three when he left. My grandmother was not surprised that there was another woman in my grandfather's life. He had never been around much, and when he was, he was distant and unkind. But he worked as a city bus driver and had always brought in money, which meant the rent had been paid and there had been food on the table. And for my grandmother, feeding the girls and making sure they had a roof over their heads was a priority over anything else.

My grandfather ended up starting a family with this other woman, which resulted in five more children. Not only did he not give my grandmother any money—he never came to visit the girls. He just left and didn't come back. He started a whole new life and never looked back toward that other life.

My grandmother was not one to sit on her ass and wallow in her sorrows. She always put herself together well, always wore a full face of fresh makeup, always donned a pressed skirt and clean blouse. She knew that she had to go out and make a living. She was sharp-witted and bright and didn't hold back her words.

If she felt someone didn't like her or thought that she should keep her mouth shut, she was known to say, "If you don't like my face, you can kiss my ass!"

She had no choice but to find ways to make ends meet and she was resourceful. Her own mother had taught her how to sew, and so my grandmother set out to look for work as a seamstress. Because she was so skilled and inherently talented, she was able to get work in factories and, at times, for wealthy private clients in Manhattan who wanted custom clothing.

Nonetheless, it was a harsh economic climate. They constantly struggled. The stress of their living conditions did a number on my mother and my aunt, who were too young to understand things. They'd had a father who was there sometimes, and then he wasn't at all. Now their mother was not around often because she had to go off to work. At times there was food in the house and sometimes there wasn't. Sometimes the lights worked, and then there were times when they had to live in candlelight because the electricity had been shut off. Because I also lived this way during my childhood, I know the ramifications. It has taken me a long time to acknowledge and to accept the struggles that I endured as a child, to sort out how and why they affected me. I could be wrong, but it seemed as if those were things that my mother never looked at, because after she left my father, she chose to go right back to them. She recreated the struggles, and, in turn, I was given the role my mother had had as a child.

When my mother was growing up, there was often support from my grandmother's extended family, but it was never financial. They did not have a lot of extra resources back then. Also, that family had weathered a lot of tragedy, so there was an additional level of grief hovering over the hardship. Both of my grandmother's brothers had served in wars overseas and had never come back. Her parents—Italian immigrants who had come over from Europe after the turn of the century—had died quite young, before my mother and my aunt were born. Her father had died of a burst appendix on Christmas Eve at age forty-five. And then, her mother died soon after from a standard illness that could have been cured had they had more help.

My grandmother had two sisters, Lily and Katie, whom she remained very close with through the years and who in turn provided young cousins close in age for my mother and my aunt. Aunt Katie was married to a violent man, so my grandmother and the girls stayed away from their house. And Aunt Lily was kept busy with running a shop and raising her own family. But they had one another. And there was always love. My mother and her sister also had each other, and their bond remained very strong. Both as feisty as their mother, they would protect each other in the schoolyard and on the harsh city streets, sometimes beating up boys and girls who went after one or the other of them. This was the Bronx, and there were gangs and hoodlums; they were constantly surrounded by crime. They lived in a tenement apartment building. Their father was gone, and their mother was working. They were fearless and tough because they had to be.

When my grandmother first went off to work, she would leave the girls with a neighbor in the building whom she paid a very small sum to look after them. After some time, the family began to lean on the Catholic Church in their neighborhood, Our Lady of Mount Carmel. The girls were sent to Catholic school as charity cases and spent a lot of time with the nuns after school, until my grandmother came home from work. The nuns were like surrogate parents to my mother and my aunt. They even took meals with the nuns if my grandmother had to work late. They got help with homework and always had somewhere to go, which kept them off the city streets and out of trouble, especially as they got older.

My mother liked to reminisce about her favorite nun, Sister Mary Frances. "She was so kind to us," my mother would say. "She loved us as if we were her own," she would tell me. Unlike my aunt Joanie, my mother has remained a devout Catholic throughout her life. Always a set of rosary beads at her bedside. Always a small bottle of holy water at the ready. Always photos of patron saints hanging in her room. When I would lose something, she would say, "Pray to Saint Anthony!" She didn't go to church very often. But every night, she recited the prayers that she had learned as a young girl. When I heard her whispering to herself at night, I knew that she was praying.

At a very grave point when they were barely even teenagers, without my grandmother knowing, my mother and my aunt traveled alone by bus from the Bronx to East Harlem. They went to their father's family bakery to ask for money so they could buy food. My grandfather's family ran a successful and well-known bakery that remained in the family for many decades. But it was my mother's aunts and uncles who ran the shop, so they were there that day behind the counter. My grandfather was out on a delivery, as he delivered bread to restaurants around the city. The aunts and uncles gave the girls a few loaves of bread. Nothing else. They were shooed away, told to go back home.

Being turned away like that by her own blood relatives ruined my mother. She told that story many times, and when she did, the narrative was so loaded with despair and also anger. I always wondered what would have happened had my grandfather been there that day. That remained a giant wound burned into my mother's heart. The thought that maybe, just maybe, their father would have seen his two beautiful girls and would have taken them into his arms, apologizing for leaving them without resources. That he would have saved them from the suffering. But he never did. Even though they did see him over the years, it was rare and intermittent. He was never their father. He was more like a distant relative, a phantom presence that loomed large in their hearts.

When they finally made it back to the Bronx, defeated and exhausted, the girls confessed to their mother what they had done. My grandmother scolded them for taking the bus alone.

"And don't you dare step foot in that bakery ever again!" she had said to them.

***

When my mother was married to my father, there was security on the surface at least and there was happiness. And there were plenty of necessary resources; so all basic needs were met. My father made a good wage as a union member in the graphic arts. He was what was then known as a cameraman, which meant that he operated a very large camera in a cavernous darkroom, photographing images that would be turned into chromes and then used in magazine advertisements. Both of my older brothers started their careers working in the graphic arts; my brother Mike continues to work in the field, but more on the white-collar corporate side, and even I ended up spending a decade in advertising and design.

My father had a firm blue-collar ethic, and he loved to work. In addition to a career in the graphic arts, my father is a jazz trumpet player, and most weekends he would gig at weddings or other events. That supplemented his paycheck and provided pocket money, as my dad would say. There was always food on the table, and bills and mortgages were never left unpaid. There were four kids to feed and clothe, and my three older siblings went to Catholic school so there was tuition. We got what we needed and that was it; there were never any extravagances.

The problem was that my mother had the

opposite disposition from my father when it came to money. If she had money, she would want to spend it. She wanted to get rid of it as quickly as she could. Because my father also came out of the Great Depression, he also knew what it was like to struggle and to suffer and to go without—but he took a different stance about money and was frugal, conservative. I remember being in my twenties and asking my dad if he wanted to go grab some lunch at the diner.

"Why would I want to do that, Ana?" he said. "I have cold cuts at home."

Most of my parents' disagreements over the years were about money. Or about my mother spending too much money or spending money that they didn't have.

Throughout the seventies, when my family still lived in Queens, we had a lot of caring neighbors and friends. It was a tight-knit Irish-Italian Catholic community. There were frequent gatherings: men playing cards, women going to church basement bingo, kids playing in the alleyways and parks until dark. For years, my mother was involved in a local bowling league, winning awards and garnering recognition. There is a great color portrait of my mother and three other middle-aged women from her league, their hair set and their makeup perfect. My mother has her chin high up in the air, her lips puckered; she is clearly proud.

But that strong sense of community was abandoned when my father moved us out of Queens and into the suburbs of North Jersey. We left in the late summer of 1980. I was about to go into second grade, my brother Mike was about to start his senior year in high school, and our two oldest siblings were enrolled in community college and working. Our mother did not want to leave Queens. She had lived in that house, on that block, next to the same neighbors, for over two decades. I was too young to give much of a shit, but I don't think anyone other than my father truly wanted to leave. But my father's extended family had started migrating to Jersey from Brooklyn, and we were the only ones still left in the city.

***

In addition to buying the house out in Jersey, a few years before we left Queens, my father had purchased a small summerhouse upstate, which we would often cram with aunts and uncles and cousins and friends. That country house was a crucial part of my childhood—some of the happiest and sweetest times of my life were spent there. As a young kid, I could spend countless hours sitting alone on a large rock by the stream that ran adjacent to our tiny white-and-green two-bedroom cabin that had been named "The Robin" by its previous owners. All the houses up there had names. I would stare into the moving stream and think about ideas, all the while noticing the subtle details of the rocks and the moss and the critters in the water. The seeds of a future thinker and writer were certainly germinating. And I relished the long walks in the woods that my father would take my cousins and me on after dark, my father buzzed on martinis and all of us toting flashlights, our hearts jumping out of our chests. He would tell us we were on the lookout for the rare species of snipe. We had no idea what a snipe was, and my father would laugh and say we would know one when we saw one.

Only later in life did I figure out that my father's version of "snipe" was fictional; for years I had pictured it like the colorful toucan on the Froot Loops cereal box.

"I saw one, Dad!" I would scream.

"Oh yeah, Ana!" he would say. "See? I told you there were snipe out here."

There was a fire station, a country store, a community center, and a huge, mountain spring–fed community pool—all within walking distance on unpaved rutty roads from The Robin. I would swim in that freezing-cold pool until my lips were blue and my teeth were chattering. I remember climbing out of the pool and onto the burning-hot, rough concrete, hopping and finally reaching the grassy area where my parents were sitting with some relatives, my mother wrapping me tight in a fluffy towel until I warmed up. After only a few minutes, I would jump back in. "There she goes again," my mother would say before lighting up another Benson & Hedges 100.

My mother would make huge pasta dinners in the evenings, and my brother and I claim to this day that, for some reason, the food always tasted better up there. You could say it was the clean air and water, or you could say that it was because we were happy and there was so much love. Maybe it was a combination of both. On any given summer weekend, we might be hosting neighbors from Queens, family from Brooklyn, or, eventually, my own school friends from Jersey. I remember dozing off on the top bunk to the sounds of the crickets outside the open bedroom window and being startled awake by eruptions of laughter from the adults who were playing cards at the kitchen table.

When I got a little older, I was allowed to walk the dirt roads to the country store without an adult. A cousin or a friend and I would sit at the faded Formica counter eating rich chocolate ice cream cones before grabbing a loaf of bread from the musky store shelves. We would return past the array of old cabins, some well kept and charming, some partially abandoned and creepy. Toward the tail end of our heyday in Mountain Lodge Park, during the mid-eighties, I would say, people began buying up the cheap cabins, insulating them, and making this once-rural vacation enclave into more of a full-time place to live. That turned off a lot of the summer residents. Houses began falling into disrepair, and things got pretty trashy.

The community center and the pool eventually closed, and while my father did his best to keep up The Robin, nobody except him and me wanted to go up there anymore. After my folks divorced in the early eighties, my mother never went back.

"That was no vacation for me," she would say. "I still had to cook and clean and take care of everybody while your father drank martinis and listened to the ball game."

After my father met and married my stepmother, Diane, he tried to coax her into enjoying the country house. Diane even bought a nice set of cocktail glasses with cats printed on them and matching swizzle sticks for entertaining guests. But Diane never really took to the house, so the glasses sat in the living room collecting dust for years.

By that point, the area had deteriorated, and more and more of those cabins remained boarded up for the winter, never to be opened again. My father would pack a few sandwiches and a cold beer and drive up alone for the day, a portable radio blasting either jazz music or talk radio by his side. Sometimes I would tag along with him and post up at the stream while he would putter around the property, raking leaves and eventually crawling under the house to turn off the water for the season. It took some time for him to make peace with it, but my father knew that he had to sell. It was hard for him to let go of that place—it represented a lot for my dad. There had been so many good times there, and I think it broke his heart that The Robin went to shit like his marriage to my mother had gone to shit.

***

After twenty-five years of marriage, four children, and two houses, my mother decided to give up. I jokingly say that she threw in the dishtowel, as if the only reason she was done was because she was sick of raising kids, sick of cooking, sick of being a wife. But it is my understanding that the final straw had something to do with my parents' conflicting feelings about money. I don't think my father trusted my mother and she knew it. He may have started to hide money from her. He may have asked one of my aunts to forge my mother's signature on a check. Whatever the case, one night during my fourth-grade year, my uncle Sal, my aunt Joanie's husband, drove out to Jersey from Connecticut. My mother and I left the house with him that night. I remember my father silently nursing a cocktail in the den. I also remember feeling tremendous sorrow for my father. And then I remember being out of my body as I sat alone in the cold vinyl backseat of my uncle's car while we drove in the dark.

My mother and I stayed at my aunt and uncle's beautiful house in the wealthy suburb of New Canaan, Connecticut, for a full two weeks. I know it was the middle of autumn because the leaves on the trees and on the ground in my aunt and uncle's sprawling backyard were orange and red. It was during my fourth-grade year, and I had been taken out of school. While we were there, my father moved out of our house and into his mother's—my grandmother's—apartment a mile away. My three older siblings did their best to tend to their lives. It's strange because when I think about this time, I think of me and my brother Mike and our parents as key players. But I draw a blank when I think about my sister, Dani, and my oldest brother, Anthony. I just don't remember them being around much, and it's as if they were cast as silent extras. I believe it has to do with the fact that they were in their twenties and had jobs and relationships, whereas I was only eight or so, and my brother Mike was just out of high school and had not yet fully launched. I also think Mike felt slightly responsible for me, that he felt a pull to make sure that I was safe. We had always been pretty tight. But he had his own life too and eventually moved out of the family house.

During those transitional weeks in Connecticut, I had known that something strange was going on and that it involved my father. I knew what divorce meant, mostly from television shows because at that time all of my friends at school and all of my cousins had both parents at home. But nobody discussed anything with me. My two boy cousins, whom I adored and who were right around my age, would leave to go to school during the day. My uncle Sal, a big sweet bear of a guy who collected vintage sports cars and looked and dressed like a seventies-era Peter Sellers, took the train into the city to work at an ad agency. I had to stay home with my mother, my aunt Joanie, and my grandmother, who lived with them.

My aunt and uncle had a warm home filled with antique furniture and collectibles and all kinds of toys and bikes and sporting goods for my cousins. Since my aunt was always very talented with decorating and keeping house, it was a comfortable place to stay even though things were about to change in my life below the surface. My aunt had clearly gone in the complete opposite direction from my mother in terms of domestic order and managing money. She ran a tight ship, the refrigerator and pantry were always stocked, and the house was always kept clean and smelling good, if maybe a bit messy, making it inviting and cozy. My aunt and uncle had a huge finished basement where my mom and I slept on opposite sides of a huge sectional couch. The second day we were there, my aunt went out and bought me a pair of red-white-and-blue-striped roller skates at a thrift store, and I spent countless hours roller skating on the back deck while the three women sat at the big farmhouse kitchen table and drank coffee talking all kinds of shit about my dad.

This was the first time in a very long time that my mother, my aunt, and my grandmother had all lived under the same roof. Even though I was a kid, I could tell that they were colluding on some front and that it was the three of these women against my father. There was nothing about the way that they spoke of my father that I liked. It was catty and upsetting. I now know that my father may not have been an easy person to be married to—but at the time, I thought that he could do no wrong. For many years, I believed that everything shitty about my life, most especially in regard to the divorce, was because of my mother and all that shit talking.

One crisp autumn afternoon while my cousins were at school, I left my roller skates on the back deck and walked upstairs to play with the G.I. Joe guys in my cousin's room. Because there was thick spongy carpeting on the stairs and throughout the halls, my mother, who was sitting on the bed in my aunt's room talking on the phone, did not hear me approach. I stood in the hallway and listened to her conversation.

"Yes, Sunny. I understand," she said. "I'm doing what I can to get him out of the house."

"I know, I know," she repeated over and over.

"The check was signed by someone else," she said.

I would later learn that Sunny was one of her attorneys. From that day forward, the layers of mistrust for my mother began to form a shell around my body.

After two weeks had passed, my uncle drove my mom and me back out to Jersey. It was autumn 1982, and the light had a deep Technicolor glow. When we pulled into the driveway, the double garage doors were open, and my brother Mike was standing inside next to his vintage red Mustang in a white T-shirt and well-worn Levi's jeans. I jumped out of the car toting a translucent orange cage containing two fuzzy teddy bear hamsters that my mom and aunt had bought for me the previous day.

"Look what I got!" I said to my brother.

"Get those disgusting rats away from me!" my brother screamed.

I could tell that he was upset, like he might cry, which caused a sharp twinge of pain in my stomach. He walked over to talk with my uncle Sal and my mom, while I headed alone into the house. I put the hamster cage on the kitchen table and immediately ran upstairs to my parents' bedroom. I quickly opened one of my father's dresser drawers. The drawer was light and hollow and empty. All I saw was wood grain, no more clothing.

My dad is gone, I thought. He no longer lives here.

***

It turned out that my hamsters were one male and one female, not two females as we had thought, because one morning I looked inside, and the cage was littered with a pile of tiny bald rodents. It was exciting and we let them be, but soon they started disappearing one by one. At first, we blamed the father—maybe he was psychotic and jealous—but when my mother called the pet store, she learned that a mother hamster sometimes eats her young. It was the mother that went nuts. In turn, I took more to the male, a fluffy brown teddy bear hamster whom I named Mikey after my brother. I wanted nothing to do with the female; she was a killer. And as I went back to school and tried to catch up with the other kids in my fourth-grade class, I also wanted nothing to do with my mother. I firmly believed that, like that female hamster, she turned on her kids.

When I think about the reasons my mother might have had for leaving my father, I have my own narrative. I also learned a lot from my brother Mike over the years. He has told me many stories about epic battles between our folks. That my mother constantly ripped up and hid unpaid bills. That she cashed in a bunch of savings bonds that my father had stashed in the closet. That she overspent at the department store on my father's credit. Of course my father would eventually find out about my mother's sloppiness, and a huge upheaval in the house would ensue. I was too young to have remembered, but my brother Mike was around most of the time. He would see the way my father treated my mother, which at times could be harsh and verbally abusive. Mike told me that one evening he witnessed our mother asking our father if she could go to bingo with the ladies on the block.

My father yelled at her for overspending that week and smacked her hard across the face. She ran upstairs and slammed her bedroom door. My brother says this happened at the same exact moment a firecracker went off in the park up the street. We laugh at that, but mostly out of a desire to hide the sadness.

Though I hardly ever witnessed that violent side of my father, I do know that he could be stubborn and demanding. You were to see it his way and only his way. I butted heads with him many times. But he could also be a kindhearted, funny, jazz cat with a liberal slant. He has influenced me in a lot of ways. He could be affable and charismatic. But underneath all of those good qualities, there was a man raised on the rough streets of Brooklyn during a very challenging time in American history. He lost his father pretty young, when my grandfather was in his early fifties. As my father was the oldest of four siblings, his role became patriarch. There was a lot of strife between the two sides of his fiery Brooklyn Italian family, which he was always in the middle of, often brought in to play the role of peacemaker.

Neither of my folks had easygoing temperaments. There is a lot of wild Sicilian fire running through the veins of our family. And like many people who were raised in the Great Depression, my parents had a lot trauma around scarcity and loss. I have very few memories of my parents being together. I do remember them giving me a bath at our house in Queens one night when I was around five years old. I see the maroon-colored tub and the mustard-yellow tiles. I see my mother sitting on the toilet seat, while my father scrubs behind my ears with a washcloth.

"Have you ever heard of soap and water?" my father asks me jokingly. "Did you know that potatoes grow in your ears if you don't wash them?" he asks me, and I giggle.

And then as I sit in the tub, my father turns to my mother and gives her a big kiss on the cheek. She turns away from him. He gives her a kiss on the other cheek, and she turns away again. He walks out of the bathroom.

***

Our father was the eldest son and grandson in a large Brooklyn Italian American clan. His father, my grandfather, who had come over from Italy, was a fishmonger. My grandfather passed away before I was born, so I never got to know him personally, but I do know that he was a striking man who was chock full of personality and wit. He was known around the Bensonhurst, Brooklyn, neighborhood as Tony Fish. My grandfather drove around Brooklyn selling fish out of a truck until he had enough capital to open up a proper fish market. Once he had the store, my grandmother worked the counter and kept the books. Within a few blocks range in their neighborhood, there were many aunts, uncles, and cousins from both my grandmother's side and my grandfather's, all full-blooded Italian, some right off the boat from Italy, some born first-generation American. There was a constant supply of red sauce simmering on those stovetops, and more than anything on earth, I loved going to my relatives' houses in Brooklyn. The pungent smells, the loud conversations between clotheslines, the kids running wild on the streets, everything so utterly disparate from my boring-ass town in Jersey.

Even though times were tough during the Depression, my father's parents managed to make ends meet, but money could be tight and food could be pretty sparse. My grandmother had good business sense, and they eventually bought a duplex and rented out the basement flat for extra money. My father's upbringing was a lot different from my mother's. There were the struggles of the Depression and the war for the early years, but my father had both of his parents and a lot of family members to share resources with.

So when he met my mother, my father wanted nothing more than to save her from a life of despair. As a young woman out of Catholic school, my mother had made her way to secretarial school and had been able to get entry-level administrative jobs in Manhattan. But she still couldn't afford to support herself, so she continued to live at home with her sister and her mother in the Bronx, and the women continued to struggle financially. My parents met at a friend's wedding. My dad was the trumpet player in the band. "Your mother was gorgeous," he would say. "But they lived like animals in that apartment, and I wanted to get her out of there." They got married and moved into a small apartment in Sunnyside, Queens.

There is a grainy black-and-white home movie of my mother and my father in their first apartment in Queens. My oldest brother, Anthony, is in a playpen in the middle of a very small living room with dark hardwood floors. My mother comes out of the galley kitchen wearing an apron and holding a wooden spoon in her hand. Although the film is silent, you can see her laugh hysterically, her head falling into her hands, because my father is making a silly face, and my brother is making the same silly face. What strikes me about my mother in that film is that she not only looks painfully beautiful and radiant with her pin-straight black hair and her stark European features, but she looks the happiest that I have ever seen her.

She was a newlywed and a new mother.

What propelled my mother to eventually leave my father? What gave her the desire to recreate her former life of squalor? Again, we create our own narratives. But I do think at least part of it was that my father could be a bully, maybe in some ways similar to her own father. This is what we do, isn't it? We end up with partners who are like one or both of our parents. When my mother would fuck up because clearly she had no skills at managing money—a side effect of all those years of struggle and squalor—instead of being compassionate and understanding her past traumas and getting her help, my father would punish her with harsh words.

"You messed up again, Tessa!" he would yell. "I can't take it anymore!"

And then he dragged her out of Queens, where they had lived for so many years in a wonderful community. My father claimed the neighborhood was changing, even though that enclave had never really changed. Like I said, she didn't want to go.

He moved her out to the Jersey suburbs where she had no friends and couldn't get around unless she learned how to drive. My mother did not have a driver's license; she had a mesh shopping cart, and she would walk up to the avenue for groceries and sometimes take the bus to Queen's Plaza to buy clothes. When they lived in Queens, my mother could hide all of her flaws. The rest of the family was either in the Bronx or Brooklyn, bridges and tunnels and rivers away from her mistakes. But in Jersey, she became exposed. There were eyes everywhere. And once she got there, my mother began to unravel.

After my parents divorced, my mother and I moved from our sprawling four-bedroom house with three bathrooms and a huge yard to a small one-bedroom garden apartment in a brick building set among many other brick buildings. She had to start working, and she was tired, so she stopped keeping house. There was no longer enough food or money. Utilities were constantly at risk of being turned off and sometimes they were. Dirty dishes were always piled high in the sink. The floors were never swept. There was a constant smell of rotting garbage. And I can only imagine that there was a sense of comfort in creating this familiar hovel-like habitat. For her, it became somewhere to hide. She would stay in bed for hours, days, sinking into a deep depression that she would crawl out of only when she had to. For me, it was a boarded up rathole that I was trapped inside of.

When I look back at the woman who raised me as a single mother, I do not see anybody. All I see is a vacant shell of a body. The true person who was my mother was must have left a long, long time ago—probably when she was a little girl and went looking for her father that day at the bakery, hoping that he would be able to save her from the suffering.

My mother was missing, and what I was always pining for was her return. But she never really did return. I root for bright glimmers of my mother, the good memories, but mostly all I can see are the dark ones.

TWO

I sit alone at a shiny wood midcentury dining table in a tidy craftsman bungalow in Northeast Portland, our small black terrier, Dot, resting at my feet. Drew bought the house, which was built in 1912 and had been a rental for many years, in the late nineties, for pennies. The first time that I walked into this house, I had a strong feeling that there was some meaning here for me. It was as if the house itself played a crucial part in the master plan of my life. At the time, though, the house was well worn from all those years of being a rental property in a not-yet-gentrified neighborhood. But if you looked past the worn-down molding and the doors in need of sanding and the windows needing to be replaced, you could feel something magical in the bones of the place. The house holds you, and many people have commented on that through the years, which I figure is a quality of the house itself and also the home that we have made out of it.

The winter before I moved in here was when Drew and I first met. It was January 2001. Only three months prior, I had moved out to Oregon from the East Coast with someone that I was supposed to be in love with but wasn't. Someone who I left because I met Drew. Someone who didn't deserve to be hurt but was, which became something that haunted me with guilt and despair for many years afterwards. The thing is, I never knew true love until I met Drew. And when true love comes to you out of nowhere, there is nothing much you can do other than let everything else crumble around you.

Not long after I arrived in Portland, I was hired as a project manager at the graphic design studio that Drew ran with two other partners. There was not an instant attraction between Drew and me, but there was definitely a deep connection, because after a few days working side by side while he had me organizing his contact list, we figured out that we had some friends in common. Even though Drew had grown up in California and I in Jersey, we had run in similar packs through college and post-college. A lot of my friends were skateboarders and snowboarders and artists of some kind. So were his.

"Is this the same Bob Lowry from Mountain Lakes, New Jersey?" I asked Drew.

"Yeah, totally," he said. "You know him?"

"Yes! He was super tight with a good friend of mine," I said.

And then we put the pieces together around all the people we both knew.

***

The early autumn morning light beams through the paned dining room windows. I look around the house, and I think about how now, unlike in those years of having to depend on my mother, there is no more financial stress. Even my college and post-college years were tough, but that was normal. Many young adults suffer and struggle through figuring out how to make ends meet. But life is way different now—Drew makes good money as a graphic artist, and I did pretty well working as a freelance project manager in advertising and design, a career that I recently abandoned in order to be able to travel back and forth to support my mother through her illness. I was also more than ready to get out of that industry. I found it soul sucking and stressful and knew that it was time to move on. We had a good nest egg, and we were about to start a family.

I make a steaming cup of Earl Grey tea with milk and honey, and I set out to write my mother a handwritten letter because she is no longer able to speak on the phone. As I write, my left hand falls onto my tight pregnant belly. I am suddenly hit with a very strong emotional force. Something that was tucked away in my family's vault for many, many years rises to the surface. It is something that my mother never talked about, but something I knew because my brother Mike would bring it up to me from time to time. "Mom was just never the same after that," he would say. "After it happened, she didn't get up to make us breakfast anymore. She would just stay in bed, and we would have to get ourselves off to school," he would tell me. As I am about to become a mother myself, I remember that my mother lost a baby at birth. It was three years before I came along. The umbilical cord was wrapped around the baby's neck. She was stillborn. And like me, she was named after my mother's mother, our grandmother Ana.

When our mother came home from the hospital, my brother, who was around seven years old at the time, ran to the door to greet her. "There's no baby," my mother said to him. And then she went upstairs and took to bed. In a way, she never really came back down. My father was also devastated. He refused to talk about it, my brother has told me. My father never spoke of that first Ana ever again. "The day you were born," my father has said to me over the years, "was one of the happiest days of my life." I always thought he was trying extra hard to make me feel special on my birthday, but now I realize that what he was saying was that it was such a relief that I was born healthy and that I could fill my mother back up with the joy that had been sucked out of her.

For the first time in my life, I also think about what it might have been like to have a sister close in age, a comrade in all of the hardship that I endured growing up and getting shuttled between my mom's apartment and my dad's house. The experience of moving between those two environments was confusing and conflicted. My mom had my aunt Joanie to lean on through the struggles—they had each other, and the thought of having a sister like my mom had feels so emotional and intense, so much that I can feel my heart racing in my chest. I never knew who I could lean on in order to feel safe. I think about how it would have been such a relief to have had a sister to share the burdens with, so I wouldn't have had to take them on alone the way I did. Of course I had siblings, but they were so much older, and because our dad's house was not always a welcoming place to visit, they hardly came around after our parents' divorce.

When I was sent to my dad's house on weekends, there were strict rules that my stepmother enforced that were foreign to me. In time, I began to adapt. Even though our father could be strict about certain things, we knew how not to set him off. Plus, before the divorce, our mother was around to protect us, to comfort us, in case he came apart. When my stepmother would get angry with me for putting something away in the wrong place or not doing something the way she would have liked, my father would either confront her, which would end in a fight, or he would tell me to just suck it up, that she didn't mean anything by those harsh words.

I think back to one of the first weekend evenings that my brother Mike and I spent at my dad's house after my stepmother moved in. It was the fall of 1984. I was ten years old, and my brother was twenty. Diane's three grown children were also in their twenties, and her oldest son was rumored to be in jail, but that was not discussed. He was just not around until months later—when he turned up and started living at the house. By the time my dad had remarried, which was only about two years after my parents' divorce, my oldest brother and my sister were out of the house already.

My brother and I were in the den about to watch *The Day After*, the long-anticipated television film about nuclear war. My father and stepmother were in the kitchen clearing up from dinner. Why a ten-year-old was allowed to watch such a devastating program, I have no idea, but I could feel the fear and excitement in the pit of my gut, not unlike the way I felt while standing on line for a ride at the carnival. During the final commercial break before the show was about to start, my brother Mike said, "Ana, go grab the bottle of Pepsi for me." "Sure," I said, as this was the nature of our relationship at the time. His indentured servant in the form of a little sister, I went into the kitchen, extracted a two-liter plastic bottle of Pepsi from the refrigerator, and proceeded to haul it into the den. Even though she was busy at the sink, the water running at full volume, my stepmother managed to catch me out of the corner of her eye. As I reached my brother's glass, which was on the floor in the den, Diane startled me.

"What are you doing, young lady?" she asked.

I just stared at her.

"No, no, no, not in here you don't!" she screamed.

Her tone was so harsh that I flinched and ended up spilling soda on the new wall-to-wall carpeting.

Neither my mother nor my father ever gave a shit where we ate or drank in the house. Ours had been a free-for-all messy house with an open-door policy where friends or family could walk in any time, day or night, and help themselves to anything in the fridge. There had always been a few half-empty glasses on the coffee table, always dirty dishes in the sink, always a stinky dog in need of a bath underfoot. But clearly our stepmother had another way of keeping house, because at the sight of the soda spillage, she let out a howl so loud and so sharp that you would think someone had taken a knife and stabbed her in the heart. My father ran in from the kitchen and, in a calm voice, tried to console his distraught wife.

"Don't worry. It's only a little soda," he told her, placing a hand on her shoulder.

"I'll clean the carpet, Diane. Don't worry," he said.

As a nuclear bomb was about to go off on television, our stepmother—a relative stranger in our lives, a blond-haired, fair-skinned, slim woman so inherently different from our own messed up but kindhearted round and dark and definitely protective mother—came completely apart at the seams. Their fight lasted for many, many long hours, or so it seemed at the time. Diane dragged suitcases down from the attic. She screamed and she ranted, and she threatened to leave our father right then and there.

"Dad just sat in the kitchen and read the paper," my brother told me later. "He let her yell her head off until she wore herself out," he said.

In the midst of the explosion, my stepsister came home from work and tried to calm her mother down to no avail. Her son was out with his girlfriend, and my own brother had taken refuge in his bedroom cave in the back of the house. I had already managed to escape from the downstairs war zone and had taken shelter in my stepsister's bed. This was the bedroom that I had shared with my own sister for a few years after we had moved from Queens. Back then, I'd had my own twin bed and my own closet and my own dresser. There was a corner where I had stored my Lite-Brite and my Holly Hobbie oven. Now I arrived on Fridays with a small weekender bag of belongings and took to this room like a guest. While my stepsister, who was twelve years older than me, the same age as my sister, worked late closing up a jewelry store, I would go to sleep on the right side of her lumpy queen-sized bed. On weekend nights, she would come home from work, flick on her bright makeup mirror, change out of her modest work clothes and into a skintight minidress, spray her bleach-blond hair into even more of a high puff, add to an already thick layer of makeup, and then leave to go out to the Jersey Guido clubs. She would come back home some time early in the morning and crawl into the bed next to me, waking up only a few hours later to get ready for work. While it was still dark out, she would put her makeup mirror back on. She would blast the radio and spend about three hours sipping lukewarm coffee and doing her hair and makeup while I tried to sleep.

As strange as it felt being surrounded by my stepsister's horrid messes of clothing and shoes and makeup and jewelry, as weird as it was that it smelled so different in the room, way muskier, more fragrant—there was also familiarity. I was in a womb of safety. This had been *my* room. That night, I repeated to myself over and over again, like a mantra, "This was my room, this was my room," as I covered myself with blankets, doing what I could to drown out the screams from downstairs. And then, suddenly, I felt a part of myself leave my body. I began shaking and crying uncontrollably. I lost track of my surroundings.

My stepsister, Lisa, found me in something of a trance.

"What's wrong, Ana?" I heard her saying in a shaky voice. "What's wrong? Why are you not talking? Why are you staring like that?"

I stared at her.

She was saying, "It's okay. It's okay."

But then she began crying, too, which kind of snapped me out of it. I knew that someone was sitting on the bed next to me, but I really didn't know where I was or who I was in that moment. And then together we rode out the waves of her mother's screams until they finally weakened and then dissipated. The bomb had gone off, and now the survivors, however many there were, needed to get on with things.

For the next few months, I had repeated nightmares of being alone and abandoned behind the supermarket in our town. I would wake up screaming, waking the whole house with my cries. And then one night my father sat me down at the kitchen table, poured me a bowl of cereal, and in a low, calm voice, told me that everything was okay now. He told me that I didn't have to wake up screaming anymore. He told me that I was safe.

"You wouldn't come to me that night," my brother told me years later. "You only wanted to be with Lisa."

"I guess that I felt torn between sides and needed a way to survive over there," I told him. "I went to Lisa because I knew that she could protect me, because she had leverage with her mother."

My brother Mike lasted only a few months in that house. The environment was too tense, and he had a way out, whereas I didn't have a choice, at least not on the weekends. After Diane reprimanded him for using the washing machine incorrectly, that was it for him. It was also too odd that it used to be the home that our mother lived in, even if only for a few years, so there was all this sadness around the loss of our family wrapped up in that big house.

My brother moved in with a good friend in our old Queens neighborhood. Over the years that followed, my brother would come out to Jersey every once in a while. The times when he did come by, he would take me to the mall to play arcade games, and we'd always catch a movie. I cherished those weekend escapes with my brother.

I have a photo of the two of us flanking a guy in an oversized mouse-gray Chuck E. Cheese costume, my chubby brother in a fitted black bomber jacket and white T-shirt, his black wavy hair in a big tuft on top of his head, and me in a denim jacket and a pair of eighties-era upside-down glasses, my own dark wavy hair cut short in a bad mall haircut that leaves my bangs in an awkward cowlick. I am twelve and my brother is twenty-two. After our dates, my brother would drop me back off at my dad's house, and he would drive back out to Queens, leaving me with a deep hole of sadness that I could feel but never thought had a real name.

Following the aftermath of *The Day After*, I latched on to my stepsister, Lisa, and didn't let go for a few years. And as much as she cared for me during that time, it pains me that I had to share a bed with a grown woman, that I didn't have somewhere to at least put my clothes, my books, my things. At the time, I just did what I was told to do because I knew, if I spoke up, that Diane might yell at me, that my dad might call me out for being difficult. I could tell that my stepmother felt that children did not have a say—that kids were supposed to just do what the adults told them. And more than anything, my dad didn't want the boat to get rocked too much. It was obvious that in order to survive, he wanted peace, and as a result I was silenced in that house. Diane called me "young lady." "Young Lady, you need to wash your hands every time you use the bathroom!" "Young Lady, you need to finish your milk!" "Young Lady, you need to hang your towel up to dry after you take a shower!"

And the thing is, there were many lessons to be had, things that my mother didn't give a rat's ass about, mostly around keeping house, learning how to take care of myself, and being respectful to others. But those so-called lessons came out as harsh reprimands, and so I was continually made to feel like I was doing something wrong. When I was under that roof, I walked on a thick layer of eggshells, always hovering on the edge of doing something wrong, constantly waiting for a scream to erupt out of nowhere.

But in a way, it became something of a refuge from my mother's apartment, because it was a clean, well-kept house, and there was always plenty of food. My stepmother made a healthy, balanced dinner every night. And more than anything, I enjoyed hanging out with my dad.

My dad worked nights because he had bad eyes, and driving when the sun wasn't so harsh was better for him. So he would be around the house during the weekdays, while my stepmother was at work. Diane worked as a surgery technician at a local hospital and would not get home until late afternoon. If I was around on weekdays, during school holidays or summer break, daytime at my dad's house before he went to work and while my stepmother was at the hospital constituted the golden hours for me. It would be this clean, quiet house with plenty of food, and my dad was so easygoing and fun to be around.

***

We sat at the round, wooden kitchen table, my father and I each hovering over a steaming bowl of elbow pasta with stewed tomatoes and fresh basil from the garden. My stepsister was in the den in a pair of ratty sweatpants, a tank top, and a sweatshirt cut away at the collar. She had on no makeup, and her dyed-blond hair was pulled back into a bright pink scrunchie. This was her day off from work, and she was watching soap operas. My dad poured himself a short glass of soda water from a plastic bottle, took a sip, and belched.

"Well, excuse me," he said, in a deep, funny voice, before ripping off a small chunk of Italian bread and wiping it in his bowl.

He took a big bite of the bread. Talk radio was blaring in the background, so we didn't say much to each other. My father grated more cheese into his bowl and tried to grate some on my pasta, but I said, "I don't want any more, Dad."

"I don't know what's wrong with you; this is Locatelli!" he said. "It's from the local deli," he told me, laughing. I ate my pasta, and I watched the clock radio above the refrigerator, as there was only another hour and a half until my stepmother came home.

We finished eating, my father loaded the dishwasher while I wiped the counters, and then he went upstairs to put on his support socks and a funny pair of black shoes before leaving for work. On the way to work, my father dropped me off at my mother's apartment, where things could not have been more different. I hovered on the edge of something inexplicable, and I didn't feel safe in the world. But at my mom's, the edges were nearer to what bill she didn't pay that week and which neighbor she borrowed money from that day and how we were going to make the food stretch until payday. But at my mom's, I knew that I was loved. I mean, she was just this big soft ball of love—she loved her own children so much. There was always so much affection seeping out of my mother, for me sometimes too much, and I would reject her. But that was all she had to give, and when you are a kid, the other stuff of life—the clean clothes, the lunch money, the working phone—all that counts just as much as the love.

**

Surrounded by a well of heavy emotion in remembering the loss of that baby sister, I continue to write a letter to my mother. I open up to her in ways that I never have before, the tears falling as I gasp for breath. There was such a lack of trust when things were so shitty when I was a kid. The worst of it was the period of time after my mother and I got back from those two weeks hidden away like refuges at my aunt Joanie's in Connecticut and before we settled into the post-divorce apartment. When I think back to that time of my life, that purgatory, I can feel a sense of heaviness in my chest that I can only describe as a fear. My mother was not well mentally. She definitely had what then would have been called a nervous break, yet she never sought help.

After our parents first split, my three siblings and I stayed with our mother in the big house in suburban Jersey, and my father lived with his mother, our grandmother, in an apartment nearby. Our parents were working out the divorce agreement. My mother would sit at the kitchen table smoking, the phone cord stretching from the laundry room a few feet away, talking crap about my dad to my aunt and my grandmother. And since my father was not around anymore, the house began to fall into disarray and disrepair. There was a layer of grime covering every surface, the lawn was overgrown and dry, and the trash bins were constantly overflowing. We lived in a tidy housing development in a straight-down-the-middle-income suburb, and hardly any houses or yards in the neighborhood were unkempt. Since ours was not being taken care of, I felt a lot of shame and embarrassment when I had friends over. My mom had become so unstable and strange, and if I didn't want to be around her, I figured that my friends wouldn't either.

***

One day, when we were still living in the big house, I was upstairs in my bedroom fussing with a giant Barbie doll bust, putting curlers in her hair and spraying her shiny yellow plastic mane down with my sister's aerosol hairspray. I heard the iron railing squeak and could tell that my mother was coming up the stairs. She hovered in the doorway.

"Ana, I need to tell you something," she said.

"What, Ma?" I asked, distracted, annoyed.

"I am going to be marrying my lawyer," she told me.

I didn't look up at my mother. Instead, I put a coating of blue eye shadow on the big doll's eyelids.

"Ana, did you hear what I said?" my mother asked.

"Huh?" I said.

"I am going to marry my lawyer," she said. "And then we will move into his house."

I felt the tears come, but I held off until she was back down the stairs and in the kitchen smoking, when I could feel her fingers pounding on the phone buttons. I knew that there were two lawyers that she talked to on the phone—one was a woman whom she spoke to in a certain way, and the other one I knew was a man, because she spoke to him differently. My sister had been in the bathroom with the door shut, drying her hair and getting ready to go to work at a department store called Stern's in the mall. She was now in our bedroom rooting through a clear plastic zipper case. She had told me that the employees' purses had to be clear and the contents visible because of security reasons. As she was about to go out the bedroom door, I clung to her legs.

I screamed, "I want to go with you I want to go

with you I want to go with you. I don't want to stay here with Mom!"

I knew that once my sister left, it would be just me and my mom in the house, and that thought made my stomach hurt really bad.

My mother never married her lawyer. She never mentioned it again. Although she did date a little bit over the years, she never remarried. For about a year, she hovered in that state of instability, until we were finally settled into our own apartment after the divorce. After she told me that she was going to marry her lawyer, my brother told me that he came home that night from work and found our mother sitting on the couch in the living room laughing at the television.

"But the TV was not turned on," he said.

"She was just sitting in the dark and laughing," he told me.

***

What saved me during that transitional year were dates with my father in Manhattan. My dad made a point of spending one-on-one time with me. We would walk through Central Park or the Museum of Natural History and then either we would go to a red sauce Italian restaurant, where I would always order ravioli, or he would take me to the Clam Broth House in Hoboken. I loved the urban landscapes; they reminded me of my early years in Queens, when things had felt safe and intact. And then we would take the big train back to our Jersey suburb, and I'd stay at grandmother's apartment with him for a night.

There were a few times when my mother would

not allow me to go out with my dad. She was obviously punishing my father, but really, she was hurting me more.

***

It's like you go through all of this suffering as a kid and young adult, and then you grow the fuck up, and all you want to do is run as far away as possible. And then there you are, left wallowing in the shit for years and years. Even though you *have* left it behind. Even though you are in charge of your own shit. But then one day something wakes you the fuck up, and you realize that in so many ways—you are still living in that shitty apartment with the torn-up old couch. You are still living in that eggshell palace that your stepmother created. But in actuality, you are somewhere new and safe where you don't *have* to hover on the edge of the cliff. Your body still thinks you are about to fall off of the cliff because you are this living photograph of yourself as a kid. In many ways, you are still living in squalor even though you shop at Whole Foods, and your bills are paid, and your house is clean, and the laundry is folded, and everything around you smells fresh and good.

What I am saying is that it's all still there. The times when you went without lunch or got yelled at really bad—they stay buried deep inside your body until you make the choice to heal the cuts. Just as it was for my mother during those years with my father, on the surface, my life looks peaceful and happy and safe. But deep down in my neurobiology, in the tissues inside my body, there is this darkness, and there is this tremendous fear that everything could change back in an instant. I often panic about where my next meal will come from, even though all I have to do is decide what I want to cook or where I want to eat. When I pay for things at the grocery store, I always think that my debit card will be declined even though there is plenty of money in our checking account. So I have had to learn how to sit with the pain. I pry myself out of bed and into a yoga class. I sense when my nervous system is getting triggered, and then I calm myself the fuck down with breath and Chinese herbs.

I put my hand on my heart and say, "It's okay."

I truly believe that my mother never sat with her pain. Instead, she chose to hide from it under a blanket of sleep and cigarettes and prayer. You could just see the pain and the suffering from my mother's life beaming through her dark eyes. And then it turned into so much fat, and then it turned into soiled clothing, and then it ended in a big blob of fucking cancer.

In the letter, I share with my mother about how I am feeling about becoming a mother myself. How I never took to kids, that I could care less about babies, but that when I fell in love with Drew, I knew that I wanted to have a child with him. "But I am also very scared," I write. I say that I will not know what to do. That I will not know how to care for the baby. That I will not have my own mother there to help. "I wish you could be here to help me get the baby room ready," I write. I tell her how excited we are, too, how it is such a beautiful, sweet time, gathering and washing and folding all these little bits of clothing and linens. "You would love this part," I say. I picture my mother sitting on my vintage rust-colored couch in an oversized housedress, barefooted, a cup of coffee that has gone cold beside her, the television blaring nonsense in the background, as she folds baby things and organizes them into separate piles, just like she used to categorize her shopping lists.

"We will miss you here," I write.

"I hope you will get better."

"So we can talk again," I write.

I fold the letter into a card with an owl on the front. My mother always admired and collected owls—it was their beauty and wisdom and power that were a constant inspiration through her life. While my husband is still in bed, I mail the letter to my mother.

UHAUL

THREE

My brother Mike and I stood in the middle of our mother's living room in a state of disbelief. The blinds were drawn, and the pullout bed was still out, stained and mismatched sheets and pillows and blankets in a pile of disarray at the foot. That familiar horrible combination of stale air, musky body odor, and garbage surrounded us.

"What the fuck?" I said.

"Are you fucking kidding me? She didn't even pack," my brother said.

"Ma, you here?" I yelled across the living room.

The toilet flushed.

"Just a minute, sweethearts," our mother yelled from the bathroom.

We were there to move our mother out of the apartment that she had lived in for the past seventeen years. We had to get her and her shit out of there in a matter of a few hours; otherwise, she would get fined. She had thrown some things haphazardly into boxes, antiques from a shelf, a few art books, pots and pans and dishes—but that was all. Now she was in a bit of a tizzy, sitting in the kitchen and staring out of the window like she always did when something was wrong, when she needed money, when she was worried that it was getting late and I was not home yet.

My brother and I proceeded to go into full Harvey-Keitel-as-The-Wolf-in-*Pulp Fiction* mode. As our mother anxiously wandered around the apartment like a lost child, we packed up the whole fucking apartment. Seventeen years of a person's life were being wrapped up in newspaper, taped into boxes, tossed into lawn and leaf bags, and hauled down the stairs and into a rented box truck.

I took a break and roamed into my old bedroom. My body tensed at first, and then a huge grin fell across my face. This would be the last time that I would have to step foot in here. This apartment where I had spent most of my childhood and the usual post-college-need-a-place-to-crash-for-a-while period. Where I had kicked and screamed and fought my way through a thorny, unstable adolescence. My mother and I had moved into this apartment, a spacious one-bedroom second-floor unit with wood floors, a living room, a dining room, and a small galley kitchen, soon after my parents' divorce was finalized. In our building, as in all the others in the complex, there were twenty-five units in total. When my mother would have to tell someone our unit number, she would say, "D three, D as in David three." Now it was D as in done with this fucking place.

***

Upon our arrival in the early eighties, I had been given the only bedroom in the apartment. It had a huge walk-in closet and a built-in air conditioner. My mother could not afford a proper two bedroom. So she had taken to a pullout couch in the living room. She kept her clothing and shoes in a cavernous closet next to the bathroom, and her makeup and costume jewelry spilled over into the smaller closet where linens and toilet paper were kept. Even after I left for college, my mother never bothered to move herself into the big bedroom. While I lived there, she would stash the pullout bed away during the daytime and then, at some point, when I was gone, she just started leaving it out for good.

There was an initial honeymoon period of about two or three months when my mother had some money from her divorce settlement. She bought some new furniture. This was the first time in her life that my mother had had a place of her very own. She had gone from the tenement apartment that she had shared with my grandmother and aunt right to living with my father. When we got to the apartment, the two of us slowly became calm and contented to be settled into a new place and probably high from the off gassing from the fresh paint and brand-new particleboard furniture. The bills were paid in full, and we had tons of food for a while. I was more than happy to sit in the big bedroom on my captain's bed as I pored over and organized my extensive, smelly sticker collection.

The previous year had been utter hell. My mother was clearly unstable from the changes that came with leaving my father. In turn, I was scared shitless to be around her. But once she had landed in a place of her own, a typically suburban Jersey sprawling complex of alphabetically organized two-story brick buildings with lots of grass, a few small play areas for kids, and a communal swimming pool at the nucleus, she settled in and began to calm the fuck down. And then I felt safe again. I had sleepovers in that room with the shiny wood floors, with the big window. I couldn't wait to come home from school, so I could organize shit in my room. But that homeostasis lasted only a few months. Once the accounts were drained, borderline poverty and household neglect started to take form. And my mother had to go back to work; like on a typical 1980s-era after-school special, I became what was known as a latchkey kid.

And throughout the years, that new garden apartment turned into a shithole. The walls were no longer a fresh shade of antique white—they had turned dark and stained from my mother's incessant smoking. When my mother and I would argue and fight, I would often throw things, so there were gaping holes in the walls where I had flung an aerosol can of hairspray, where I had thrown a heavy boot, where I had punched into the drywall with my own fists. The thick white venetian blinds became dusty and were always drawn, the windows shut tight against the light and the freshness of the outdoor world. Unless I took out the garbage myself, which I hated to do because the bag was always leaky with rotting food, the place smelled like a dump. When I would reach for a glass or a plate or a fork, it was almost guaranteed to be encrusted with gunk.

"Ma, this glass is dirty!" I would say.

"No, it's not," my mother would respond.

The kitchen cabinets began to fall off of their hinges, and the shower and the toilet were eternally moldy and leaky and drippy. Because she was always late on rent, my mother hesitated to call the super to have anything repaired.

"Your mother doesn't give a hoot," my aunt Joanie told me years later in regard to my mother's lack of domestic prowess. "She could care less!"

My mother worked all day tending to the needs of corporate executives, and when she came home in the evening, she was exhausted and ready to plop down with a pack of smokes. She would take off her stockings and blouse and skirt and bra, and she would change into a flowery housedress that she hardly ever washed. The sight of such a stained and stinky garment would sometimes push me into a downward spiral of anger and disgust.

As the years progressed, and as the apartment began falling into more and more disrepair, my mother's personal hygiene also gave way to neglect. She often had a musky body odor that my brother and I would joke made her smell like a small barn animal. We had to laugh and joke. Otherwise, it was just too sad. Her teeth started falling out one by one because she suffered from an awful case of gum disease and refused to go to the dentist even though she had insurance. She began to let herself go, and went from bigger bodied and curvy to fat and eventually obese. My mother seemed to be okay living in squalor, I believe because it closely resembled the environment that she had grown up in. She created as close a reproduction as she could of the Bronx tenement apartment that she had lived in with her own mother and sister. Dark, dingy, and unkempt.

Every day after school, beginning in fifth grade, I walked about a mile or so home, first from my elementary school on one end of town and then eventually, from my middle school on the other end of town and let myself into our apartment with a loose key that my mother kept in the mailbox. We called it "the mailbox key."

"Ma, how am I supposed to get into the apartment?" I said to my mother in a panic, shared shitless because I had never been left alone at home before.

"Just use the mailbox key, honey. You'll be just fine," she told me.

"But what if someone takes the mailbox key?" I asked.

"Who would do something like that? There's nothing in here that anybody wants," she said.

Standing on my tippy-toes and opening that thin black metal mailbox to extract the mailbox key made me feel so vulnerable. Some random person could see what I was doing and would notice how easy it was to get into our apartment. I had definitely been privy to some questionable characters lurking through our small middle-class town of Lincoln Park, mostly haggard-looking men with large, hooded sweatshirts and work boots with the laces untied riding amok on crappy bikes. Later in life, I would realize that they had lost their driver's licenses because of DUIs. But as a lone kid roaming the after-school wilds of suburban Jersey, I didn't like the looks of those guys one bit.

And more than anything, I didn't like being alone in the apartment. I have always had a crazy imagination and could freak myself out super easy. I was absolutely certain that some madman would appear behind me on the stairs right as I unlocked the door. So with my hands trembling, I would rush to get myself in and would quickly lock the door behind me, panting and flushed with sheer panic as I ran like hell up the stairs and into the relative safety of the living room. And then I would realize that there was a chance that someone had used the mailbox key and got in earlier. So I would tiptoe around from room to room opening and closing closets, my heart beating like crazy. It would take me a minimum of two sitcoms and a microwave burrito to settle my nerves.

***

Every once in a while, I would be asked over to my best friend Elise's house after school. Her folks were pretty strict and structured, and these things had to be coordinated well ahead of time. Even though Elise's folks wouldn't let us just rot in front of the tube for hours, I liked hanging out there way better than being alone and bored in my apartment or walking on eggshells at my dad's. Her folks were kind but stern Midwestern transplants. They were an intact family with three school-aged, blond kids, and while they didn't have tons of money, they were loaded with stability and middle-class normalcy. Theirs was a simple split-level house with clean beige wall-to-wall carpeting and comfortable colonial-style furniture. Even though we couldn't just rifle through the kitchen, her mother would set out a nice, wholesome snack for us.

There was a teenager who lived up the street named Mo who babysat Elise and her younger brother and sister sometimes. Mo had grown close with Elise's family over the years, and so we would go up the street to hang out with her. She came from a large Irish American family. Her house was big and fun and chaotic, so when we would get bored with Elise's super structured house, we would knock on Mo's door for a little action. Mo was a short odd-looking girl who wore waist-high Lee jeans and boys' T-shirts and kept her light brown hair close cropped and feathered. Even though Mo was clearly super butch, she began going out with a much older stocky balding man, a mall cop who became the butt of many of our jokes. But Elise and I set the judgments aside one day. The mall cop owned a soft-top Jeep, and on an early fall evening, he and Mo invited us on an alfresco off-road adventure through the North Jersey wilderness. Because Elise's folks trusted Mo, they let us go on the ride, but there was clearly nothing safe about speeding full throttle on questionable dirt roads in a Jeep with a non-age-appropriate mall cop at the helm.

Elise and I hopped into the open backseat, and the four of us headed north on Route 23. We drove to the end of a street spotted with houses and onto some unpaved back roads. If Mo and the mall cop had abandoned Elise and me there to fend for ourselves alone, we would have had no idea where we were. There was even some talk of this being Jersey Devil country. Where we lived in Morris County, New Jersey, you didn't have to drive too far to get into the sticks, even though we were only about a half hour west of New York City. But once we got on a trail, the mall cop put his foot on the gas pedal and sped like a maniac through the woods. With Mo and the mall cop in the front on their own trip, Elise and I were in the backseat grasping hard on the thick crossbars, our narrow preadolescent bodies bouncing up and down on the hard seats, drool spilling out of our mouths.

All four of us were screaming and hooting and laughing. I felt full of joy. My eyes were tearing like crazy from the fierce wind, but also because I was having so much unbridled, raw fun. The wind ripping through that Jeep felt so pure, as if it was actually cleansing and purging away all of the bullshit of my life: those bizarre weeks in Connecticut without my dad, the long-drawn-out drama of my parents' divorce, my mother's fucked-up insanity, my stepmother's incessant yelling, all of the money stress, never having enough to eat—all of it was gone in those wind-fueled moments.

I remember telling myself that I needed this, that I really just needed this. I was eleven years old that fall, about to turn twelve in another two months, and already I felt like an adult, like I'd been through some heavy shit.

After middle school ended, Elise and her family moved to an affluent town about twenty minutes away. They bought a big house with an expansive yard that was surrounded by woods. I did spend some time there, and as a matter of fact, when I finally got my driver's license years later, the first real drive I made was to Elise's house. I had been studying the route and had plotted that maiden voyage for a long time. But it just wasn't the same anymore, with Elise and all her stability gone from my everyday life.

My grades began to slip, and for a while I took up with some questionable kids from my apartment complex who also came from broken homes. Without the refuge of Elise's house, I began to do what kids do when they have parents who are not watching over them—I drank, and I messed around with boys, and I stopped giving much of a fuck about school.

And then on the weekends when I went to my dad's house, where everything was spotless—vacuum cleaner lines in the carpeting, kitchen floors polished to a sheen, the fridge and cabinets organized like a library—I figured out ways to ignore the anxieties that my stepmother surrounded herself with. I found ways to adapt. I learned to tune out my emotions. I stayed out of the way whenever I could. I clung to my stepsister, Lisa, for protection, if she was around. And then come Sunday evening, I would return to my mother's apartment, and the anger and the hatred that I felt toward my mother would fester.

"Mom, do I have clean clothes for school tomorrow?" I would ask.

"No, honey, I don't have any quarters for laundry right now."

"I have a field trip tomorrow. Can I have a few dollars for lunch?"

"I'm sorry, sweetheart. I don't get paid until Friday."

And then I would freak the fuck out and call my mother all kinds of names, and I would throw shit. Sometimes I would hit my mother. I usually punched her in her fat upper arms.

When she was already sick and dying, she said to me, "You got so mad that you bit me once."

"I did?" I said, pretending that I didn't remember.

But I remembered it well. She was supposed to take Elise and me on a trip to Colonial Williamsburg. We sat on my bed for hours and pored over the brochures of the people in puffy shirts baking bread in old ovens, the two of us in the height of dorky preadolescence. But my mother did not come up with the money, and the night before, she cancelled. She even asked Elise's parents for the money. I got so upset that I bit her.

Even though most of the time it sucked pretty hard, there were actually some decent times in that shithole apartment. As much as the hierarchy of needs often went to hell, there was always so much unconditional love to be had. We might not always have had cable or sometimes even electricity or gas, but we always had running water and we had love. "Come here, sweetheart," my mother would say, and I would rest my head on her fat arm while we watched *Charles in Charge*.

"I made your favorite dinner, my Neenoo," my mother would say.

She had all these crazy made-up names for her kids, and she would bring me a big plate of homemade manicotti with a thin red sauce and only a little cheese because that was how I liked it and she knew. When I was sick with a stomachache, which was often when I was a kid—I had a terribly sensitive stomach—she would warm up salt in a pot on the stove and then put it in a sock for me to rest on my belly for relief. In the winter, when it was cold out, she would serve me hot tea in a porcelain teapot on a tray with a side of milk in a small vessel and a few sugar cubes on a plate.

After many years of struggling to make rent, and every single month not knowing if there would be enough money to cover bills, to buy enough food to make it through the week, my mother just could not do it on her own anymore. I didn't know how many times my brother Mike had bailed her out when he could, but he couldn't bail her out of this one; she was in debt way too deep. Mike made a good salary working in Manhattan in advertising and marketing, but he was married and had a wife to support. They didn't have kids, but they had their own expenses. And so mostly on the sneak, my brother would often drive from where they lived in Queens out to Jersey on a Saturday and take our mother to ShopRite to buy her a cartful of groceries. He would wire her money through Western Union to cover bounced checks. He would pay the long-overdue electric bill, so the lights would stay on. Every couple of weeks—it was inevitable—my brother Mike would get a call from our mother that he would then recite back to me verbatim.

"Again?" I would always say.

"Yup, again," he would say. "It never fails."

He and I could always tell when our mother needed money, as there would be a certain drawn-out cadence to her speech when she was in a panic.

"What's up, Ma?"

"Oh, nothing much, sweetheart," she would say between drags of a cigarette. "I just need three hundred dollars."

"Um, okay, Mom, when do you need it by?" Mike

would say.

"Tomorrow morning," she would tell him. "Otherwise the gas will get turned off."

And then it would be a mad scramble to bail her out again.

It was a mystery where her money went. I think she just blew it. I would see her blow it. She would go to bingo. She would take me out to the mall and buy me iron-on shirts, and then we would go out to dinner. She would order stupid, useless shit from those awful mail-order catalogs. She didn't make much money, and so after all these extraneous purchases, the bills would just sit there unpaid. She had a full-time job as a secretary, so she at least made a living wage, definitely enough to support herself and a kid if she'd budgeted properly and hadn't overspent. But she never budgeted and she always overspent. And every Friday, my father would let himself into the apartment with the mailbox key and would leave her a white bank envelope filled with cash on the sticky kitchen table. I'm not sure exactly how much his alimony and child support payment was, but it supplemented her income.

By the end of the weekend, without fail, the cash would be gone, her checking account would be overdrawn, and, come Monday, it would be back to living in relative poverty for the rest of the week.

"Dad, there's no food here," I would say. "Can you leave me some money?"

"Again!" he would yell.

And for years I thought he was angry with me for calling, for bothering him, even though he was just as frustrated as everyone else with my mother. And so oftentimes I would just sit in that apartment and watch television, the fridge down to a couple of rotten carrots, the cupboards bare except for some stale cereal and some old crackers, doing what I could to not think about being hungry. I recall one time after an especially grueling day in middle school, probably one of those days when I had to change in front of other girls during gym class—I always hated that because I was so flat chested and didn't wear a bra yet—I called my dad and asked if he could drop off a few slices of pizza on his way to work.

For some reason, my father was especially short with me on the phone. I thought that it was my fault, that I had done something wrong, that I was being a pain-in-the-ass kid again. My father's frustrations were aimed not at me but at my mother and her sloppy financial nature. When he got to the apartment, my father rang the buzzer and left. When I reached the landing, I saw a brown paper bag, not a white paper bag with greasy slices. In lieu of pizza, he had brought me a bunch of not-yet-ripe bananas and a dozen white eggs. I was so upset, but also so hungry, that I ate too many of those hard bananas, and I scrambled too many eggs, and my stomach wasn't right for days.

***

My life shifted once I got to high school. I did what I could to stay out of the apartment, and I hardly went to my dad's anymore. Instead, I learned to lean on friends, many of who were growing up in a similar situation. But as a result, my high school grades were awful. For those four years after middle school, I was less focused on academics and way more focused on my friends and drinking in the woods. My folks didn't seem to give much of a fuck. The good thing was that they were not up my ass all of the time and I pretty much came and went as I pleased; the bad thing was that I had no direction whatsoever and started partying and fucking around with guys.

So I don't recall anyone guiding me down any of those craggy, unpaved roads that may lead to a decent college, toward a decent adult life. There were times that I had good intentions. I would sign up for field hockey and then softball, but after a while, I would lose interest and would inevitably quit. I remember my softball coach, an athletic blond woman who seemed to really see something in me, saying, "I don't know what we are going to do with you, Ana." My art teacher, who was a tolerable and super artsy German woman who painted small peas on canvas for hours at a time, would even shake her head at me when I handed in a project late. I did have a guidance counselor whom I remember as sweet and supportive but so overworked that she couldn't offer me much mentoring time. The only class that I excelled in was AP literature. Even though my teacher did not pluck me out of the class and take me under her wing like you often see in films or read about in books, telling me that I really did have talent, that I was not the worthless piece of shit that I felt like inside, I was super inspired by what I learned in her class. For the first time in my life, I was exposed to the beauty and the joy of books. I read *The Catcher in the Rye* during my senior year in one sitting. And from that point on, I didn't stop reading.

Unlike in most of grade school and middle school, I no longer had the stability and healthy competition that my best friend Elise and her normal-ass family had provided. But I had two boyfriends who kept me pretty grounded for a while. My first boyfriend was Mike, a skateboarder with a long flop of black curly hair who drove a dark blue Buick Regal. We would drive around Jersey blasting the Red Hot Chili Peppers and looking for empty pools where he and our other friends could skate. It was more fun-casual and not a serious relationship, so when Mike went away to college, I took up with Jamie, a tall, handsome athlete who was also super artistic. We were together for about three years, during my last year in high school and my first two years of college. Things got weird and toxic toward the end between Jamie and me, mostly because we loved each other so much and we spent so much time together, so much so that we scared the shit out of each other with how we felt.

I also met a whole new crop of friends that lived in the town where I went to high school about ten minutes from mine. They became my first chosen family. Still are in a way. The bonds are deep, strong. Most of us are creative spirits of some kind, and almost all of us came from broken homes. We found one another, and we clung on tight for years, plastic Solo cups in hand, Beastie Boys on the tape deck. For me, high school was like one long drunken house party.

***

When it came to college, the only place that would take me was a crazy expensive private school not far from where I had grown up in Jersey. I spent two uneventful semesters in the dorms, mainly because I felt that I had nowhere else to go. All of my friends were leaving for college, and I didn't want to be the lone wolf still living at home. After freshman year of college, I somehow had the wherewithal to transfer to a commuter-style state school about twenty-five miles west of New York City and still close to home. Luckily, my grades were up, and it was easy to get in—there was no way they would have taken me right after high school. I got more into academics. I majored in philosophy, which was deep and interesting, and started learning about critical thinking and writing. I also took a shit ton of studio arts classes like Photography and Life Drawing and Ceramics. I studied film. I took my first creative writing course. I had finally found my place in the world. And for the first time in my life, I also attempted to live at my dad and stepmother's house fulltime.

It was the tail end of summer, and my dad and stepmother had just gotten back from a cruise in the Caribbean. While they were away, I had stayed at their house with my stepsister, Lisa. Both of Diane's sons had since married and moved out, but Lisa still remained single and living in the messy bedroom that I'd sometimes shared with her when I was a kid. Throughout high school, I had spent the weekdays at my mom's apartment and most weekends at friends' places. I'd hardly spent the night at my dad's anymore. Now I greeted my dad and Diane in the hallway. My father was his usual post-vacation bronze-tanned self, and even though my stepmother was still pasty white, both were in wonderful spirits.

"We were wondering if you would like to live here with us," my stepmother told me, her suitcase still resting at her feet.

"Really?" I asked.

"You can have the back bedroom," she told me, a big smile across her usually stern face. "You are a college student now, so we can make sure you have a desk and a chair," Diane said.

"Okay," I said, skeptical.

And then my father whistled and snapped his fingers with joy as he dragged their bags up the carpeted stairs.

That same evening, when I went to the apartment to pack and move my clothing a mile up the road and into my dad's house, my mother was cold to me. She was sitting on the couch, the television blaring in the background.

"What do you think you are doing?" she asked me as I ran up and down the stairs, loading bags of shit into the back seat of my Dodge Dart.

"I'm gonna stay at Dad's for a while," I told her.

My mother wouldn't look at me

"They are giving me the back bedroom with a desk and a chair. I have to start school next week."

"Oh, I know," she said, bitter.

And then she crossed her legs, lit up a cigarette, and stared out the window.

***

In the weeks that followed, my dad bought me a

better car, so I could commute safely to school, a brand-new medium-blue base-model Volkswagen Fox. When I got the refund from my student loan check, I bought a killer TV/VCR combo and a word processor and made the back bedroom into live/work space. Most evenings, I rented dollar movies at ShopRite and got super into foreign and independent films. A friend from high school got me a weekend job as a hostess at a new restaurant called Chili's Grill & Bar. I focused on my classes and managing hour- or two-hour-long weekend wait lists at Chili's. My high school and now college boyfriend, Jamie, was away at UMass, and we were fighting on the phone constantly, neither of us knowing what to do about being apart for so long.

Only a month after taking residence at my dad's house, things turned to absolute and utter garbage. I was nineteen years old.

Here's the thing—I did some really fucked-up things. When I was a teenager and young adult, the glass face on my moral compass was cracked. Did I know that what I was doing was wrong? Probably. And I didn't do the worst shit; I did stupid shit. I would borrow my stepsister's clothes and jewelry without asking. If she left money around, I would take it. I would spit gum out onto the driveway instead of throwing it in the garbage. I would keep people awake cry fighting with my boyfriend on the hall phone. I would write my papers the day before they were due so my printer was running its head off late into the night. But I was confused as fuck. I didn't have a sense of myself, and even though a part of me knew that I just needed someone to at least talk to me like I was a human person, I couldn't imagine who that person would be. Ironically, my folks sent me to a therapist in our town for a while whose approach was to sit silently while only the client spoke.

When my stepmother confronted me, I would deny everything.

"Ana, did you eat the spaghetti that I put aside for my lunch?" Diane asked me one day in a loud, stern voice.

I was standing in the middle of the kitchen and immediately shut down. I went somewhere else entirely.

"No," I said, in a soft voice, even though I most certainly had eaten the spaghetti that she put aside for her lunch.

I lied to her in order to avoid getting yelled at, even if it had to do with a stupid Tupperware container of macaroni. My father never confronted me. He avoided conflict, whereas my stepmother lunged at any opportunity.

And I do not know why I stole shit from Lisa, but I did. I could rationalize and justify this with all kinds of reasons, like because I never had enough, because I always needed money for something. No matter what, it was fucking wrong, and I felt like shit doing it, but I couldn't help myself. For a brief period, I shoplifted, too. I've since read that stealing provides some kind of control for the perpetrator. I would go into the dressing rooms at Macy's and layer myself up with bathing suits and blouses and casually walk out of the store. The only time that I got busted was when I stole a box of tampons from the A&P grocery store in our town. A kid from my high school's mom caught me at the door. I opened my deep, colorful Guatemalan bag that I had bought on Eighth Street in Manhattan, and she let me go when she saw what I had put in my bag. She had such a sorrowful look in her eyes that I never shoplifted again. You poor thing, it felt as if she were saying to me. When I would her around town, I would walk in the other direction.

I knew that things were really falling apart at my dad's house when Diane took a load of my wet laundry out of the washer and put everything in a black garbage bag in the garage. It was during a winter snowstorm, and when I finally made it home safe from a night shift at Chili's, my nerves rattled, and went to recover my load of laundry, my clothing had frozen. At first, I thought Diane was pissed that I hadn't stuck around to put my clothes in the dryer. But then I saw that on the top of the pile of laundry was one of Lisa's sweaters that I had borrowed. It was light pink cotton with a ribbed texture and a wide neckline. It had frozen like a rigid Steak-umm. They were punishing me for borrowing without asking, and after that laundry incident, Lisa began to turn on me too. I didn't say anything to anyone that night. I drove through town in the deep snow and went right to my mom's apartment and stayed there until I knew that Diane would be in bed. My father would not be home from work until after midnight.

Then I made a habit of doing that every night until I had enough money to get my own apartment. I would sit with my mother in the living room, and we would watch television like when I was a young kid. After ten or so, I would go back to my dad's house and would hide out in the back bedroom with a few VHS tapes from ShopRite. My mother never said anything to me about why I'd decided to live at my dad's or why I would come there at night and stay until late.

I quickly moved up the ranks at Chili's from hostess to waitress to bartender like it was some broken-ass corporate ladder. I knew I had to get the fuck out of my dad's, so I worked my ass off slinging sizzling fajitas and frozen margaritas.

When I had enough capital to live on my own, I somehow ended up in a should-have-been-condemned apartment in Jersey City with some roommates. I wanted to be closer to the city, and at the time, Jersey City was way more affordable than the city. I had started taking the bus into Manhattan when I was in high school and couldn't get enough of the art-house cinemas and the cheap ethnic food and the galleries. I would spend countless hours sitting in Washington Square Park or Tomkins Square Park nursing a Snapple Iced Tea and smoking Camel Lights, just watching, observing.

Rent was super cheap, but the apartment hardly resembled anything close to a home. It was a place to sleep and shower and eat ramen, but the decrepit flat was bitter cold in winter, and every once in a while, a rat would run across the kitchen floor. Somehow, I lasted a solid few years in that dump, first commuting out to Chili's in the burbs and then finally scoring a killer bar gig at Uncle

Joe's in Jersey City. I remember the day that I was hired. It was the tail end of spring—I started on Memorial Day weekend. I went to talk to Rob Farrelly at his retail shop on Franklin Street.

"Do you guys need any help?" I asked.

"Not right now," he said.

"How about at Uncle Joe's?" I asked.

I had started hanging out at Uncle Joe's after I moved to Jersey City, sipping brandy and going to shows with friends from college.

"Yeah, we need a bartender. Come by tomorrow at four."

When I met Rob at Uncle Joe's, the place was empty except for a young girl with ponytails cutting fruit for cocktails. He took me behind the bar and had me pour a pint of Bass.

"Can you start this weekend?" he asked.

And so I did.

***

After a while, I'd had enough of that decrepit apartment. It was about to be winter, and I couldn't deal with the barely habitable living conditions anymore—the lack of heat, the rats. I think what got me in the end was the ecstasy-loving raver roommates that I lived with and their endless thumping techno soundtrack. So I borrowed a friend's truck and moved back into the bedroom at my mom's apartment until I could find a way more decent, affordable place to live.

Living with my mom as a grown-ass adult was exponentially different from living with her as a kid and then a teenager. Spending some years out on my own, struggling to pay bills, having only myself to blame when I had to subsist on bagels and pasta, was crucial to the unfolding and understanding of my past. I bought some furniture at IKEA and made my old room into a studio apartment of sorts. To freshen shit up, not only for me, but also for our mom, my brother Mike paid my friend Ray from Uncle Joe's to paint the apartment. The place hadn't been painted in at least ten years, maybe more, and my brother and I looked at the repainting as if it were a christening, a new beginning.

A few days after he started painting, Ray said to me, "Where does your mom even sleep?"

We were working one of our usual busy Friday night shifts at Uncle Joe's, me behind the bar and Ray on the floor waiting tables. It was during the two-or-so-hour window of time after the band had started playing in the back room, when the front room emptied except for a few tables of baseball-hat wearing locals eating burgers and red-faced regulars hovering over cigarettes and pints at the bar. The jukebox was playing Jon Spencer Blues Explosion.

Between drags of a Camel Light, I asked, "What do you mean?"

"She's got nothing of her own in the bedroom," Ray said.

"I just don't get it. It doesn't look lived in," he said to me.

"Try to figure it out," I said, laughing.

And then, on Monday, Ray called from my mother's house phone and said, "I just solved the mystery. When I got here, the couch was pulled out into a bed."

"Yup," I said. "You figured it out."

"She never uses the bedroom?" Ray asked.

"Nope," I said, laughing.

It took a lot for me to let Ray so close into my inner world, into the depths of my mother's apartment. When I was a kid, I hardly let friends come over for fear that they would be repulsed by the stench, the moldy bathroom tiles, the lack of snacks. But I was desperate to make the apartment habitable and trusted Ray.

It was under that roof, at Uncle Joe's, and behind those doors that for the first time in my life I was able to see myself. For most of my life, the mirror had been smudged, dirty, fogged. And then there came a sudden sense of clarity into who I was as a person. I was surrounded by so many creative types: musicians, artists, writers, performers. Bands played in the back room most nights, traveling from all around the country, from all around the world, and of course the music itself was inspiring and transformative.

When I got home in the early-morning hours after a long shift at the bar and a grilled cheese at the diner with some coworkers and a couple of local cronies, I would often sit up in bed and write pages and pages of strangely terrible poetry. The words would come pouring out of some dark pit in the inner depths of my psyche; they would write themselves. And as a result, I came into myself, and even if it would take many more years for me to fully commit to the actual process, to trust the truth, I came to the realization that I was a writer.

I lasted at my mom's for about a year, wrapping up classes at the college and driving into Jersey City on the weekends to work at Uncle Joe's. There were times when I would crash in Jersey City with friends, but mostly I drove home in the early-morning hours so I could sleep in my own bed. There was something soothing and healing about driving west down Route 3 alone in my Volkswagen Fox with R.E.M. on the tape deck and that blue light of early dawn over the New York City skyline behind me. I could feel a strong sense that there was still so much ahead of me.

Though we never discussed anything about the past, living together as two working adults broke through a thick layer of old pain. I was making lots of cash at the bar and was able to buy food for the apartment. My mom managed to keep up with the bills and kept the place pretty clean because she finally embraced and accepted what that meant to me, which was a lot around feeling safe in the world. Maybe she had healed a bit once I was out of the apartment and not under her care. She had raised four children, and then she was alone with herself for the first time ever.

***

I stayed at the apartment and graduated from college with a nonsensical degree in philosophy. Nonetheless, I was proud and felt no concern about my future. After I did some traveling around Europe with two guy friends from high school, my brother scored me a nine-to-five entry-level in Manhattan. His friend ran a direct mail company off Hudson Street, and she paid me $250 a week to answer the phones. I walked about a half a mile from the apartment complex and commuted by train into downtown Manhattan. The structure and the rhythm of going into the city every day suited me.

Rob Farrelly had recently sold Uncle Joe's to a suburban investor who tried and subsequently failed to make it into a brewery, so I was moving away from that scene. Those were some strange times. Luckily, the in-house booking agent and a local business partner took ownership. But it just wasn't the same anymore. I would grab shifts here and there, but mostly to spend time with friends.

And then I made my way to the Jersey City brownstone. My family was not supportive of the move out of my mother's apartment. Living there had simply expired as a respite between graduating from college and starting a career in the city. Plus, boring-ass suburban Jersey was not for me. It never was, and it never would be. I have always been an urban person at heart. But my dad felt that I was making an impulsive decision. I didn't give a fuck what anyone thought. I was a twenty-three-year-old adult, and I made my own money. Their thoughts were unsolicited. I packed up and moved to Jersey City.

In time I went from sleeping on a futon in the living room of the main unit to my own small bedroom upstairs and then finally into the one-bedroom apartment downstairs. There was a rotating cast of characters consisting of current and former Uncle Joe's peeps that moved in and out of the brownstone. We lived like a typical dysfunctional commune in the sense that we all cared about one another, but there were times that personal shit got thrown in the mix that none of us really had the skills to properly address. But all the bullshit of life aside, there were some killer times on that big crumbling stoop. And as much as the place was often in some type of disrepair because our landlord never really fixed the place up, it was our home. And it felt like a true home; I felt safe in a way that I had never felt before. There might be a discrepancy on a phone bill to talk about, but the bill would get paid in the end, and nobody would yell.

To say that life in my twenties—living in a super chill house with amazing friends and working in Manhattan—was epic would be a grand fucking overstatement. It was certainly not as challenging as having to depend on parents who had a bunch of rusty, unused tools in their toolboxes, but there were some super hard times because I was in the throes of learning how to be a real person. The worst part was that I couldn't manage a decent intimate relationship, and so I was lonely as fuck. My most recent boyfriend was the guy I had dated in high school and part of college. I would have these super intense flings, lasting a few weeks if I was lucky, but nobody stuck around in the end. I was too much. I was too fucked up emotionally, and it was as if there was a red flag stapled to my forehead. It was all or nothing, and so mostly it was nothing. But there was also a sense of peace in knowing that I had my own back, that I didn't have to depend on anyone.

I had just picked up a Thursday night hostess shift at Uncle Joe's for some extra money, since I had rent to pay. After only a few months of answering phones, I had decided to quit the direct mail company. The woman who ran the company was a screamer, and it was just too triggering for me after those years growing up with my stepmother. Again through a friend of my brother, I had gotten a better-paying job at an advertising agency in the Flatiron District. So I had to get up for work early in the morning. My paycheck from the ad agency was supposed to post at midnight, and my plan was to pull a couple of twenties out of the ATM machine so I could take a cab home.

It was the middle of winter and cold as shit outside. I was bone-tired from the stress of trying to learn my new job at the ad agency, and my feet hurt from running around seating people and clearing tables. I ran downstairs to the basement office to punch out on the time clock and then sidled up to the bar with a Camel Light and a Rolling Rock.

Bob, a local whom I'd known for the past decade or so, was sitting next to me. My housemate Pete was working the closing shift behind the bar. The pace had slowed; maybe there were ten people left in Uncle Joe's, including the two cooks and the door guy. I joined Pete behind the bar, so I could make a phone call to my bank to make sure there was loot in my account, as it was now past midnight. Fuck. There was still only $8.35 left in my checking account. I went into the cabinet where we stored our things and looked in my wallet. Two dollars and some loose change. I kept calling my bank. My balance had not changed.

"Who are you trying to call?" Bob asked.

"Oh, I'm trying to get a cab, but the line is fucking busy," I said.

"Do you want to just take my truck?" Bob said. "I'm pretty lit, so I can't drive you home, but you can take my truck."

"No, it's cool," I said. "I'll get a cab here soon."

There was cash everywhere. On the bar. In the register. Spilling out of the tip jar. I thought about those times when I had rifled through my stepsister Lisa's room for cash that maybe she had forgotten about: in her jeans pockets, on her night table, at the bottom of her purse. And I could not even muster the humility to ask one of my good friends if I could borrow ten bucks for a cab on a bitter cold night. Something in me had shut down. It was all those years when my mother would borrow two dollars for a pack of cigarettes from the neighbor and then they would call asking for it back. "I'll give it to you tomorrow," she would say. It was always tomorrow, and it was never, and I just couldn't allow myself to be anything close to that person. To do so would mean that I would have to confront the shame that I was not ready to confront. So instead I said good-bye to my friends in the warm bar and walked a mile down Franklin Street in the freezing-cold darkness. I waited a good long while for the train home.

Only a few months after moving to Jersey City and settling in, I got a call from my brother. I was in my cubicle in the city, sipping an almost-cold deli coffee and nibbling on the crumbling remains of a hard roll with butter.

"We have to move Ma out of the apartment," he said. "She got evicted and needs to be out in a few weeks," he told me.

"Holy shit," I said. "Are you serious?"

I thought my brother was joking, that he would just start laughing hysterically in my ear, but he didn't. He was silent on the line for a few moments.

"Yeah, Ana, she's done. She's gotta go to Dani's," he told me.

And then I got off the phone and cried at my desk.

My mother had fallen very far behind in rent and bills—she was hardly even going to work anymore. I honestly think this was when the cancer started growing. Even though my mother hadn't smoked in years, she had this eternally wicked wet cough that she constantly claimed was allergies. "Ma, why are you coughing like that?" I would ask. "Oh, it's just allergies, Neenoo." It seemed to me that she didn't feel well most of the time. She would stay in bed for days on end and began to get really heavy. When I would call to check on her, she never sounded good.

"What's wrong, Ma?" I would ask.

"Oh, nothing, honey," she would say.

***

We couldn't fit everything in the truck. All the larger pieces of furniture had to be left behind. These were things she wouldn't need at my sister's small condo. We took only our mother's personal belongings, essentials, like her clothing, the tattered art books that she would pore over hoping to someday visit the works in person. The dining room set that she had gotten from my aunt Joanie, which we had used on so many thrown-together and festive holidays; that filthy, rotten couch with the cigarette burns and the food stains; the kitchen table where she would sit for hours, smoking and picking at her eyelashes—it all stayed behind, and a few weeks later, she got a bill from the management company saying that she had to pay for the removal of junk furniture. This upset my mother.

"That was not junk furniture," she said. "That was my furniture."

The truck was packed, and the three of us piled into the cab of the U-Haul, like three low-rent criminals. It was me in the middle, my brother in the driver's seat, and my mother staring blankly out of the window and holding on to the overhead handle. We proceeded to haul down the New Jersey Turnpike, south toward my sister's rented condo in central New Jersey, where my mother lived in a converted dining room adjacent to the kitchen for most of the rest of her life.

THE CANCER WARS

FOUR

When I found out that my mother was sick with the cancer, I was working as a project manager on temporary contract at an ad agency in Amsterdam. Drew and I had rented out our house in Portland. He had come over to Holland and was working remotely for a few months. When I got the call from my mother that she was ill, I knew that I had no choice but to return to the States. I also knew that I was done with working in advertising. As much as I have talked all kinds of shit about it throughout the years—the inflated and needy egos; the maddening, stress-inducing deadlines; the sickness and disease of capitalism—my time in the cubicle had served its purpose when I needed nothing more than a large dose of stability, a sturdy desk, and rad people to go to lunch with. But I said good-bye to that chapter of my life, left Holland in the pissing-down rain with a pocketful of euros, which thankfully ended up funding the following year of my life. I made nine cross-country trips from Portland to New Jersey. This journey began in 2006 when I found out that my mother had stage 3A lung cancer. And, in a way, it both ended and began in 2007 when I gave birth to my son.

After a very challenging year for my mother and for her four grown children, after, lot of both physical and emotional pain had been endured, my mother left her body in the early-morning hours of September 12, 2007. I was seven months pregnant at the time. And as much as I have made many attempts to make peace with losing my mother right before I became a mother, as many times as I have picked through the narrative for hidden clues, as much as I have tried to edit the frames so that they created a more cohesive and linear motion picture, what my personal story—not just that one year but all the years leading up to it and following—has offered me more than anything is a giant shot of inspiration and a tremendous dose of healing.

***

It was late in the afternoon on Christmas Day. My mother's four children, her six grandchildren, her sister, some nieces and nephews, and a few significant others were crammed around two large folding tables in the living room of my sister's rented condominium in central New Jersey. I was still somewhat jet-lagged and most certainly culture-shocked from having spent the last six months living in a natural light–filled sixteenth-century flat on a narrow cobblestone street in central Amsterdam. It had taken me a few hours to adjust to these surroundings: a dark apartment with wall-to-wall carpeting in desperate need of a steam cleaning. But now that my nervous system had settled and accepted, I felt comfort in being there with my family as we gathered around the woman who had always been the central figure in many of our lives.

Dani and I had been chopping and cooking and cleaning in her dated and run-down galley kitchen since morning. At one point earlier in the afternoon, my mother had sat upright in her bed while I prepared to sauté a carton of white button mushrooms. I had been standing a few feet away in the kitchen, only steps from where my mother slept in a twin bed up against a gold-speckled mirrored wall in the converted dining room. It was the first time since the cancer diagnosis that I had been able to see that my mother was not physically well, that she was unable to stand up to cook. This felt more than strange because my mother was usually at the control panels in the kitchen even when someone else was cooking, dipping her fingers into sauces, adding salt, commenting on flavor, making a giant fucking mess.

I could see that the radiation treatment that she had started about one month before was clearly weakening her body, even though the tumor that had been choking her was shrinking considerably. And although my mother had instructed me otherwise, I took the plain white button mushrooms, put them in a metal colander, and rinsed them under the faucet. My mother saw this and snapped at me.

"I told you not to wash them!" she yelled, her black and gray hair flat and matted on the side that she had been sleeping on most of the morning, her voice crackly and wet from the sickness that lived in her lungs.

"Just brush the dirt off, Ana!" she snapped.

I ignored her orders and stood at the sink and kept washing the mushrooms. She was too weak to do anything about it. My mother was powerless.

Now there were two large round plastic platters of presliced carrots, celery, cauliflower, broccoli, green and red peppers, all surrounding a cup of ranch dressing in the center of each platter, one on each side of the long, improvised holiday table. There were smaller plates of cubed white and yellow cheese, crackers, and sliced Italian bread. A few days earlier, my sister had bought colorful Christmas-themed paper tablecloths, paper plates, paper napkins, plastic silverware, and plastic cups at the Dollar Store.

"Can we at least use good plates?" I had asked my sister that morning.

"The paper ones always get soggy," I had said.

"We won't have enough," she had told me.

"You sure?"

"Wait," she had said.

And then she had taken out a box from the hall closet. I had set the table with the good plates that my sister had gotten when she was married, even though she was long divorced.

"That looks so much better," she had said, as the two of us stood in the living room looking at the table that was supposed to hold twenty people.

Now my sister and I brought trays of food to the table. We were sweating profusely because it was hot in the kitchen from running the oven all day and from all of the bodies that had filled the small living room. At one point, we looked at each other and started laughing hysterically. Nobody had offered to help. They never did. In my family, when you host, you hustle, and everyone else sits. And even if they had offered to help, there was no room for another ass in the kitchen.

"This is so sick," Dani said, as she walked from the kitchen into the living room, an apron tied around her waist, like my mother on those other holidays.

Lasagna, smoked sliced ham, breaded and fried chicken cutlets, mushrooms sautéed in butter, steamed broccoli with lemon, a salad that my sister-in-law had brought. There were multiple conversations going at once, voices firing in all directions.

My brother Mike was about to make a toast. I sat on the arm of one of my sister's couches, which was only a foot or two away from where everyone else was sitting at the table.

"Ana, sit," my oldest brother, Anthony, said, pointing to an empty chair.

"I'm fine here," I said.

"You sure?"

I nodded. I preferred to sit and observe from that perch rather than be a part of this thing that I felt did not yet have a name. The energy in the room was tense, heavy, thick with heat and sickness. We toasted to something about all being there together in that one room. My sister ran into the kitchen sobbing, black mascara running down her face. She has to live with this every day, I thought to myself. She has had to live with my mother for the past seven years. It's not been easy, and it's not going to be easy.

Mike said, "Let's eat."

And we ate.

When the tables had been cleared of people and

holiday detritus, my sister and I folded them and put them in a closet where they would be stored until the next family gathering. We put the living room back together. My sister vacuumed the carpets. I took garbage and the recycling outside to the dumpsters and then began spraying and wiping down the counters. My mother was sitting in her room off the kitchen wearing an old light blue nightgown and a pair of cheap reading glasses. The television was going in the background, and she was holding the makeup-stained cordless phone in her lap. There were rust-colored translucent bottles of pills lined up on her nightstand next to a small plastic container of holy water.

My mother looked pale and exhausted, tired and drained in a way that was so different from when she used to say she was sick and call out of work.

"That was so nice, wasn't it, Ana?" she asked in that crackling voice. "Yeah, Ma," I said.

"The mushrooms came out good," she said.

"I know," I said.

"You and Dani did such a good job," she said.

"Hey, Ma. So Dani will take you to radiation this week and then Mike the next. Then I'll be back in a few weeks," I told her.

"Okay, honey," she said.

"Don't kill yourself traveling," she told me. "Drew needs you," she said.

"He's fine, but I haven't really been home in months," I said.

What I didn't say was that we had been trying

to start a family. What I didn't say was that my life over the past year had made that difficult.

***

It was early morning, and I had just flown into JFK on the redeye from Portland, completely sleep deprived and jacked on bad coffee. But it was inspiring in a strange way to be running on fumes, mostly because there was something beautifully shocking about being thrust into the bright, bright sunshine of a clear blue New York City winter sky. I headed into Brooklyn on the subway with my bags between my legs, and a deep well of emotion came over me. I wept silently, not necessarily out of sadness about my mother's health but more around an intense feeling of coming home, of finally arriving. For most of my adult life, maybe even into childhood, I had longed to return back to my family's roots in Brooklyn and to make a home there.

I had once consulted an oracle about this longing to live in Brooklyn, where my grandparents lived after leaving Italy, the borough where my father and his siblings were raised.

"It's so painful—this pull," I had told her. "Like it's deep in my guts."

"It's your ancestors calling you home," she had said. "You just have to tell them to wait."

And so I had told them to wait, and even though the pull was not as strong anymore, I could still feel the significance of home in my body when I was there, traveling on an elevated train through the stark winter landscape.

"You seem different when you are here," a good

friend had once remarked when we were walking through the leafy Carroll Gardens neighborhood one fall afternoon a few years earlier.

"What do you mean I seem different?" I asked her.

"Oh, I don't know; you just seem more energetic and happy," she said.

"I think this is where I feel the most full," I told her.

"My grandfather lived in this neighborhood after he came from Italy," I told her. "He died before I was born, so maybe this is the way that we get to connect," I said.

"Why don't you just move here then?" she asked me.

"It's complicated," I said. "Drew doesn't want to leave Portland. I'd move here in a second if it were up to me," I told her.

**

I got off of the subway in Williamsburg. Droves of twentysomethings and early-thirtysomethings were heading toward train to go to work in Manhattan. Good black shoes, side bags slung over their shoulders, white paper coffee cups in hand. I thought to myself, I used to be that person. As I walked down Bedford, I considered what might be next for me. I had recently left my last job in advertising, an industry where I had worked, often begrudgingly, for a decade and had promised myself never to return. And now that my mom was sick in Jersey and I was still living in Portland, I knew that I would be uprooted and uncertain for who knew how long.

I watched a woman around my age, early thirties, walking on the other side of the street. She had on fitted jeans and trainers, a wool pea coat, and a thick wool scarf around her neck. She ducked into a café. I thought about her as I continued toward South Third Street, where my friend Donna lived, where I would spend a few nights before heading to Jersey. As much as I was that woman, could still be that woman, I didn't want to be that woman anymore. I felt a sense of wholeness come over me. I had made the right decision to quit my job, to leave that career; I was doing the right thing by being able to be there for my mother.

And then I didn't get off of Donna's couch for two days, other than to walk up to Bedford Avenue to pick up takeout and DVDs. It felt like the past six-plus months of my life had finally caught up with me. Living abroad in Holland and working a crazy stressful job. Trying to figure out if I wanted to relocate to Amsterdam, as I had been offered a much longer contract, and discussing this with Drew: Could he find work there? Would he want to live there? And then finding out that my mother had cancer and trying to manage so much fear and having to make sense of all that. When Donna got home from a photo shoot in the city, we cracked open a decent bottle of Côtes du Rhône, crawled under the covers and watched *Kramer vs. Kramer* and *Ordinary People*, two films that I had picked up from the video store earlier.

"What is wrong with you?" Donna asked, laughing.

"I need 1980s and depressing right now," I said.

"It's comforting. And nostalgic."

***

A few days after I'd arrived in Brooklyn, Donna drove me to Queens to pick up my car, which I'd had shipped out from Oregon. I wanted to be able to drive my mother back and forth to the hospital for her cancer treatments, and my brother's friend, who owned a shipping company, had offered to ship the car gratis. We arrived at the shipping facility, and my white 1989 Honda Civic hatchback from Oregon was rolled off a ramp and into a parking area. Seeing the car that my husband had bought for a thousand bucks off his buddy back in Portland parked there in Queens, the place where I was born, was jarring. It was this bizarre convergence in the form of an old car with green moss in the cracks and a familiar grassy mildew smell.

After I had signed some paperwork, Donna left to go into the city to shoot photos. I felt a little sad, like a little kid left to fend for herself at camp. But then I collected myself. I got in the car and rifled through the glove compartment. I pulled out a case of CDs. I put on *Out of Time* by R.E.M. and headed toward New Jersey. Now I was in this familiar car on these familiar roads with this familiar music. A true convergence of my new life in Oregon and my old life in Queens and Jersey.

I thought about the year when I worked at Uncle Joe's and lived at my mom's apartment, trying to make my way through college. How I would drive home in the early-morning hours listening to R.E.M., with the New York skyline behind me, not knowing what was ahead of me in life but feeling a pull to be somewhere different. That was before I decided to leave my roots and forge new territory in the Pacific Northwest. Now it was ten years later, and Michael Stipe still sang on the track "Country Feedback," "I'm to blame. It's all the same. It's all the same." But what I knew now that I hadn't known then was that I was not to blame and it was not all the same.

I had run the fuck away to Oregon with someone that I wasn't meant to love. And after I had left that guy in a huff because I had fallen in love with Drew, I walked around wearing a heavy woolen coat of guilt for years. I had always thought that I was a bad person. Not only for fucking over a really good person but for being a fucked-up kid, for stealing and lying and messing around and doing bad in school when it seemed that everyone else around me was thriving and living epic lives with no mistakes being made.

As I headed south on the New Jersey Turnpike in a ratty hatchback from Oregon, I blasted the music of my youth. I came to the realization that it was really not my fault. None of it was. Life is just super fucking messy and unpredictable, and you grow though this shit, you really do. You build strength and character.

And nobody is to blame.

***

I arrived at my sister's condo complex, parked the Civic in front of the building, and walked up a short flight of concrete stairs. I had to think for a minute about what the unit number was because my sister had lived in the same building when she was married, but then had moved into a rental unit once she divorced. I rang the buzzer and was immediately buzzed into the building, so I walked onto the landing, and suddenly that familiar mix of moldy carpeting and cooking odors caused my synapses to fire. Ever since she'd moved in with my sister and her two kids, it had always been my mother who had greeted me when I visited. She would hang her head out of the open door, usually with a dishtowel in hand, as I walked down the stairs toward their ground-level unit.

But my mother was sick in bed, and so she did not greet me at the door. My sister had buzzed me in and walked off, and so I let myself into the apartment. It was immediately apparent how very much it sucked here. My mother was lying sideways in a twin bed in her small room off the kitchen, wearing nothing but a flimsy polyester nightgown that was torn at the hem. Her hair was in tangles, her skin clammy, pale, and her mouth sunken. As often as I had seen my mother lying in this manner pretty much all of my life, the sight of my mother in bed because she was broke and depressed was much different than the sight of my mother in bed because she had been poisoned with cancer drugs. It shocked my nervous system into a state of fight or flight. I did not want to be here. I had to be here.

So I bent down and greeted my mother with a quick kiss on her cheek. She patted me on the head.

"Hi, my sweetheart," she said in a choking, wet voice.

"Hi, Ma," I said.

It smelled awful in her room—not just the usual body odor and staleness that surrounded my mother, but also a chemical tinge, a toxicity that was palpable.

I walked into the living room and found my sister, Dani, sorting through a pile of bills and paperwork, drinking coffee that she kept getting up to zap in the microwave. My sister, who was in her midforties, always did her hair, ironed her clothes, and put on a face of makeup when going out in public, just like our mother. But at home, also like our mother, she let her guard down. Dani's medium-length dark brown hair was pulled into a ponytail, her layered bangs falling onto her wide pale forehead. My sister had not changed her hairstyle since the 1980s.

"Dani doesn't like change," my mother always said.

My sister's nerves seemed more rattled than usual, her breathing extra shallow and heavy. She had always been an anxious person. But she was also very kindhearted and warm and loving; you could see it with the young children that she worked with as an assistant kindergarten teacher in her local school district. When I went to the grocery store with my sister, it never failed—at least one kid would run up and give her a giant hug. "Hi, Miss Dani!" they would say. Even awkward, pimply teenagers that she had taught years before. She knew all their names and would end up in lengthy conversations with the parents. As our mother had been back when I was young, my sister was a single mother trying to get by on a measly salary and child support. Money was always tight, and even though my mother contributed her Social Security checks and a small pension each month, they could never seem to make ends meet. As usual, my brother Mike would be called upon for a bailout. "We need two hundred," my mother would say. "By when?" Mike would ask. "Tomorrow morning." "Jesus, Ma. Couldn't you give me a little notice?" he would ask her. "Nothing has changed," I would say when he called to tell me. And with our mother sick and the endless additional medical costs, it was more dire than usual.

I sat on the couch in the living room and stared at the television.

"Don't you ever turn this thing off?" I asked my sister.

"I like the company," she said.

Dani told me I could spend the night in my nephew's room. Her son was thirteen years old, and her daughter was seventeen, both of them in the throes of teenagerdom. I grabbed my bags and walked into my nephew's room. A panic washed over me. I cannot fucking stay in here, I thought to myself. Something about the small captain's bed with the mismatched sheets and the dingy off-white walls in desperate need of a paint job, something about the stained tan carpet in need of a steam cleaning, something about the overall muskiness and messiness of a preteen boy, something about all of this was throwing me way too far over the edge of what was okay for me. My shoulders tensed and my stomach clenched because it felt as if I were back in my mother's shithole apartment. My mind knew that I was here, but my body thought I was back there.

I walked back into the living room and told my sister that I needed to make a phone call.

"Okay, honey," she said.

I went into the main hallway of the building and sat in the unheated stairwell, shivering from the cold, my head resting in my hands. I called my brother Mike, who was at work in Midtown Manhattan.

"Hey, Ana," he said. "What's up?"

My voice was shaking as I said, "I'm freaking out right now. It's grossing me out too much to stay here."

"O-*kay*," he said slowly, blowing out a long breath.

And then his voice perked up, and he said, "Why don't you just get yourself a hotel room? There are tons of places off Route 1," he said.

I remained quiet.

"I could never stay there," he said. "So I get what you are feeling," he told me.

"Really?"

"Yeah, listen. Just go online and find a deal on one of those websites."

"Okay, I will," I said.

We got off the phone, and I sat in a warm spot of sunlight. Fuck it, I thought. I'll get myself a hotel room. I have my own money. And then I thought about how my husband, Drew, would never have spent money on a hotel room. He wouldn't have thought twice about crashing at my sister's. But he hadn't grown up in a shithole apartment like I had. He had grown up in a nice ranch-style house in California. It wasn't always clean and orderly, because his dad and stepmom are super casual on the domestic front, and we relate on that level, but his place wasn't nearly as shitty as my mom's. It was a bit dirty and stinky with dog funk, but there was always food, and bills were always paid.

I can afford this splurge, I thought to myself. I worked so hard these past six months, I rationalized.

***

When I walked back inside, my mother was out of bed, sitting with my sister at the dining table. She was making a categorized food-shopping list in her usual loopy script. The small, round four-seat table was crammed into a corner of the living room, next to one of those halogen lamps that everyone had in college. Standing, I looked at my mother and my sister.

"I'm gonna go stay at a hotel," I said.

"I need a little space," I told them.

My mother looked up through her glasses and said in that tumor-strained voice, "Awww, honey."

And then right away my sister asked in a concerned tone, "Are you sure?"

"Yeah, I'm just tired and need some alone time," I told them.

"All the traveling," I said.

A tremendous wave of guilt washed over me and ripped through my core. This was my family, and they loved me, and yet I was such a snob that I was not even comfortable staying in their home. As I stood in the middle of the living room, I knew that I had to go. Otherwise, I would not be able to withstand what was ahead of me. I would not have the strength to face the realities of a sick mother and the harsh cancer treatments and all of the interpersonal dramas and fears that were to come. I needed temporary reprieve.

***

I drove down a mile-long road that at one time had been farmland but was now lined with condominium complexes. I parked in the lot of a supersized grocery store to pick up the things my mother had on her list. When I walked inside, the culture shock of being in an environment like this slammed into me like the extra-giant shopping carts that were violently being smashed into one another by a greasy-haired teenage boy in his red smock. It had been a while since I had been in a store like this, as I had spent most of the last six years of my life in either Portland or Amsterdam, where I shopped at smaller-sized natural grocery stores and outdoor green markets. In here the bright-colored food packaging and waxy produce were so strange and unnatural that I became slightly dizzy and confused. I wandered from aisle to aisle in this state for a good hour, somehow managing to find everything on my mother's shopping list. I wanted to please her, because I felt like half an asshole for needing to check myself into a hotel.

I got back and hauled five doubled-up plastic bags out of the hatchback and into the apartment.

My arms were strained, and I was overwhelmed.

"What's wrong, my honey?" my mother said.

"I just don't understand why they still use these goddamn plastic bags," I said adamantly.

"Next time just see if they have paper, sweetheart," my mother said in the same tone that she had used when I was a kid having a fit about the specifics of my Halloween costume, about my homework, about the dinner that she had attempted to serve me but wasn't what I expected.

"Okay," I said.

I sat on the couch. I noticed that my heart was racing, and my breath was super shallow. In my mind, I knew why I was feeling this way, but my body could not catch up with my thoughts. I thought about all those years of being around my stepmother, who had never been satisfied with how I did things, with where I put things. And all those years of being around my mother, who had been so physically unkempt, how our apartment had always been so dirty and uncomfortable. This toxic combination of environments had made me what I now knew was hypervigilant. With an over alert nervous system that was easily triggered into a fight-or-flight state. And now that I was being reminded of all of that, my nephew's room, the crisis of my mother's health, the overly lit and over-stimulating big-box grocery store, had made me feel out of control and anxious.

When I started to feel more grounded and calmer, I unloaded the groceries onto the kitchen counter with my mother hovering beside me, making sure I didn't leave anything out. It was approaching evening, and so the light was growing darker beyond the cheap mini blinds. You would have never known the day was coming to an end, since my mother and sister tended to close out the world, hardly ever cracking a window to let in the fresh air. When I opened windows, they closed them. "You don't know who will come in here!" my sister would say in a fearful tone. My sister's two kids were in their rooms, each with a neighbor friend. The television in the living room emitted loud voices and bright colors in the background while my sister and I put together dinner. A rotisserie chicken and some steamed green beans and mashed potatoes. My sister heated up a can of gravy in the microwave, and I decided not to give her shit about the sodium content or the use of the microwave as opposed to heating in a pot. No more difficult child, I told myself.

The kids were called to the table, the friends left, and we all sat down in the living room to eat together as a family. I picked at my food, while my sister and her kids showed one another the chewed-up food in their mouths and laughed at each other. My mother, who had filed many complaints over the years to my brother Mike and me about how my sister had chosen to raise her kids without a lot of boundaries, scowled at the three of them.

"Not at the table!" my mother said, firm.

"Mom, just leave us alone!" my sister fired back.

This had been their dynamic for the seven years they had lived together as an extended family. Like a stranger, I hovered somewhere outside of this circle of dysfunction and chaos. I had left Jersey six years earlier and run away to Oregon. When people asked me what took me out west, I usually said it was because I'd wanted to live somewhere different, that I'd wanted to snowboard, that I was a fan of the filmmaker Gus Van Sant. But really, really, I'd needed to get the fuck away from all of this. And so I fled, and now, in a way, I was back, and it was not feeling very good.

I brought the dinner dishes into the kitchen and put them on the counter. My mother took to her bed, the kids went to their rooms, and after she'd loaded the dishwasher, my sister retreated to her perch on the corner of the couch. And then I left to go to my hotel room.

***

I drove toward the outskirts of Princeton and parked my crappy Civic in the hotel parking lot next to a bunch of brand-new rental cars. I grabbed my bags and headed through the glass doors. Ashamed that I was not clad in business attire like all of the people wandering about the sterile lobby, concerned that I would be scrutinized because I had purchased my room on a discount website, feeling lesser because I was wearing jeans and a weathered hoodie. When I got to the counter, I handed my credit card to a young guy with wire-framed glasses and clean-cut dark brown hair. I could feel the judgment as he typed away, but I also knew that I could easily judge him back.

"Do you need help with your luggage?" he asked, as I looked down at the battered small wheeling suitcase that I had wedged between my feet.

"No, I'm good," I said.

As I dragged my bag to a room on the second floor of this nondescript, corporate-style hotel, I felt super sad and alone. Here I was in Jersey, the state where I had lived for the majority of my childhood and adolescence. But it all felt so foreign and strange to me now. There was no longer a home to come back to, as my mom's shithole apartment was gone, my dad and stepmother's house was still so frigid and unwelcoming, and my sister's place was now crammed with sickness and teenagers and dysfunction. I was feeling like a lost, sad child, kind of how I used to feel when I was a kid home alone after school.

When I walked in, I could see that the climate-controlled (emphasis on control) square room with the shiny wooden desk and the neatly folded, bleached white towels in multiple sizes and the endless cable channels would become my savior. I did not know it yet, but these hotel rooms would be one of my biggest refuges during the time that divided me from the person I was then and the person I would later become. I took a hot shower, crawled into bed, and watched *The Golden Girls* on Lifetime until I passed out cold.

The next morning, when I woke in my hotel room, I could see the early-morning blue light through the thick drapery. I put on a morning show, washed up a bit, and took a fistful of Chinese herbs that my acupuncturist back in Portland had given me so I would stay healthy while traveling. I was feeling way better, my nervous system no longer on high alert. I had had a good night's rest and felt stability in knowing that there was somewhere safe to retreat back to for the next few nights. I departed from the confines of the hotel compound in the Civic and drove into downtown Princeton. I sat for about an hour in Small World Coffee, a warm and lively café off of a side street in this lovely and historical upper-crust university town. I worked my way through a few cups of strong coffee and some steel-cut oats while I reviewed my mother's care notes and insurance information and personal finances using a flimsy spiral notebook with a bright green cover that I had bought at Walgreens during my last trip out to Jersey.

***

Even though she had seen me jotting things down in it, my mother had not yet asked about the intention of the notebook. I knew she knew it had something to do with the cancer, and I had a strong sense that it made her feel safe. She never asked to see it, never asked what I was writing in there, what I was reading over. All she knew was that her youngest child of four, the baby of the family, had a special notebook. Months later, during a very grave period of her illness, there was a moment when my mother was half-alert in a hospital bed while I was flipping through my notes.

When a nurse came to check her vitals, my mother said, "My Ana has a notebook."

***

After I left the safe, liberal bubble of the café in Princeton, I headed over to pick up my mother for her radiation treatment. My sister and the kids were at school, and so my mother buzzed me into the building. When she met me in the hallway, she was in bare feet, no stockings, and wearing an apron over a blouse and skirt. Her face was pale and clammy, and she hadn't put on her usual outside face of makeup.

"Ma, you're not ready? We have to leave soon," I said.

As we went inside, my mother was saying that she was too tired, that she didn't feel good, that she didn't want to go to radiation.

"We're going," I said.

"No, honey."

"But I came all the way over here to take you," I told her.

"Just call and see if I can come a little later so I can rest a bit," she told me.

"Okay," I said.

When I called, the radiation-scheduling person patiently told me that they could not see her later.

"We'll come," I said.

And then my mother begrudgingly put on stockings and lipstick and a thick beige winter coat. I shoved her into the passenger seat of the Civic, and we drove about a half hour on a four-lane road through Central Jersey to a hospital in Trenton so she could get zapped near her heart.

"You okay, Ma?" I asked as she hung on to the overhead handle like she always had, as she panted like a dog needing air like she always had.

"I guess," she said.

***

When I got back to the hotel, I called my husband in tears to catch him up on the state of my mother's health. After that day's radiation treatment, my mother had become very weak. I had seen firsthand the havoc that radiation was wreaking on her body. "It just burns a little," my mother had told me after she came into the waiting room, about to change back into her blouse. I had been nervously flipping though a five-year-old *Time* magazine.

"You need help?" I asked my mother as she sat in a changing bay with the curtain not yet drawn.

"It's okay, honey," she said.

I didn't want to help my mother back into her blouse, so I was relieved. I didn't want to see her worn-out bra, her sagging breasts, that tattooed x and that small red burn mark on her chest.

I told Drew that my mother was so weak, that she was so sick. I told him it was not the treatment itself but the anticipation of having to muster the energy to get ready to go when all she wanted to do was stay in bed with the TV blaring because she didn't feel well. And I reminded him that she was cohabitating with a large tumor in one of her lungs. I told him it was the aftereffects, how the treatment zapped her of energy and leveled her for at least a day or two. I told him how I had taken her home and hung around until my sister and the kids came home. I told him how my mother had immediately taken to bed. That she hadn't wanted anything to eat, which was not like her, as she would usually prop herself up in her room with at least a bowl of greasy potato chips or salty pretzels, crumbs everywhere.

"You want tea and toast, Ma?" I had asked.

"No, honey, thank you. I just want to rest for while," she had said.

***

"Are you ready to let her go?" my husband, Drew, asked me.

I was huddling under the blankets in the starchy hotel bed. It was not like Drew to say something so serious and sobering; he existed within a no-worries-it's-all-good type of reality. If he was being serious, the situation had to be serious. I'd been in such a whirlwind state since her initial diagnosis, living in Holland and then moving back to America, now traveling back and forth between coastlines, that the truth, the reality of it all, hadn't caught up with me. I'll never forget the moment when I found out that she had cancer. I was in my simple bedroom on the top floor of a sixteenth-century row house on a cobblestone street in Amsterdam.

"You're not gonna like it," my mother said to me across continents.

I had just gotten home from a long day at the ad agency and had sent my husband out for a bottle of wine so I could be alone to call my mother. She had gone for tests the previous week, initially for an allergy test, as she was continually short of breath and chronically battled a postnasal drip.

"It's can-*cer*," my mother said to me that evening.

I didn't tell my husband for over a week.

***

"I don't know if I am ready to let her go," I said between sobs.

We remained quiet on the phone.

"I gotta go," I said.

"Ok, hon. Try to get some sleep," he said.

All I could do was hide in my blanket cave and weep and shake like I had when I was a young girl and my stepmother was screaming her head off because I had spilled soda on her new carpet. And then I began to picture my mother's fat body sailing up into the sky like a float in the Macy's Thanksgiving Day Parade. But those floats are tethered to something, I thought. What is my mother tethered to anymore? I asked myself. It's the love for her kids, I thought. That's all she's ever had, and that's all she's got left in the world now.

***

There had been many times I'd wished my mother away. I had hoped that she would just leave me to live the rest of my life in peace. Those were the times she embarrassed me with how she looked, with the musky, pungent way that she smelled. Those were the times she embarrassed me with the way she borrowed money from people. Those were the times she embarrassed me with the way she promised to take me somewhere after school and then backed out last minute. Those were the times she upset me with the way she sat and talked on the phone gossiping for hours on end. Those were the times she smoked and smoked and smoked and ate and ate and ate and coughed and coughed and coughed. There were so many times that I had wanted a different mother. A mother who took care of herself and took care of our home and took care of me. There were so many times that I had wanted a perky lady in a tidy station wagon who would send me off to school with a healthy packed lunch. We all want what we don't have, and I had the warm mother with the traumatic past who loved me in the only ways that she knew how. And no, no, no—of course I was not ready to let her go. I had finally found a way to live far enough away that my mother could still be in my life but not taint me with all of her buried illnesses. I had finally found a way to keep my mother in my life without feeling so goddamn strangled by her. But now she was being strangled by a big blob of tangled-up cells. And there I was, hiding away in a blanket cave at a sterile, corporate hotel because I was afraid to watch her float up into the skies. I was afraid because I knew that, once she was gone, I would have to take a long hard look at my own past.

I was not ready to let her go.

FIVE

The past two plus months of intermittent radiation treatment were wearing my mother down. The first obvious sign was weight loss. She was no longer an obese lady in a ratty housedress, swollen belly protruding, arms and breasts melting into the sides of her body. She was now a bigger-bodied woman with an unhealthy pallor. There were many complaints. It hurts to sit this way. It hurts to lie this way in bed; please get me a pillow. There was a lot of nausea, and there was even more moaning.

There was my mother in a twin bed, in nothing but an old polyester nightgown, a worn blanket pulled over her legs and feet. As she rested on her side, her body protruded from the bed like a mountain. The television was the only source of light in the room, bright flashes of blue and white, the sounds droning and chaotic. There was her cordless phone on a round side table, the handset smudged with foundation makeup and encrusted with food particles. There were her rosary beads and her small marble owl statue. There were the framed photos of Catholic saints. The air was stale, and there was an old saucepan next to her head, positioned strategically in case she had to vomit. She tossed and she turned and she groaned.

When I saw her like that, I thought she was a fraud, faking the pain and the nausea in order to get attention, special care. There had been far too many instances when I was a child when my mother had called out sick from work, starting the day horizontal on the pullout bed with the puke bucket. Later, when I came home from school, she would be parked in a chair alongside the cracked kitchen window, chain-smoking cigarettes.

"I thought you were sick, Ma," I would say.

"Mind your own business, Ana," she would answer back nastily.

***

When I had taken my mother for her latest radiation appointment, the doctors had told us that the treatment was shrinking the tumor. I felt good about driving out to Brooklyn to stay with my friend Donna, a reprieve from cancer and from the corporate hotel and from the familial dysfunction at my sister's that festered as my mother's tumor shrank.

But then my cell phone rang at almost two in the morning. I was sharing a bed with Donna, so with my hands shaking, I quickly grabbed the phone and ran toward the living room so as not to wake her. As I rushed down the dark hallway, I saw that it was the home number at my mom and sister's. When I reached the living room, my heart was pounding.

I whispered into the phone, "Yeah, what's up?"

My sister was crying hysterically, saying, "Mom wants to go to the hospital. . . . I don't know what to do here, the kids are sleeping, I can't do this anymore, I just can't. . . ."

She trailed off, and I waited patiently on the line until she calmed down enough to tell me what was going on. My understanding was that our mother was unable to breathe. And that my sister had been begging her to please calm down, to please not go to the emergency room at that hour, in the cold dark of winter. She had been telling my mother to please just wait until the morning, and then she would call the doctor first thing, once the kids were off to school.

I was on the edge of the couch in the bright living room, bright from the streetlights along Berry Street, bright because the long white curtains that lined the tall windows were translucent. I could hear activity outside of this upper-floor apartment, the sounds of taxis speeding full throttle toward the Williamsburg Bridge into Manhattan, a few people cavorting in doorways and on stoops, people walking dogs, people just walking. It was the middle of night, in the middle of winter, in New York City.

"If Mom cannot breathe, you need to call the paramedics," I said to my sister.

"But she just needs to calm down and go back to sleep; it's probably just anxiety," she told me.

"It's not up to you to decide right now," I said, firm.

"Okay," my sister said. "I'll call now."

When we got off the phone, I held my breath for as long as I could, and I tried to see what it felt like to be my mother in that moment. And then I laid myself down on the couch and pulled a blanket over my body and tried to get some sleep, even though sleep never came. My mind raced.

What I did not know was that in the upcoming months, there would be so many days and nights of existing on the edges of couches and chairs, there would be so many times when my hands would be gripping on steering wheels, and there would be so many moments when my ears would be pinned to phone receivers. In the years to come, I would think a lot about that night in particular, how afraid my mother must have felt not being able to breathe through a tumor-infested lung and how she must have struggled with needing her children so much. I would think a lot about how our mother leaned so heavily on my sister, way more than on me, way more than on my brothers.

"It's different with daughters," my mother always said.

"What do you mean, Ma?" I would ask.

"Daughters take care of their mothers," she would say.

In the years to come, I would think a lot about the fact that my mother came from the old school and the old school taught that daughters took care of their parents.

I would think about my oldest brother, Anthony, my mother's firstborn, who has always existed on the periphery of the rest of our immediate family. I don't know my oldest brother that well—we are fourteen years apart—but I do know that he has been in and out of recovery for alcoholism for most of his adult life. I know that when I hug him, he's tense and thin and I can feel his bones when he pats me on the back in an awkward way even though I'm his kid sister. It's hard for me to truly know my oldest brother, because I don't see him often, and we never talk on the phone. Sometimes we write emails and we send texts. He has lived in the Philadelphia suburbs for many years, far enough away from the rest of the family to exist outside the fold. He had two children with his first wife, sweet, loving kids who are now adults, his son an alcoholic in recovery like himself. With his second wife, he had a daughter, my goddaughter, and he adopted his second wife's son from a previous marriage. See, I know facts but I don't have a complete narrative. Through the period of time when our mother was very sick and then dying, my oldest brother came around, but he wasn't in the thick of things like my brother Mike, my sister Dani, and me. It was okay, and we didn't complain, because we got it; there was this silent understanding. There would be a time when we would have a quiet family dinner, months away from that night when my sister called me at Donna's, very close to the end of my mother's life. Our mother would be extremely weak, and she would spend most of the day in bed, but we would all be together, her four children, all of her grandchildren. My older brother Anthony would spoon-feed our mother warm coffee, and our mother would take little sips, saying, "Ahhhhhh" after each serving.

I would think a lot about my brother Mike, the sibling nearest to me in age at ten years older, my closest comrade during The Cancer Wars. During that time, we spoke daily, if not a few times each day, regarding the status and next steps of my mother's illness.

I would think a lot about how my sister had such a hard time with all of this, the worst time out of all of us, really; she suffered through so much emotion and exhaustion and instability. She already had enough caregiving duties, what with raising two kids as a single mother. I would think about how she and her kids had been living with our mother before she got sick, always struggling to make ends meet, never having enough to live comfortably. I would think about how my mother could be so critical of how my sister raised her kids, how she would try to intervene, and how my sister would reject our mother's requests. You take my sister, and you take her kids, and then you take our mother, who was being choked to death by a tumor, and then you take the fact that they were all subsisting on my sister's measly assistant teacher's wage plus a bit of child support from her ex-husband plus my mother's shitty Social Security checks, and then you take the fact that nobody in that house had the tools to deal with anything adverse, most especially sickness and death. And I do think a big part of why my sister's parenting style bothered my mother was because of the way my mother raised me. It was certainly a reflection, a trigger.

And then I would start to unravel some aspects of my own inner world. I would begin to understand the relationship I had with my mother. Not until I became a mother myself, soon after my mother was gone, did I understand who we had been as mother and daughter. After she left my father, long after she had already raised a family of three children, she had been left to raise me. She had pretty much raised me alone, and she had been worn out and tired by then. I knew that she loved me, but I also knew that she didn't want to do it anymore, and I could feel that. So really, in so many ways, I raised myself, and I don't think that I did a very good job.

***

When the clear winter morning light began to fill the living room at Donna's, I peeled myself off the couch and I washed and dressed. I had hardly slept, so I was running on nerves and fear. I bundled myself in a warm jacket, a scarf, a hat, and I walked up to Bedford, the bitter cold stinging my face. I got a hot coffee and a muffin in a white paper bag. I went back to the warm apartment, and I sat with Donna at her dining table. We chatted a bit before she had to go into the city for a photo shoot and Donna expressed her concerns about me and of course about my mother.

"But I feel strong," I said to her. "I know that I have to be strong; otherwise I will fall," I told her, but it didn't seem like she believed me.

Fueled up on caffeine and carbohydrates, I drove from Brooklyn to the hospital in Central Jersey where my mother had been taken in the middle of the night. When I arrived in the emergency room, after I checked in at the front desk, I found my mother situated behind a curtain at the end of a row of patients. The hospital was in an urban area outside of Trenton. There were cuffed inmates and homeless people probably in desperate need of a warm bed and a hot meal, as I could not imagine that anyone would last a night on the streets in the dead cold of winter. And then there were people like my mother, people who could not breathe on their own, people who were in tremendous pain, people who were infested with cancer. I felt so much suffering swirling around in the horrific, stagnant air.

When I opened the curtain, my mother was sleeping. My heart skipped a beat, and a wave of energy ripped through my core. She looked awful; the skin on her face was gray and lifeless. This was certainly the worst that I had ever seen her. I had hardly been able to look at her when she was obese and tumorless, sitting on a chair eating potato chips, crumbs falling all over her housedress, hiding in the creases of her fat folds, leaving stains. I had hardly been able to look at her when she would laugh with her toothless mouth wide open, exposing raw gums and food particles, the phone resting on her ear. I had hardly been able to look at her when she would be in bed during the day, dressed in a stained nightgown, a pile of cigarettes in an ashtray at her side.

I was finding it so hard to look at my mother. She was in a hospital-issued gown, a thin white sheet covering her midsection, legs, and feet. Her head was tilted to the side, half falling off of a pillow. Her skin was not only gray in color but also clammy. A few long black hairs were sprouting through on her chin. Oxygen tubes were jammed into her nose, and some clear fluid ran through ports sticking into her arms. Her straight chin-length black hair was in knots at the back of her head. Her belly was distended, and her breasts fell to her sides, sloping toward her armpits.

This was my mother. I had lived in her.

I stood motionless in the middle of the

emergency room floor, all this activity going on around me, phones ringing, voices echoing, people in wildly patterned scrubs rushing by. As my mother slept a liquid-drug sleep, there was a buzzing in my head, and a wave of something intense was working its way through my chest cavity. I thought about Drew, saying, "Are you ready to let her go?" And then something in me shifted gears.

***

I started having a recurring anxiety dream. In this nightmare, I was trapped in the ward of what seemed to be a hospital, except that instead of beds and doctors and nurses and clear bags of medicine, there were metal torture devices, and there were super-sick people strapped to big metal chairs. They were sticking their tongues out and howling and flailing their limbs. In this dream, I was not being tortured, and I was not strapped to a big metal chair, but I was trapped in the bowels of this dingy hospital ward. I was always caught in a stagnant stairwell or in an elevator, and I was always unable to make my way out of so many extensive winding corridors. The worst part of these dreams was the horrific fluorescent lighting, which made all of the suffering and devastation hyper-visible and disturbing.

When I woke from these nightmares, I knew that I had these dreams because the fears needed to go somewhere. There was so much fear buried deep inside of me, programmed into my cellular structure, nestled in the warmth of my tissues. Not everyone has the same response to childhood experience, a therapist told me years later. "What do you mean?" I asked. "Oh, it's just that you had your own experience of your childhood," she said. "You are a sensitive being, and you felt everything around you, whereas some kids may have been able to tune out all those things, so it wouldn't affect them in the same way." When she said that, I told her that I felt lesser than, a failure, a fucking loser. "But that was your individual experience, and you need to honor that in order to heal," she said. "You are being really hard on yourself," she said. Another trait of the hyperaware, hypervigilant person is self-criticism and perfectionism.

***

One day I allowed myself to fold. I had taken my mother to one of her scheduled radiation appointments. I had gotten her out of the house, and we had managed to get to the hospital on time, so I was feeling heroic. I had dropped her off at the hospital entrance and then parked the Civic. As I always did when I took her to these appointments, I thought about just ripping out of the parking lot and leaving her there alone, abandoned, and worried about what had happened to me. When I was a teenager, she would sit by the window in our apartment with the lights off waiting for me to get home. When a friend would drop me off after a night of partying in the woods, I would see her silhouette, and it bothered me how much she worried. Leaving her there was only a fleeting thought, and it was not serious, but it was a thought nonetheless. And then I had her in the wheelchair, and I was acting all silly, walking too fast, taking turns like we were running from the hospital guards.

"Ana, stop it now!" she snapped at me.

And then right before we were about to get on the elevator, she craned her neck around and said, "Honey, will you walk down to the radiation area and tell them I won't be making it today?"

"What do you mean?" I asked her.

"I don't feel good now," she said. "It's my vertigo."

"C'mon, Ma, we came all the way here. Can't you just try?"

"No," she said adamantly. "We need to go home."

I was so angry with my mother. It took a lot to get her out of the apartment and into my low car and then out of the low car and into a wheelchair, if there was even one available, and into the hospital and then all the way down to the radiation area. My emotions in that moment by the elevator definitely set off some rogue shit from my childhood, from when she would promise me something and then not follow through. I don't know how many times she had promised me a trip to the mall for an iron-on, three-quarter-sleeve band T-shirt, and, one time, I know for certain, she had promised to buy me an adding machine from Sears, one where numbers got spit out on white ribbon, like a store receipt. I was obsessed with adding machines and calculators and cash registers, fucking dork that I was in my preteens.

There would be these promises, and then she would back out last minute because she had already spent the entirety of her paycheck. Maybe it was overdue bills, or maybe she owed money to a neighbor. Nonetheless, my whole world would be shattered.

"We can't go to the mall today, honey," my mother would say.

"Why not?"

"I don't have any more money left," she would tell me.

And then I would slam my door and freak out on my bed.

So there I was, wandering through the shiny, sterile hospital corridors in this preteen, arrested-development state. It was as if I were twelve again, donning a head of wild cowlicks and a pair of greasy upside-down glasses. I left my mother in a waiting area in the wheelchair with her purse resting on her lap, and I stomped down to talk to the radiation people. When I got there, working the front desk was this sweet, pudgy Italian man with gray hair and a bushy gray beard whom I'd met before and whom my mother knew and adored.

"Heya there, honey," he said. "Where's your mom?"

"She's here in the hospital, but she doesn't want to come . . ."

And then I just lost it, tears flying out of nowhere, uncontrollable and unleashed from the depths of some super-dark place, from as far back as fourth grade. It was all the iron-on, three-quarter sleeves, and it was the adding machine, and it was the fake blue contacts, and it was the hot-pink Guess Jeans, and it was the trip to Colonial

Williamsburg.

It was all of these things that used to get me through the day and then be yanked out from under me, like they had never existed in the first place. I was sobbing. And like an adoring uncle, this man pulled me into his soft, warm chest.

"You gotta know, it's really, really hard, honey," he said. "It's just really, really hard."

***

And then there I was, a few days later, back at the same hospital. I was in the emergency room, the site of my horrific recurring nightmare. Now, my sister was sitting on a plastic chair next to my mother; both women were curtained off from the rest of the world, inside a cocoon. I noticed that my sister was looking haggard: black lines of mascara were running down her swollen face, her hair was all over the place, not in its usual state of suburban-Jersey, hair-sprayed neatness. I didn't want to stay there in the tainted cocoon; there was no room for me. My mother had been administered something to calm her nerves. She had been given a flow of oxygen to breathe, so she was in and out of sleep.

I walked off to get my mother a can of Sprite and my sister a cup of coffee at the hospital cafeteria. It was the errands and the minutiae that kept my feet planted on the ground beneath me. When I returned to the ER, a drink in each hand, I saw an older Catholic nun with a round pale face in a habit whisk open the white curtains and exit my mother's area. Whoosh!

The nun proceeded to walk briskly toward the administration area. Something in her body language exuded seriousness. I walked closer and I saw that my sister was floating in a pool of tears; her hands were covering her face, and she was quietly weeping. My mother looked asleep in the bed, her head still slumped, her slack mouth wide open.

"What's going on?" I asked in a concerned tone.

My sister shoved her hands over her face in an *I can't talk right now* gesture. In a split second, I realized that my mother was minutes from death. I realized that the nun had come over to give my mother her last rites. This was a Catholic hospital, after all—wasn't that what they did? I looked at my sister.

"Dani, what was that nun doing in here?" I asked her.

Through her tears, she choked, "I don't know. She just came to check on Ma. They do that," she said.

"Holy, shit!" I said. "I thought it was last rites," I tell her.

In these moments—when you are trapped in a brightly lit emergency room because your mother is being choked by a cancer tumor and your sister breaks down and cries every ten seconds—a giant dose of comic relief is a massive fucking treat. My sister could not stop laughing, and she was still crying, and she was trying to tell me something but was struggling so hard.

"It's the priests that give last rites, not the nuns," she said.

Now I started laughing so hard that I put my head between my knees and my eyes welled up with tears.

"Then why were you crying?" I asked her.

"It's just so hard to see her like this," she told me.

***

My sister and I had been in the emergency room all day, taking short breaks from our mother's bedside to procure inedible food from the hospital cafeteria or to ask nurses at the front desk for updates on the tests they were administering. They never had answers. Going down the hallway to the bathroom had become a highlight, a reprieve. Every couple of hours, our mother was hauled away on a rolling bed to get some kind of test. We were constantly updating our brothers as best we could, even though everything seemed uncertain and super unclear.

At midday, my sister left to pick up her kids at school, and so without her rogue emotions to get in my way, I decide to go full gangbuster. I need to find out what the fuck was going on with our mother, why they were holding her in the emergency room all these hours, giving her all these diagnostic tests, and what the fuck the doctors were planning on doing with her next. All day I had been trying to figure out whom the attending ER doctor reminded me of, and then while I was sitting there next to my mother, who was falling in and out of consciousness, it finally hit me.

"Hey, Ma," I said, startling her awake.

"What is it, honey?"

"Don't you think the doctor looks like Woody Allen?" I asked her.

Sounding as if she had got a dead frog trapped in her throat, my mother said, "Yeah, I guess so, honey."

"I'm gonna go talk to him to see if any of those tests came back yet."

"Okay, my sweetheart," she said before falling out of consciousness again.

I approached where he was standing, near the circular front desk area, and could tell straight away that this doctor person was not going to be easy to talk to. We still had no clue as to why my mother could not breathe other than the fact that there was this asshole tumor stuck inside her lung. Here I was in the middle of the ER pit of this urban hospital. It was rough and it was raw. There had been a constant influx of inmates in their shackles, and there were a plethora of what appeared to be mentally ill patients who were either howling or slumped on chairs, clearly on the opiate nod.

I walked up to Woody Allen and stood awkwardly in front of him, hoping he would take notice of my presence. We were practically the same height, at eye level with each other, but he would not look at me. He was looking down at his clipboard, and then he sort of half acknowledged me with a chin nod.

"I'm really sorry to bother you, but can you please let me know what's next for my mother?" I asked him.

I pointed to her bed, so he would know which patient I was referring to.

"*Oh, her,*" he said sarcastically.

He rifled through his clipboard.

"Yeah, well, she's got a bunch of fluid around her heart, so we have to take it out," he said.

And then he shook his head from right to left and let out this *PSSSST* sound before walking away, his New Balance running shoes squeaking dramatically on the polished floors as he flew through the swinging double doors.

I remained standing in disbelief about the doctor's dismissive tone and the fact that there was some kind of fluid around my mother's heart that needed to be removed. What does that even mean? I was super pissed off at Woody Allen's "Oh, her" comment, which made it sound as if my mother was somehow lesser than, as if she somehow deserved this fluid, this cancer tumor, as if she had done something wrong and now she was being punished by getting fluid around her heart. I felt protective of my mother, and at the same time, I was ashamed of something.

For so much of my life, I had been aware that I was of a lower socioeconomic class than many of my schoolmates. When friends' mothers who drove Mercedes-Benz wagons and carried Coach purses would ask me where I lived, what my father did for a living, where I planned to go to college—I would shrink into myself. I never knew how to answer them. I would shut down.

And so talking to this doctor and being blatantly disregarded, hearing him say, "Oh, her," really meant *Oh, her—you mean, that toothless fat lady on Medicaid who was stupid enough to smoke cigarettes for too many years and clearly didn't take care of herself and got cancer, and now she has this*

*fluid around her heart because of all the radiation,
and now, now I have to waste my precious time
extracting it.*

Yeah, her, I thought to myself.

***

Later in evening, my mother was transferred from
the ER to a hospital room. She was awaiting final
clearance for surgery the next day, as Woody Allen
had been scheduled to siphon the strange fluid out
of her. After my mother was settled in a room,
chatting to one of the nurses, I explained that the
doctor had been a little gruff with me, and the nurse
informed me that although he was known around
the hospital to not always have the best bedside
manner, he was extremely talented.

"Oh," I said.

"He's a good doctor," the nurse told me.

"That's good," I said.

My brother Mike had driven down to the
hospital from Manhattan after work, and my sister
was now back home with her kids. Our oldest
brother, Anthony, was in Pennsylvania, unable to
get off of work. I kept trying to rehash the day with
Mike, trying desperately to get him to laugh with
me about my thinking that the nun was giving our
mother last rites, hahahahahaha. But he was not
laughing with me. I knew that my brother could be
very distracted, constantly looking at his watch,
moving far away from the present moment when he
felt pressured in one way or another.

We made sure that our mother was settled in
her room for the night. She was nestled between the
rails of a hospital bed, tethered to the oxygen tank

and medication drips, her cheeks now getting more and more rosy with color. My brother petted her head and stroked her face, coddled her in a way that was a bit awkward for a grown son, yet it was endearing. She appeared comfortable and safe in this clinical igloo; the nurses were in and out, doling out sleeping pills and tucking all of their sick babies into bed. My brother and I parted ways in the bitter cold of the darkened hospital parking lot.

"Good night, Ana," he said. "Be safe."

"Good night," I said.

He kissed me on the cheek and got into his Ford Explorer. I felt like a kid again, like back when my brother would come to Jersey on a Saturday and take me out for pizza and a movie. When he dropped me back off at my dad's, I would feel so alone again. I got into the Civic, and as it warmed up, I shivered from the cold, remembering all the winter nights that I had left a friend's house, maybe a boyfriend's place, late at night and driven the dark Jersey roads alone. And then I pulled onto the four-lane road that would lead me to another night in another one of those strange and sterile hotel rooms.

***

It was late morning, and my sister and I were back at the hospital, waiting for our mother to get out of surgery. We were sharing an uncomfortable couch and watching shitty daytime television in a small bright waiting room. A few nurses and family members shuffled in and out, but mostly it was just my sister and me and our rattled nerves.

After what felt like ten hours but was probably about an hour, a young nurse walked into the waiting room. We'd met her a few times before; she knew my mother from radiation, and they had a nice rapport. This nurse usually came off as silly and fun, often joking with my mother.

"You two have to come with me," the nurse said in a serious tone. "And please take all of your things."

"Okay," I said, starting to shake.

A wave of electricity ripped through my body. This was going to be one of those waiting-room scenes. It was obvious that my mother's heart could not handle the invasive surgery. In a matter of minutes, someone would say, "There was nothing else we could do to save her." And then the nurse saw my facial expression, and she read my sister's body language.

"Oh, no, girls!" she said. "Your mother is fine."

"Really?" I asked.

"Yes, she's just being moved to another part of the hospital, and I need to take you there."

"Holy shit," I said.

"Oh my God," my sister said.

We quickly gathered our purses and coats, and we were led out of the waiting room. And then out of the corner of my eye, I saw my mother being wheeled away on a gurney. I could see a lump of a person and a few bleach-white sheets, and there was my mother's black head of hair. We did not make eye contact, but I knew that it was my mother. I didn't say anything to my sister. And next to my mother, tucked into the bleached-white sheets like a newborn baby, was a large clear glass jar containing the cranberry juice–like fluid that had been extracted from around my mother's heart. I gasped.

"What's wrong, Ana?" my sister asked.

"Oh, nothing," I said as I watched my mother and the jar being loaded into a large elevator.

***

When my three siblings and I exited through the glass hospital doors, leaving behind the stale air and the smells and the sounds of human suffering, we were thrust into the middle of a clear bright winter afternoon. I looked up at the open blue skies and took a long deep breath. I was carried far back to my Jersey youth when the sharp bite of winter would force me to be fully present to the environment around me. Remembering walking home alone from school, trying to balance on thin sheets of ice beneath my feet, and letting myself into my apartment, I wrapped my gray woolen scarf tight around my face and neck and pulled my brown knit hat over my ears. And as I walked alongside my three much-older siblings through the busy hospital parking lot, cars circling anxiously to find spots, I thought about what it could have been like had I never moved west. But I had left and taken up with a man who had grown roots in Oregon. And now in a lot of ways, my two brothers and my sister did not really know me, and I did not really know them because years had passed since we had spent this kind of intimate time together.

While our mother convalesced post-op in a quiet sunny room, we took a short reprieve from the hospital and from the fears. The past few days had us all reeling. We could have lost our mother. It really did feel like she had come close to the end. The radiation treatments had burned a hole in the sack around her heart, and she had been drowning in the fluid that developed there, a nurse had explained to us after our mother was taken to a recovery room. It would be a while before she could resume cancer treatment, we had been told. She might not be back on her feet for a while, the nurse had said. Now we were in my brother Mike's car, heading to a nearby diner for lunch. Mike was driving, my brother Anthony was in the front passenger seat, and my sister, Dani, and I were sitting in the back. I felt nervous and agitated about being in this contained space with my siblings, as I was simply not used to us all being together like this. I leaned toward the front seat.

"Hey, so when do you think was the last time the four of us were all in a car together?" I asked my brothers.

"Oh my God," my brother Mike said. "It was probably some time in the late seventies, when Dad would drive us all out to Brooklyn to have Sunday supper at Grandma's."

"You're probably right, Mike," Anthony said.

"It was definitely back when Mom and Dad were still together," Mike said.

"That's crazy," I said.

"Jesus, I know," Anthony said, blowing out his breath.

"I can't believe it," our sister said. "You're right, Mike."

We drove the rest of the way to the diner with

my brothers chatting in the front. My sister rested her head on the window with her eyes closed.

I don't remember too many of those car trips, all six of us together as we drove out to Brooklyn to see my dad's large extended family or up to Connecticut to visit with mother's sister and her family. But I do remember the way it felt for my immediate family to be together in a car, our two parents and us four kids.

Our father would be at the wheel, casually whistling and snapping his fingers to jazz music and not paying much attention to the road. He has always been a terrible driver, distracted and swerving and without much sense of direction. Our mother would be in the passenger seat with her right hand grasping the overhead handle, a nervous wreck about being on time and prattling on about the tray of lasagna that was bouncing up and down in the trunk. I do remember sitting on my brother Mike's lap in the middle of the expansive backseat of our seventies-era Ford LTD, Anthony and Dani flanking us on either side.

Every once in a while, everyone would erupt with laughter over something that was way over my head, or there would be a loud argument over directions and which way to turn.

"Go *that* way," our mother would tell our father.

"Which way is *that* way, Tess?" my father would snap back.

I do remember what it felt like to finally arrive at one of our relatives' houses, the six of us spilling out of the car and into warm houses that smelled of huge pots of what my family called gravy, a thick red pasta sauce made with various kinds of meats, that had been on the stove since early morning. "Here Ana, have a meatball," my grandma Nora, my father's mother, would say. "You need to fatten up; you're skin and bones," she would say. "Tess, does this kid even eat?" my grandmother would ask my mother. "Yeah, Mama, she eats fine," my mother would say. And then I would run off to play with my cousins in the back alleyway, long lines of laundry flapping overhead and the sounds of an inner city swirling around from all directions. But that's about all I remember, mostly just sensory memories, nothing too specific.

***

When we got to the diner, the four of us piled into a big vinyl booth by a window. We worked our way through large platters of burgers and fries and cups of acidic, weak coffee. Throughout the meal, I sensed a tension from my brother Anthony. He did not seem at ease in our company. He was the oldest and had also been the most removed from the family, even though he lived only across state lines and I lived on a different coastline. To break the tension, Mike brought up a few old memories from when they were kids in Queens, when I was still just a baby. The three of them laughed hysterically, and even though I had heard a lot of these stories before, I could not relate; the setting and the scenes were just so foreign to me, almost seeming fictionalized. They had had inner-city childhoods filled with neighbors and friends and a park up the street and stickball in the alleyway. They had had parents who were together at least until they were out of high school, and my parents had gotten divorced when I was in grade school. They were from an intact family with three kids, and I was an only child who came from a broken suburban home. They talked about the times that our parents and our aunts and uncles had all rented cabins at a resort upstate. They talked about those summers when our small country house was crammed with friends and relatives. And they didn't talk about the years after we left Queens for Jersey, because after that, they had been older and there had been no more good times.

"You really got the short end of the stick," my brother Mike told me many times. "We had so much fun when Mom and Dad were together."

When we returned to the hospital, our mother was sitting upright in bed sipping ginger ale through a straw and nibbling off a tray of food. The room was filled with sunlight, and the spirit that had been drained out of her during the past few days, when she hadn't been able breathe, when her skin had been gray, and when she had been filled with anxiety and fear, seemed to be filling her back up again. She saw us all walk in together and gave us a huge toothless smile.

"Hi, my sweethearts," she said. "I feel so much better now."

"That's great, Ma," my brother Mike said.

"Thank God," she said.

***

After this, our mother was transferred to a single room in an area of the hospital that was designated for patients who were fighting in The Cancer Wars.

When walked into her new room, I noticed that she was comfortable and relaxed and most certainly doped to the gills. The cancer wing at this hospital was quite pleasant, actually. It was dim, warmly lit. There were lots of mauves and tons of beige, plus the staff was as kind and calming as the color palette. But when I walked down the hallway and curiously peeked into the rooms, I could see that there was so much grave illness in this wing, the suffering too visible. I saw a middle-aged woman in nothing but a flimsy gown sitting up in bed, all skin and bones and a perfectly shaped bald scalp. Sitting next to her like a beloved pet was a brown-haired wig cut into a perfect bob. I saw an older gentleman making his way through a mountain of bleached-white washcloths, creating a tidy pile on his side table. When I asked a nurse later why he was folding washcloths, she told me that it helped his anxiety to create order, which meant he didn't bother them as much.

As our mother went on and off the opiate nod, my brother Mike and I sat anxiously in a room at the end of a long hall of rooms that was set aside for family to hang out in while their loved ones were very possibly dying of cancer. The Family Room, as it was called, tried desperately to mimic a den in a nice suburban house, clad with bookshelves and comfortable Shaker-style furniture and flouncy drapery. We were waiting to meet with our mother's oncologist, a stoic and inaccessible middle-aged woman who wore a wig because she too was undergoing cancer treatment. How could I not wonder if she had caught cancer from her patients? Mike and I waited for what seemed like ten hours, flipping through dated magazines, until the wig-wearing oncologist came in about forty-five minutes past our appointed time.

"I'm so sorry that I am late," she said.

"We understand," my brother said.

She sat across from my brother, opened a tattered manila folder and scanned through the contents. Without hesitation or warning, she looked up at the two of us.

"I would give your mother about six months," she told us.

Before this point, my siblings and I had pretty much been in the dark about the status of our mother's illness. We had become privy to her cancer stage (3A) and type (small-cell lung cancer, otherwise known as "the smoking kind") at initial diagnosis. But none of the health care providers had given us an actual timeline. I had done some online research, mostly when I first found out she was sick, but I had found the information too anxiety provoking and confusing, and so I had stopped.

As I listened to the muddled and drowning sounds that were coming out of the doctor as she informed my brother and me about the state of our mother's cancer, as I sat where so many scared people had sat before, on the edge of the overstuffed couch, I felt a strange sense of relief wash over me. My mother might be around for only six more months, I thought to myself. When the doctor finished her incomprehensible talk—I knew she had lost me about midway through—she asked if we had any questions. My brother and I both sighed audibly. She probably realized that we were in shock, and so she gave us a few moments. And then she told us that it might not be a bad idea for our mother to move onto the hospice floor upon release.

"They have a great massage therapist up there," she said. "It's really nice."

"Good to know," my brother said.

She handed us a brochure before shaking our hands and breezing out of The Family Room.

After the doctor was gone, my brother and I didn't break into tears. I leaned back and let my body relax into the shitty couch, while he checked his phone for work messages. There was an inevitable end to the suffering, and as much as we wanted our mother to be a little too fat and annoying again, we knew somewhere deep down that she was a very sick woman who had been enduring a tremendous amount of pain. A part of me believed that our mother had also been in the dark about her illness. The topic had never been broached between us, not yet at least. And so my brother and I made a pact to not relay the prognosis to our mother after our meeting in The Family Room.

"Yeah, fuck telling Mom," my brother said. "It's just a number."

"She's better off not knowing," I said.

SIX

During one afternoon, while my mother was still on the cancer floor, I sat by the window reading a book while she slept a deep opiate sleep. She had become incontinent since the surgery and now had to wear adult diapers at all times. There had been a period of resistance at first, when she would coerce my sister to help her to the toilet if the nurse's aides were not available. But once it was deemed that it was unsafe, that someone could fall and get really hurt, that my sister was not trained to support that kind of weight, our mother had given in. Now caregivers came in to change her diapers regularly.

It was hard for me to witness my mother in such a raw, vulnerable, exposed state. The intimacy frightened me. I hadn't seen intimate parts of her body in many, many years. When I had lived with her as a kid and a teenager, she hadn't had a bedroom of her own, and so she would often change in the hallway near the bathroom. Her big walk-in closet was down there, and sometimes I would be going into my room, and I would catch a glimpse of her in a large beige bra and a silky, skirtlike slip. I knew that it made her just as uncomfortable as it made me, and she made sure to keep herself covered up most of the time that we lived together. But now that she was so physically sick and had lost most of her autonomy, now that she had given in to allowing strangers to take care of her personal needs, this exposure had bled over onto her adult children. There had been times that my brother Mike had

had to set her down on the toilet. So many times my sister had lifted nightgowns over our mother's head, unlatched her bra straps, taken down her knee-high panty hose, even cleaned her up after a bathroom accident.

So as I was reading, the steamy heater clicking away in the background, my mother woke up from an opiate nap. After a few moments, she sat up in bed. Her hospital gown was fully open in the back; it was only covering her breasts really, and they were clearly visible under her armpits. I saw so much of her skin, and I realized how much weight she had actually lost in the past few weeks. And for the first time in my life, I noticed the actual shape of my mother's figure.

"Your mother knocked me out," my father had once said about my mother when they first met and married. "She was so gorgeous."

As sick as she was, my mother was very beautiful. It was just that she had been hidden away in emotional pain for so many years. I had never gotten to witness her true beauty until she got really sick.

"What is it, honey?" my mother asked me in a groggy voice.

She must have caught me staring at her body, so she attempted to cover herself up with a blanket.

"Nothing, Ma," I said.

"Can you go ask one of the aides to come change me?" she said.

"Sure, Ma."

My mother remained for a few weeks in the

hospital's cancer center, where she was closely monitored after her surgery. She was very well cared for not only by doctors and nurses but also by some of the most compassionate caregivers. I couldn't believe what these nurse's aides did on a daily basis. It was next-level kind and rather sobering. They tended to all her personal needs, including diaper changes. At one point, an aid noticed a drop of blood in my mother's adult diaper, which freaked me the fuck out.

"We have to call for a gynecologist," the doctor on call told me.

"Where do you think the blood came from?" I asked.

"We're not sure," he said.

It made me uncomfortable that she had to undergo such a personal exam. I wasn't sure if my mother had ever had a gynecological exam, because this was not something we discussed with one another. Of course she had, as she had given birth to five children, but the vagina was not something that my mother and I had ever talked about. I had never told her when I got my period at fourteen. I had managed pads and tampons on my own somehow just to avoid the conversation. And then I started going to Planned Parenthood for pelvic exams and birth control pills and condoms when I was sixteen, without her knowing. She may have known—maybe she saw my pills—it's just that she never broached this subject with me. And neither did my father or stepmother or older siblings for that matter. I figured things out on my own.

I never found out the source of the blood in the

adult diaper. I could have probed, but I needed to put it out of my mind. I did tell my brother about it and we both figured it was the result of internal bleeding and figured if it came up again, we'd deal with it then. We left it at that.

***

One hot late summer afternoon when I was around fifteen, my father told me that boys have a hard time when girls say no. We were rooting around in his backyard garden, surrounded by that familiar weedy smell of the tomato plants and hot composting soil. He was picking leaves of basil and putting them into a small plastic container.

"They don't want to stop once they start," he said to me.

"Okay," I said.

"You know that, right?"

"Yeah," I answered shyly.

I didn't really know what the hell he was talking about until many years later when I remembered the awkward conversation. Who knows how long it took him to muster up the courage to bring up the topic of sex to me—maybe it was impulsive. That I'll never know.

"Dad never talked to me about sex and about being a man," my brother Mike told me once.

"Really?" I asked.

"We had to figure it all out on our own," he said.

***

When my brother and I waltzed into our mother's hospital room after our meeting with the oncologist, we sat down next to her bed and, like a couple of salespeople, we gave her our spiel on the option of transferring up to the hospice floor.

"The doctor said they have a good massage therapist," I told her. "And it's more like a home environment than a hospital."

"Oh, that sounds pretty nice," she said.

"But you wouldn't be able to do any more treatments," my brother told her.

"Then no," she had said. "I'm not done."

And so that was the end of the hospice floor. When I left the hospital that day, once I was in the safe bubble of the Civic, I was finally able to begin processing the conversation that my brother Mike and I had had with the wigged oncologist. Before I drove off to my hotel, I found a mixed CD my husband had made a few years before when we drove from Portland to San Francisco on the 101, before we were married. It reminded me of the time when I was still new to Portland and, had just gotten together with Drew. We would just drive around, exploring that gloomy, not-much-going-on city, not giving much of a shit about anything but a few killer thrift store finds and a strong cup of coffee. And there I was, back in Jersey, weighed down heavy by the fact that my mother would not be around too much longer.

"Holy fuck!" I yelled at the top of my lungs.

My brother and I had left that meeting in total shock that, based on the current state of her cancer, statistically speaking, our mother probably had only about six months left to live. And so when we were presented with the option, we had latched on to the idea of our mother going into hospice not because we wanted to ditch her on the side of the road but because we were so scared about her enduring more and more suffering. We knew that the idea behind hospice is all about keeping the patient as pain-free and comfortable as possible. Since our mother did not have a spouse, so much fell on her four adult children. We were responsible for her, all of us in different ways, but all of us in this together nonetheless. We also knew that Dani did not want our mother to go back to her apartment. Dani had been too scared since my mother had such a hard time breathing that night. She also wanted to protect her kids from the trauma of witnessing a terminal illness so intimately. That was her choice, and as much as it was very frustrating for my brother Mike and me, we had to accept her position and respect her feelings. And so the concept of hospice meant that our mother would be taken care of for the duration of her disease, in a homelike environment with a massage therapist on staff.

But she wasn't ready to give up the fight. And we couldn't make her go.

I knew that we had a lot to think about in terms of our mother's health and what might emerge in the upcoming months. I also knew that for the time being, she was stable and safe and clearly in super good hands. Before too long, it would be time for me to head back to Portland. I needed to chill at my house, and I needed to spend some time with my husband. We were still in the process of trying to start a family.

"Do you think it's a good time with my mom sick?" I had asked a friend.

"I think it's the perfect time," she had told me.

***

My life in Oregon is nothing like my life in Jersey. It never has been. Since I moved west, I have become two people, split between opposing coastlines, like the left and right hemispheres of a brain. My friends in Portland do not know me like my friends back in Jersey or Brooklyn know me. "They are my people," I say, referring to the friends I grew up with or came of age alongside. When I am in Portland, I wear a mask, and beneath that shield is the kid who first grew up in Queens and then moved out to Jersey. And the person I am now married to knows only the masked woman, the one who simply grew up back east, has a certain outward personality and nothing more. He knows only the masked woman because he doesn't want anything to do with the person underneath. It's not because he doesn't care; it's just that it would be too hard for him, maybe because he cares too much.

I was home again, hidden away in my safe bungalow, protected from the cold rains with my husband, Drew, nestled at my side on the couch. On a good day, he would ask me how I was doing even though he didn't really want to know how I was doing because he knew that I was falling to pieces. Now that I was here and not in Jersey, I could hide. And I did hide, because if I took off the mask, I would be exposed in ways that I was not ready for. Thoughts about my mother, the dire state of her health, my conflicted feelings about how she had raised me and how she had neglected herself, swirled through my head. I kept them hidden from view.

"I would give your mother about six months," the oncologist had said. And then she had breezed out of the room, her wig still as a stone, not moving like natural hair moves. This image stayed with me as I sipped wine with my husband, as we smoked weed and biked around, as we spent countless hours in bed. Even though the reasoning part of my intellect knew that my mother might not be around to meet my child, my body still wanted to make a baby.

"We're not *not* trying," I told the gynecologist at my annual checkup.

A somewhat curious and sometimes personal but firm bleach-blond woman in her midforties with two young kids of her own, she always asked if I was thinking of having a baby. I was now in my early thirties, inching closer and closer to the age when it gets harder to conceive, when it becomes riskier to carry a child. She asked how I was doing.

"I'm decent," I said. "I've been traveling a lot to the East Coast."

"For work?" she asked.

"This will be a little cold," she told me, and then in went the plastic speculum. My breath went shallow.

"My mother has cancer," I said, the words hardly able to exit, as I was cringing in discomfort.

"Oh," she said.

She inserted a swab into my vagina. Her bright blue eyes met mine, and she said, "That must be hard."

I remained silent until she finished the exam.

"Okay, Ana," she said, snapping off the latex gloves. "We're all done here."

After I dressed and left the treatment room, I passed by the doctor's office. Her desk was a chaotic mess of thick manila folders and loose papers and shiny drug brochures. She was holding a sturdy ceramic coffee cup with "Zoloft" printed in white type. She took a sip from it.

"Good luck with everything," she told me.

"Thank you," I said.

***

For the next couple of weeks, I did what I could to lead a semi-normal life. When friends asked how things were going with my mother, I gave them empty answers. "Oh, you know," I said. "We're just hoping for the best," I told them. Nobody pried too hard. Everything was glazed with a thin layer of weed and red wine, a carry-over habit that had formed when I was living in Amsterdam and working under stressful conditions. I checked on my mother a few times a day, either making direct contact on her hospital extension or liaising through my siblings.

"How's Ma today?" I asked my brother Mike over the phone.

"She's pretty good," he told me.

"They're talking about releasing her soon," he said.

"Where do you think she'll go?" I asked.

"I have no idea, because Dani doesn't want her

back home," he told me. "And I don't think she'll be able to be on her own, for a while anyway, because she's still very weak."

***

When it seemed that I might be needed, that there was a transition about to occur, I made plans to head back to the East Coast. The travel was starting to wear me down, my checking account dwindling. But I knew that this was something that I needed to do. Something about putting in the effort was healing, an indirect way of showing my mother that I did really care for her, that I might actually be capable of loving her, that I might be able to forgive her. I could tell that my siblings and my mother found me cold at times, a stoic. I knew that I was judged for this.

But I also knew that this was my protection, something I had learned at an early age. How to tuck my emotions away into a locked cage. I had learned to task and busy my way out of difficult feelings. "You're strong," my mother told me. "My Ana has a notebook," she said. And so I knew she appreciated what I had to offer, while my siblings were able to coddle and comfort her. After all, a much different mother had raised them.

When I landed in Newark, it was a mild, early spring afternoon. It was such a relief that the bitter winter cold had passed since my last visit. Those long, dark, cold months when my mother's health had been so grave, her life so fragile. I gathered myself and then made my way to Central Jersey on a bright, mostly empty commuter train. It was not yet rush hour, so it was mainly moms with young kids, some students, and a few other airport people. By the time I had taken a window seat and mentally settled into being there again—in that glowing yellow sunlight, the urban then turning-suburban landscapes—the outside world had become a familiar late-day blueness that had saddened me as a kid. I thought about my mother huffing and puffing up the stairs and finally making it into our apartment in the evening hours after a long day at work, too tired to parent me even though I had so many needs. I rested my head on the window, people chatting around me, and let the train lull me into a deep sleep, a quiet respite until I was thrust into my sister's apartment, the kids, the stress, the unknowns.

After convalescing in the cancer wing of the hospital—a slow recovery from the delicate surgery that had extracted a large glass jar worth of red fluid from the sack around her heart—my mother had been deemed not physically strong enough to return home. Upon release from the hospital, she had been transferred via ambulance to a rehabilitation facility outside of Princeton. After a half-assed attempt at sleep on my sister's couch, I spent the following day with my mother, cruising around rehab, sipping on kombucha tea, and getting the lay of the land.

She was up and running to some degree, getting closer and closer to becoming capable of taking care of herself again. Before she could be released, the caregivers told me, my mother needed to obtain muscular strength in her arms and legs, something she had lost because the radiation had basically zapped it out of her.

At her daily physical therapy session, I watched as my mother got up and down from a low vinyl-covered padded table, something that the physical therapist thought was a tremendous feat, so much so that there was a little clapping. The fanfare seemed a bit patronizing to me—this was a seventy-one-year-old woman and not a child—but I played along because my mother seemed to be enjoying the attention.

I watched as my mother methodically placed forks and knives and wooden spoons and spatulas into the drawers of a mock kitchen, pots and pans and stacking mixing bowls into a mock pantry. This was part of the therapy process, so she could redevelop dexterity in life's simple tasks. She had clearly never been one for domesticity, my mother, so this was the one time in my life that I had witnessed her being orderly around the kitchen. I found it fulfilling. I got a sense that she too found it satisfying and not demeaning at all. I thought about all those years when our apartment had been dirty and disorderly, and now suddenly everything seemed to have a place.

It was bright and sunny in this corner of physical therapy, an expansive and airy gym-like room that seemed far away from the sick and the sad, even if it was just down the hall. There was a strong positive energy within the space, most especially for me since my mother was back on her feet, no longer horizontal and super sick like she had been a month prior. We stood shoulder to shoulder for the first time in a long time. As I observed and coached her in her kitchen duties, she continued to put things where they belonged, and again, received praise from the staff.

"Tessa, you are doing such a wonderful job!" a therapist cheered from the other side of the room.

I could tell that she really liked these people, that she felt safe, seen. Something about having the physical strength to perform these otherwise simple tasks, to have purpose, to do things right in my presence, provided my mother with tremendous joy.

"Ma, why do you always put the dishes away all messed up?" I used to ask her when I would try to find a bowl for cereal.

"Oh, it doesn't matter, honey," she would answer.

"But I can't find anything," I would tell her.

"Stop it now, Ana," she would say, plopping down on the couch and lighting a cigarette.

***

There was a lot to consider at this juncture, most especially whether she would truly be able to continue with the next course of cancer treatments.

"I wanna do chemo," she kept saying.

"You sure, Ma? You sure you're up for it?" I kept asking.

"Yup," she kept saying.

We needed to consider where the best place for her to live would be moving forward. And so as a family, we needed to formulate an alternate housing plan on the quick. We had also just gotten word that our mother's insurance company was about to stop paying for rehab. And they might or might not contribute to an assisted living arrangement, the billing coordinator had recently told my brother.

"What if we get a nurse to come in every day?" I had asked my sister, thinking my brother Mike and I might be able to kick in for a home health aide.

"I just can't do it," my sister had told me.

What I was hearing was pure fear. What I was hearing was, I just can't do it again—not after that episode where Ma couldn't breathe in the middle of the night. As hard as it was, I forced myself to understand.

***

When physical therapy ended, my mother made sure to thank the physical therapists for that day's session. There were four working the afternoon shift, and they were all young and fit underneath their scrubs.

"Go get some rest, Tessa," a young woman told my mother in a strong Philly accent. "So you have energy for tomorrow."

"Okay, dear," my mother said.

The woman helped my mother into her wheelchair, and I escorted her down a long corridor and waited as she settled herself in a chair in her room. When I put out my arm to help her, she shooed me away. Then she grabbed a cane that she had hooked on the back of the wheelchair and hoisted herself up.

"I need to learn again," she told me.

By the time she plopped down into the chair in the corner of her room, she was out of breath and her face was flush.

"You okay, Ma?" I asked.

"Yeah, honey, I'm fine."

My mother was sharing a pleasant, well-appointed salmon-colored room with an elderly woman who was asleep behind a thin curtain.

"Don't worry; she won't hear us," she told me. "She's very nice. And she doesn't say much."

My sister had decorated my mother's half of the room with framed family photographs and a few pieces of owl artwork from my mother's room at their apartment.

"It's pretty nice in here," I said as I looked at my mother's familiar artifacts.

"I don't mind it at all," she said. "The people here are good to me."

I booked myself into another sale hotel. I stayed at my sister's the previous night, but had found that it rattled my nerves too hard. And before I was completely out of the room, I turned back towards my mother. She was sitting upright and seemed calm, contented.

"Where do you want to be, Ma?" I asked her.

"What do you mean, honey?" she asked, looking up from her magazine.

"When you're done here. When the insurance runs out," I said. "They say you might only have another week or so left at the most."

"I want to be home," she told me. "I want to be with family."

***

Outside it was a mild, drizzly spring evening. I

drove about twenty minutes along once-rural Central Jersey back roads, passing Victorian homes built well over a hundred years ago, probably once farmhouses. I thought about the families who were inside making dinner, kids doing homework at big wooden tables, plates with crumbs and empty milk glasses at their sides, the smell of fresh laundry being dried coming from the basements.

I thought about what my mother had said to me—that she wanted to be home, that she wanted to be with family. I thought about how many times as a kid I had passed big, warmly lit homes and dreamt about what it would have been like had we had one of those and not an apartment that was rotting at the seams. And now, as I passed these beautiful, well-kept homes and thought about my mother wanting to be home with family, I wished that I could provide that for her, even though I knew she hadn't done a good job providing that for me.

I got into my car that was stored at my sister's apartment since my last visit and I pulled into a Walgreens about a mile up the road. I felt like I was doing something risky, something sneaky. I felt like a teenager about to buy condoms or cough syrup to get high. As I wandered down the bright florescent aisles, I was on edge, because my sister was always at Walgreens buying over-the-counter this and that, filling prescriptions. I was nervous that she could whisk by at any moment with a little white bag in hand. I was nervous because I was there to buy a pregnancy test. My period was at least a week late now. For the past couple of days, every time I wiped after peeing, I had looked to see if there was blood on the toilet paper and there hadn't been. Back in Portland, before I came out here, I had noticed some light spotting in my underwear. When I went online to research it, I had read that small spots of blood could be an indication that fertilization had occurred.

"When I got pregnant, I bled like when I first got my period," one of my friends had told me recently. "It was like coffee grounds."

Another friend had told me that she had thought she had her period and had used pads for a day or two until she realized that the flow was so light and then realized she was actually pregnant.

Not even discriminating between brands or prices, I quickly grabbed a pregnancy test kit from a top shelf, nervously knocking a few down and then having to put them back. Luckily, nobody was in that aisle, but I thought some weirdo manager was probably watching me in the concave mirror on the ceiling. I rushed to check out at the register. There were two parties ahead of me in line, a tired-looking mom with two whiny kids buying cigarettes and formula and an elderly woman with a shaky handful of coupons. Feeling like I would never get out of there, I tucked the pregnancy test under my armpit, so nobody would notice my purchase. The florescent lights buzzed, and the background music hummed.

When I finally reached the counter, I did my best to avoid making eye contact with the middle-aged woman who was ringing me up. I bet she knows my sister, I thought to myself. They are around the same age, I thought. She placed the skinny box in a small plastic bag.

"No bag, thanks," I said and took the kit out of the bag and put it into my purse. I thought about how many times a day these people had to deal with these super-awkward, life-changing purchases.

"Thank you, though," I said as I handed her the small plastic bag to reuse.

"Okay, fine" she said, giving me a crooked look.

When I finally left the store, it was raining pretty hard, so I ran through the darkened parking lot and jumped into the car.

"Fuck," I said aloud, as if I had escaped out from under something.

"Fuck, fuck, fuck!" I yelled.

I took the pregnancy test out of my purse and put it in my glove compartment. I got to Dani's apartment, and she and her two kids seemed to be in good spirits.

"How was Ma today?" Dani asked as she finished putting dinner on the table.

"She likes it over there," I said. "I think she's doing really well."

"That's so great," she said.

We ate pasta with meat sauce and Caesar salad at the table in the living room, the TV blaring in the background. While Dani and the kids joked around with one another, I considered talking to my sister about our mother wanting to come back here after she was done with physical therapy. They seemed too distracted. I helped my sister with the dinner dishes and told my family that I would see them tomorrow.

***

After I checked in at the hotel, I wandered through the dated lobby and let myself into my room. It smelled like an unwelcoming combination of cleaning solution and cigars. I welled with emotion thinking about how I wanted nothing more than to be back at my cozy house in Portland, sipping hot tea with my husband at our wooden kitchen table. Although we didn't talk much about it, Drew and I were both fully aware of the fact that we were trying to start a family. Yet we had not broached the subject of my mother being very sick and possibly close to the end of her life. We hadn't ever talked about the fact that I might be under extreme stress if I were to get pregnant. I felt like I had waited decades for Drew to come around to the idea of a baby, and even thought it had only been a few years, he was finally up for the task of baby making. I was not about to allow him to revert back to going totally silent when I brought it up.

Ever since we had first gotten together as a couple, I had wanted a child with Drew. But even though I craved it from the inside of my being, Drew wasn't near ready. "Not yet," he would say. "Maybe someday," he would tell me. Now I went into the bathroom, ripped open the pregnancy test box, tore open the wrapping, and peed on the stick. I stood there hovering over the toilet, and double lines appeared within seconds. I couldn't stop looking at the stick.

***

I stripped out of my clothes and stood under the hot shower, glaring at the dated mustard-yellow tiles around the tub. I was reminded of the yellow tiles in the bathroom at my father and stepmother's house. I thought about all of the baths that I had taken in there as a kid, during that year when my mother was crazed and manic with something I could not understand at the time. All I had known was that it made me feel scared. I thought about all of the times I hid away in that bathroom afterwards, the door closed, the fan spinning white noise. It was a temporary escape from my stepmother's screams and the incessant fear that I had put something away in the wrong place.

Now as I stood under the scalding hot water, I was lulled into a dreamlike state. I was no longer in the shitty bathroom at a nondescript corporate hotel. I was hovering in space, and nobody was sick, and nobody was pregnant, and I was not in New Jersey, and I was not in Portland. When I fell back into consciousness, I turned off the water and walked out of the shower, my legs scalded from the heat. I wrapped a starchy white towel around my warm body and called my husband.

"Guess what?" I said, plopping down on the bed. "I just took a pregnancy test, and it came out positive."

There was silence on the line. "Really?" he asked. "I guess I'm not surprised."

More silence on the line.

"Okay," he said.

"I better go rest," I said.

"Love you," he said.

"Love you too," I said.

***

Back when I first met Drew—when I got a job at his design studio—I felt that we had known each other for many years. There was something strangely familiar about his way of being in the world, how he carried himself, his general demeanor. "He's got a bad case of the mellows," one of his good friends from college told me once. "Drew is so gentle," my mother always said.

Like me, Drew grew up pretty raw. He was raised by a stern single father in Southern California, in a town that he found not only dull and uninspiring but in a cultural environment where he felt isolated for being creative and different. His mother had come to America from Germany in her twenties when she had met and married Drew's dad, who was stationed there when he was in the military.

But after a few years of being in America, she had decided to return to Germany. She stayed there for a few years and then settled down in San Francisco where she still lives. She didn't want to raise her kids, but she has always been their mother. They visited her on holiday breaks and in summer.

Whereas I ran toward the pain and wanted to deconstruct and disseminate and comprehend, Drew went in the complete opposite direction. It was too hard for him. And now that he was maybe about to have a child of his own, all he could say was that he was not surprised. To become invested emotionally would have put him at too much risk. And so as I sat staring at the double lines, wrapped in a starchy towel on a hotel bed in Central Jersey, ensconced in a moment that I had been wanting to happen for many years, I wished Drew could at least be there to hold me. Of course I am alone, I thought to myself. And when I thought about Drew's understated reaction, I thought of my father, who also had such a hard time confronting the difficult stuff.

When my stepmother would get upset with me, when she would yell at me, he would say, "She doesn't mean anything by it."

So as hard as it was sometimes with Drew, most especially during those crucial moments when all I wanted was to be heard, to be noticed, it was familiar.

***

I dressed in drawstring pants and a tank top and crawled into bed. But I was suddenly overcome with a deep hunger. Something about finding out that I was pregnant. Something about the fact that, though my body already knew, now my mind knew that I was pregnant—it was time to eat. But there wasn't any room service at that late hour. I could have driven to an all-night diner, but I was too exhausted. So I put on shoes and wandered through the endless carpeted corridors in my comfy clothes until I reached a bright wall of buzzing vending machines. I wanted a real meal, a burger and fries, grilled cheese with tomato, but I knew that I had no choice but to put a few singles into the machine and extract a bag or two of emptiness.

When I got back to my room, I turned on the TV and crawled back into bed with pretzels and crackers and a can of ginger ale. I pretended that I was a kid again, that I was home sick from school.

***

It was morning, and I was in bed, falling in and out of sleep, the TV on low in the background. "It's company," my sister always said when I asked why the TV was always on in her living room. Both my mother and my sister fell asleep with the TV on. When they came out to visit me at my home in Portland, the biggest source of anxiety had been that we didn't have televisions in the bedrooms, that we didn't have cable, how were they going to sleep? "Bring some books and magazines," I told them. Now that I had been staying alone at these hotels, I too found the television comforting, even if I was not fully engaged in a program or movie. Most especially the morning shows. Something about the well-manicured, energetic hosts and the camera shots of the screaming out-of-town people holding up signs made me feel warm inside, nostalgic for the time before I moved out west away from my family.

When I lived at my mom's as an adult and commuted into the city, I would wake up to the sound of these morning shows in the background. My mom and I would be getting ready to go to our respective jobs. She would be posted up at her lighted makeup mirror in the kitchen, with bottles of drippy liquid foundation and crumbling eye shadows and lumpy mascara on the table. I would be trying to scrape up a decent outfit to wear to work in the city, so I could at least look semiprofessional.

"You should wear a little *lipshtick*," my mother

would say to me in a funny voice.

"Leave me alone, Ma," I would say.

She was still relatively healthy then and working full-time, and because I had money of my own, there wasn't this added pressure to support me. I supported myself. That was a good time. And there had seemed to be good things ahead of me in life. We had started our days with drip coffee and morning shows.

***

My brother Mike called to tell me that he was driving down to Jersey from the city. I let out a breath of relief.

"I'm not busy at work today, so I want to go see Ma," he told me.

I was overjoyed. I got dressed and he picked me up about an hour later. I knew that I would not tell anyone that I was pregnant, not for a while, not until I saw my doctor back in Portland. I knew that I could miscarry. I knew that a lot of women did, that it was something that caused extra grief when they had already told people. "It's a secret society," a friend had told me after she miscarried. "People don't like to talk about it. And it's really fucking hard."

We stocked up on supplies at a strip-mall deli—coffee, sandwiches, soda, chips, small cakes wrapped in plastic. My brother Mike has been obese most of his life and tends to overbuy and over consume food. Because I can see how it affects him, there are times that I give him shit, but mostly I just leave him alone because he can get defensive. My sister, too. "Do you really need that?" I'll ask my brother or sister as they go for a second piece of cake. "You don't need that much butter," I'll say to one of them as they spread a thick layer onto Italian bread. "Maybe try dipping it in a little olive oil," I'll say. They call me The Food Nazi. "Watch out, The Food Nazi is coming!" I hear as I round a corner at a big family gathering, huge steaming trays of eggplant Parmesan and baked ziti and breaded chicken cutlets spread out on a folding table. I can tell that it's a deep-rooted issue for them and that there's a lot of emotion and feelings around food and eating.

We all have it in a way, and I believe that part of it is cultural, us being full-blooded Italian American, food being such a crucial part of our lives. The other part is that it's a way to stuff down the pain, the traumas, the hard stuff. Our brother Anthony and I are slim and fit and super-cautious about our eating habits, more like our father, while Mike and Dani are bigger bodied and tend to eat emotionally like our mother.

When we got to her room, Mike and I found our mother in good spirits. Her eyes were bright, and the skin on her face was rosy.

"Ma, you have such good color!" my brother said as he kissed her on the cheek.

"Thanks, honey," she said endearingly.

"I feel good today," she told us, as I kissed her on the cheek.

"Hi, my baby," she said. "Did you sleep good?"

"Yeah, Ma," I said, fearing that she knew that I was pregnant.

***

Our mother appeared to be the strongest she'd been since she had gotten hit with her cancer tumor diagnosis. Since she had started fighting in The Cancer Wars. She was sitting up in a chair with her glasses perched on the end of her nose, a scrap of paper and a pen and a tattered catalog on a side table. Her elderly roommate was on the other side of the room, again hidden behind nothing but a thin curtain. My brother gestured to that side of the room, as if saying, There's somebody here; should we be quiet?

"She just sleeps," our mother told us. "Don't pay attention."

My brother and I laughed.

"What?" our mother asked.

"You're funny, Ma," my brother said, as we unpacked the deli treats and put them onto a small laminate side table.

"Oh goodie," our mother said.

I grabbed two more chairs and put them around this makeshift dining table, creating three place settings out of plastic utensils and small white paper napkins. It was like we were picnicking.

"This is so fun!" our mother said.

"You don't get out much, huh?" my brother asked jokingly.

"Yeah, not so much," our mother answered. "But I am almost ready."

We peeled back the plastic tabs on our coffees, and my brother and I broached the subject of where she would go after she was done with her physical therapy.

"So, Ma," I said. "It doesn't seem like Dani feels comfortable having you go back to the apartment."

My mother looked at me.

"She thinks it will be too hard on the kids," I told her.

I saw my brother squirm in his chair.

"Ma, we just want to make sure you are well taken care of," he said.

And then our mother causally told us that she had heard from some internal sources that there was a really nice assisted living wing right next to this rehab facility.

"Maybe I can go there until I get better," she said.

It was clear to my brother and me that she had been giving this some thought. We unwrapped our sandwiches. My brother ripped open a small bag of Lay's potato chips and spilled the contents onto a piece of white butcher paper from the sandwiches. He and our mother started chomping away at the chips while I nibbled on a pickle.

After we cleared up from lunch, my brother and I decided to talk to some of the nurses down the hall, who helped us make arrangements to tour the assisted living wing.

"You wanna come, Ma?" my brother asked.

"No, honey, you two go," she said. "I trust you both."

"You sure, Ma?" I asked.

"Aunt Joanie is supposed to call in a little while, so I want to be here."

We left her to yack on the phone with her sister

while nursing a cold cup of coffee, like she always had. The only things missing were a soft pack of Benson & Hedges 100s and an overflowing ashtray.

***

After checking in at the front desk, Mike and I were led up a wide, winding staircase by a balding middle-aged man in brown slacks and a white button-down. Something about this man made me feel like he hated his job. As we walked behind him up the stairs, my brother turned to me and gave me a look that said, What's up with this guy? I smirked and shook my head as if I had no idea. The manager led us down a heavily carpeted hallway and to an empty studio apartment.

"This is the only available apartment right now," he told us.

"Oh, okay," I said.

"But that could change at any point, he said.

I took that to mean that someone could die soon, and then another apartment would be made available. That idea freaked me out a bit. While the manager and my brother went inside to look at the apartment, I hovered for a bit in the hallway.

"I'm gonna take a look around out here," I said to my brother.

"Okay, Ana," he said.

I walked up and down the long, wide corridor, passing the numbered rooms on both sides, passing a few small seating areas and into a larger seating area with four chairs around a large round table, two loveseats, and a few overstuffed chairs scattered around the room. Another one of those family rooms, I said to myself, remembering meeting with the oncologist not so long before. I peered down the dramatic winding staircase, and all I saw for miles was busy wallpaper and bright red carpeting and shiny dark wood furniture. I saw a lot of flouncy drapery, and I saw a lot of fluffy upholstered furniture. There was this fancy facade, like this was some kind of fantasy palace for the sick and the elderly.

This was the kind of place where you might be able to forget the truth for a minute, the truth of how life is just so fragile. I immediately saw through the bullshit filters, saw how illness and old age had clearly become a commodity in our country for those who could afford to throw down for protection with amenities. How desperate and vulnerable we could become.

When I walked back down the hallway and into the apartment, my brother and the manager were talking money and timing details. I looked around and found the apartment to be something like a nicely appointed single college dorm room, but with a spacious private bath.

"It's not bad at all," I said to my brother, as I peered out a large window, which overlooked a nice wooded area.

I thought about how our mother had lived for so many years in squalor, of course during the first part of her life in the Bronx and then all those years after she left our father and before she moved in with my sister. Something about this ridiculous place made me feel like she deserved it. All those years of her struggling financially, the past months of physical suffering, and now she was heading into who knew how long she had left to live—it made me think this was the least we could do.

My brother Mike couldn't provide a home for her all the way out in Queens—it was too far from all of her doctors. Our brother Anthony had no space in his already-cramped town house in Pennsylvania that he shared with his wife and two kids. My sister was not emotionally strong enough to handle what lay ahead, felt protective of her children, and had already done her share of housing our mother for the past seven not-so-easy years. And me, I was all the way out in Oregon. I'd thought about hauling my mother out there, thought about how I had a lovely home, how we had amazing alternative medicine options and decent allopathic health care, but I couldn't take her away from her other three children, her grandchildren, and her sister. That would have been awful. This was the least we could do, I thought. Let her live in a palace like a sick princess.

"We'll take it," my brother said.

"Great, I'll draw up the lease terms," the manager guy said in a flat, unenthusiastic tone.

He shook hands with my brother and then waved good-bye to me before descending the long dramatic staircase and then finally disappearing like magic.

"What's up with that guy?" I said to my brother.

"Who the hell knows, Ana," he said. "The guy probably hates his job."

"You think?"

"Would you want to do his job?" he asked. "It's

like the roach motel. You check in and you don't check out."

We wandered around the small studio apartment.

"But Mom said that she wanted to be home with family," I told my brother.

"I know, Ana," he said. "I wish Dani would have her back there. But it's not gonna happen, so this is the best we can do."

"I wish she could just go back there."

"Listen, we'll set her up nice," he told me. "There are people here who can take good care of her when she needs help. She can go down to the dining room for all her meals, and she can even go back to bingo."

"They have bingo?" I asked.

"Of course they have bingo."

***

When we got back to our mother's room, she was sitting up in bed wearing a housedress and snacking on potato chips leftover from lunch. A can of ginger ale with a straw sat on a side table. It was like the past few months had never happened. I don't know how many times over the years I had found my mother in a housedress eating potato chips and sipping soda in bed, crumbs and grease down her front.

"Ma, we got you a beautiful apartment in the assisted living wing," Mike told our mother. "You're gonna love it!"

"Oh yeah?" she asked. "That's wonderful, sweetheart."

I had a strong sense that my mother was conflicted and that my brother thought our problem was solved. I could tell that she would have much rather gone home to my sister's, and I also knew that my brother tends to rush through things, that he often ignores what is below the surface of things.

"You sure this is okay, Ma?" I asked her. "Do you want to see the apartment?"

"No, honey, it's fine. I trust you," she said.

"It's very bright. Lots of natural light. And there's a big window that overlooks the woods," I said.

"That sounds so lovely," she said.

"You need anything, Ma? Ana and I are gonna take off," my brother said.

"I'm fine," she said.

"You sure, Ma?" my brother asked.

"Yeah, sweetheart, I'm fine," she said. "But when are you gonna tell Dani?"

"I'll call Dani on the way home," my brother said.

We said good-bye to our mother and planned to catch up about details the next day. I was planning to spend a few nights in North Jersey at my dad and stepmother's house before I returned to Oregon.

As I drove up the turnpike north, I remembered that I was pregnant. It was as if I had forgotten. Holy shit, I thought. Is this real? It might be and it might not be, I thought. And then I thought about how my mother would soon be living alone in that clean, bright studio apartment, how there were caregivers on site, three hot meals daily, a housecleaner. She wouldn't be able to see through the fancy; she'd actually embrace the glitz. It's gonna be okay, I said to myself. She's gonna be okay, I told myself. Even though I knew her wish was to be home with family. This is the best that we can do for now, I thought. And maybe she would even get some of her strength back, so she could go back to my sister's, so she could be with family. I did some calculations in my head around how long my mother needed to live in order to meet my child. I didn't have a proper due date just yet, but I figured that she needed to live at least eight more months.

**

At my dad's house, I sat on the floor in the living room while he and my stepmother, Diane, sat in their chairs watching the news, not talking toward each other or me but at the television set. They didn't ask me too much about my mother, and I shared only a few basic facts.

"How's your mother?" my father asked.

"She's doing good right now," I said.

"That's good," he said.

"She's moving to assisted living in a few days," I said.

"I see," my stepmother said.

"Who's paying for that?" my father asked.

"Mike will," I said. "And I'll pay the utilities. We thought insurance might cover some of the rent, but they probably won't."

They turned back to their program, and I went out for a walk. As I wandered through the familiar suburban landscape, I felt a combination of repulsion and comfort. It was all so familiar. Every house, the location of every fire hydrant, the shape of each sidewalk. Not much had changed since I was a kid. I had spent so many hours riding my bike up and down these streets, through small parks and wooded areas. Either out of the joy of adventure or to escape out from under the tension that always lurked at my father's house.

***

The next morning, I left my dad and Diane to watch the news in their chairs. I went to Target and bought things for my mother's new apartment. A large box filled with some basic kitchen essentials. A small coffeemaker. A microwave egg cooker. Sheets and towels. A bath mat. Cleaning supplies, toiletries. I found a small antique kitchen table and two chairs at a thrift store. My brother would buy her a reclining chair, and she would take her bed from my sister's apartment. It felt like we were sending our mother off to college.

Everything was loaded into the hatchback of the Civic. I drove down to the assisted living palace, grabbed a set of keys from the bald manager guy, and put everything I'd bought into the studio apartment. "I'll come back again soon," I told my mother when I say good-bye to her before getting ready to head home to Portland.

She was in her usual spot, sitting in a chair in her rehab room, in a housedress and slippers with her reading glasses perched on the tip of her nose. She was picking at a tray of food.

"Don't worry, honey. You go home and rest for a while," she told me. "You've done so much," she said.

"Okay," I said and kissed her on the cheek.

"How do you feel about going to that new apartment?" I asked.

"It's going to be wonderful," she said.

SEVEN

Early spring in Portland is a sweet, sweet time. The rains that come in autumn and get heavy in winter start to let up just a little bit. But it's drizzly and wet, still keeping you safe inside. There is this positive vibration in the air, because you know that the sun might just come out to warm your skin. People at the grocery store become rather cheerful, even friendly, not as grumpy and vitamin D deprived as in the middle of winter. You start to see more of your friends, as winter hibernation requires catching up afterward. All of a sudden, there are coffee dates, dinner plans, walks around the neighborhood. When the sun does come out, even if just for a few moments, when you feel the first warmth on your skin, when you begin to notice the glorious little buds on the trees, you feel hopeful for the first time in many months.

As the outside world around me was budding and thriving, so was my own physical body. There was this small hard place in my belly, so full of potential, so full of the makings of a new kind of life, not unlike the firm pods on the lilac bush outside the French doors that led to my bedroom. But I felt stomach sick most of the day. It's not so bad, I told myself. The doctor says it will pass, I said to myself. Gentle yoga helped. Walking helped. Naps helped. Comfort food helped. I saw an acupuncturist who poked me with needles and gave me soothing herbs. Only the acupuncturist and other medical professionals knew of my condition. And my husband, Drew, of course, but he had left for a two-week rafting trip down the Colorado River with his brothers and his father. Before he left, I had asked him, "What if something happens with the baby? Will I be able to get in touch with you?" "Not really," he had said. "We're really out there. But you'll be fine," he told me.

After I got back to Portland from my last visit back east, I had gone to see my gynecologist for an exam and a blood test. "Yup, it's positive," she had said enthusiastically when she returned to the cold examination room.

I had been shivering in a thin gown, but when she gave me the news, something in me warmed, relaxed. She even gave me a due date of November 30, which fell only a few days after my own birthday.

"What if something happens?" I asked her.

"What do you mean?"

"Like, what if I miscarry?" I said.

In a very firm, matter-of-fact way, she looked at me and said, "You cannot predict that. If it happens, it happens."

"Okay," I said.

On my way home, I made an appointment with a group of nurse-midwives who worked out of my local hospital—I craved a bit more warmth and compassion. I had already had my fill of firm, emotionally disconnected doctors during the past months, and the last thing I needed was another one.

**

With Drew away on the river, being alone felt like medicine. This was the first time I had felt truly home in many months. Before I found out that my mother was sick with the cancer, I had been living overseas, working in Amsterdam. Being there had been chaotic and stressful, but also very humbling and inspiring. My heart cracks open at the thought of the North Sea evening light shining down on those beautiful crooked buildings.

"It's what inspired the Dutch masters," a friend from the ad agency told me one night when we were at a pub drinking cheap wine.

When I decided that it was best to leave Holland so I could be closer to my family—as hard as it was to leave my friends and a career—my life did not settle. I hardly had a rest. Right away, it was all about traveling back and forth between Portland and New Jersey, riding the ups and downs of my mother's illness.

So for the moment, I felt peaceful and reflective. There was a lot to think about at that juncture, a lot to consider. There was just so much to prepare for mentally and emotionally, in regard to becoming a mother as I was losing my mother. So, hovering over all of this springtime glory and these bursts of warm sun, there was a cloud of cold darkness. I sat on the couch by my front window and called to check in on my mother, who was due home from chemotherapy. After spending those weeks in rehab, building up her strength, she had gotten the green light to begin a new course of cancer treatment. "You sure you are up for this, Ma?" I had asked her many times. "I want to do chemo," she would respond. And now she seemed to be responding well to the treatments, so there was a slight glimmer of hope.

"Hi, Ma," I said. "Did you make it to chemo?"

"Yes, your brother took me," she said. "He's about to go back home to Queens."

"Oh, okay."

"How are you, honey?" she asked.

"I'm good," I said. "Do you feel sick?"

"A little nauseous," she said. "But not that bad."

I wanted to say, Me too, but I couldn't. We were both nauseous right then, and the dichotomous forces made me feel dizzy and like I might vomit.

"I'll call you later, Ma," I said.

"Okay, my baby," she said. "You all right?"

"Oh, yeah . . ." I said. "But I gotta go."

"Okay. I love you," she said.

"Okay, bye, Ma."

As I rested on the couch, breathing through deep waves of nausea, I wondered if the news of a new baby would give my mother more of a reason to fight. And then for the first time since I had learned I was pregnant, I truly felt what it might be like if my mother was not around when I became a mother. It was as if I could feel her presence and also her non-presence. There were so many times that I wished her gone. I wanted the sheer responsibility of her to go away forever. She had such a hard time taking care of herself, so much so that she had clearly been unable to take very good care of me. But I also knew that she had always loved me. And it began to set in that the love was gold. Most of the time, my mother hadn't been able to provide much else but love, and even if she was not around to be a grandmother to my child, the love that she had for me would become the love that she would have for her youngest grandchild.

I fell asleep on the couch, and when I woke up, the nausea had lifted, and the sun was shining down on my face through the window. I was comforted with the thought that whatever happened in the upcoming months would be okay.

***

Now that our mother was settled into a routine at the assisted living palace, now that she was undergoing chemotherapy treatments, there was a feeling of hope surrounding our family. My brother Mike shelled out for my mother's rent, and I managed the rest of the bills, covering anything out of pocket that my mother's meager Social Security checks did not. We had hoped that Medicaid would pay some, but it did not, and we were making it work. My sister went to see our mother almost every day, ran any necessary errands, and shopped for her and took her to chemotherapy. My brothers visited when their busy work schedules permitted. I was still in Portland and not mentioning my pregnancy to anyone, not until I reached the second trimester, when there is less of a chance of something going wrong.

Our mother seemed to be acclimating well to her new living space, making friends at the assisted living palace, going to bingo, and now going bald from chemo. But she was fully up and running again, mostly on her own, albeit always tethered to an oxygen tank and grasping a walker for support.

As much as she was still such a gravely sick woman, as much as she was almost certainly in the last part of her life on earth, it did seem as if she was in something of a recovery phase. Her mental state was good, and my siblings and I were finally relieved that our mother was getting some care other than from a hospital and other than from us. We were able to relax a bit, at least for the time being.

Parked for countless hours on my couch at home, still stomach sick from a growing baby, I was suddenly feeling anxious for my husband to return from his river trip. We hadn't spoken in a couple of weeks, and even though I was used to us living apart—we had been away from each other for a few months when I went to work in Holland and also when I had taken a few freelance assignments in New York—we spoke on the phone most days when we didn't see each other. Now I pined for his presence, how he sat and talked to me while I bathed in the tub, how he got me a glass of water when I woke from a bad dream. I remembered that it was exactly this time of year, this early wet part of spring when the bush outside our bedroom window began to burst with bright yellow flowers, when the sun would finally peek out and warm our skin, that Drew and I had begun to love each other.

That time of my life five years before had also been very conflicted, confusing but also very hopeful, not unlike this time with my mother sick and me being pregnant. Then, I was falling in love for the first time in my life, so I was blissed out and full of love hormones, but I would also weep like a mourner at the thought of not living close to my family and friends anymore. I know that I was abandoning my east coast roots, and there was this massive sense of loss. Similarly, now, as I waited for my husband to come off the river so we could share the joy of starting a family together, I also felt a heaviness at the inevitable loss of my mother.

And it was not about the loss of some epic mother-daughter relationship, because my mother and I clearly had a difficult past. It was more about the sadness and loss around what she had never gotten to have in life. When she was with my father, she had been provided for; all of her basic needs in life had been met. But I knew that she would soon die with so much buried trauma. And that made me begin to mourn the loss not of what we could have had but more of what she could have had for herself, what she should have had, if she had learned how to sit with the pain. I thought of my mother in bed on a beautiful sunny day. I thought of my mother smoking cigarette after cigarette after cigarette. I thought of my mother telling me not to answer the phone because there was yet another bill that had not been paid. And now, every month, I made sure that all of her bills were paid, and it made me feel good to take care of her even though there had been many times that she had been unable to take care of me.

***

A few weeks had passed since Drew had returned from his river trip, and I didn't feel baby sick anymore. The relief had come on quick, almost on the exact day that I transitioned into my second trimester of pregnancy. It was as if a literal curtain had been drawn. And now that I was feeling much better and had a nice-sized, healthy lump growing in my belly, Drew and I decide to fly back east together to celebrate my mother's seventy-second birthday. The group of nurse-midwives that I had been seeing regularly had been very kind and supportive, continually telling me that the pregnancy was going well. They knew that my mother was sick with the cancer, so I felt like they offered me a little more care and attention.

My siblings and I made plans to throw our mother a party in a community room at the assisted living palace. We invited all of her grandkids and her sister and her nephews and their families. I would share the news that I was pregnant, a plan that was giving me tremendous anxiety. For my whole life, I had done what I could to hide who I really was from my family, because I was so riddled with shame from years of feeling invisible and unworthy. In a lot of ways, I had never really known who I was, so how could I have shared myself with people?

"I'm not going to tell them until most people are gone from the party," I told Drew.

"I don't want it to be about us," I said. "I want it to be about my mother."

"That's fine," he said.

Before getting swept into the Jersey madness, Drew and I flew into Newark and headed right into Manhattan for a night. I had scored one of my infamous web deals on a hotel close to Battery Park.

It was a glorious spring day in the city. After we

checked in, dropped our bags, and washed up, we headed over to the park and grabbed a bench overlooking the Hudson River. It was almost too much for me. And like so many times since I had left the East Coast to move out to Oregon, I was overcome with this intense urge for New York to be my home again. So many of my roots were planted here. My mother's in the Bronx, my father's in Brooklyn, our family's in Queens. But it had never been Drew's home, and as much as he enjoyed visiting the city, going to see art, and eating good food, he was just a tourist. There was no intimate connection. So he always pushed back with how expensive everything was, how there were too many people, how it was just not that cool anymore. As much as he might have been right on the facts, he was wrong in the heart.

As I looked across the Hudson toward Jersey City, the place where I had become a real person after so many years of emotional and financial struggle, I began to cry out of confusion, desperation. I thought about the brownstone where I had lived in Jersey City. How it was the first real home that I had made for myself, how nobody had made it for me. How I had finally been able to support myself by working an entry-level job at an ad agency in the city, taking in a meager but somehow livable salary. How I had lived in this brownstone surrounded by good friends from Uncle Joe's. How they were like family. How we had all loved one another even though we were all still coming into ourselves. It was the tail end of the nineties, and after years of being alone, far from dateable, sick with anxiety and love obsessions as the nineties were coming to a close, in those salad days of amazing music when things still felt relatively safe. That was before New York got brutally injured. That was when I had moved out to Oregon with someone who I ended up hurting.

Watching a motorboat speed down the river aggressively, I wiped away my tears with a deli napkin stained with coffee.

"I want to live close to family while my mother is still around," I said.

Drew took a deep breath, but didn't say anything.

"I want to raise our child here," I told him, the tears now uncontrollable.

I could tell he was embarrassed at the thought that someone might see me crying. I sat with my head in my hands as Drew stared into the Hudson, his body still as a statue. He remained silent. It pained me that he didn't feel what I felt. It frustrated me that he couldn't empathize with me, that he was incapable. I was his wife, and I was carrying his child, but he was afraid to feel what I was feeling. And he didn't feel the cosmic pull from this river, the magic that seeped out from under these old sidewalks like I did. He could not relate to me. And then there was a switch. I could tell that he was thinking about what it might actually be like to live here.

"But what would we do?" he asked.

"We'd do a lot," I said. "There's a lot to do here."

***

Drew and I spent a nice quiet night in the city. We

walked up to our favorite Korean restaurant in the East Village. I didn't bring up a move to New York again. I let my feelings pass. Tucked them away for the time being. We've been here before, and we'll be here again, I told myself. Nothing will change, I thought. I would have to change it myself, and at that point, my energy was all going into growing a baby and managing the concerns I had about my mother.

We woke up the next morning to another bright spring day, and I was feeling hopeful, positive. That emotional release had been cathartic, and I had let some of the anxiety that I had been feeling spill into the river. I felt more ready to be with my family, to tell them about the pregnancy.

After a late breakfast at the hotel and another walk along the Hudson, Drew and I headed down to Central Jersey by train to pick up my car at my sister's.

We were walking around Princeton in the warm sweet sun. I brought Drew to Small World Coffee, where I had spent many mornings sipping strong coffee and reviewing care notes about my mother's health, sorting through her bills. I brought him to the Princeton Record Exchange. We bought Neil Young's *Greatest Hits* on CD to play in the Civic. And then I went into a store on Nassau Street and bought my mother a large basket of nice lotions and soaps for her birthday. She had always loved these kinds of smelly products, and I enjoyed spending a lot of money to buy them for her. When I was a kid and we would go to the mall on payday, she would lather herself with all kinds of samples at the department stores. It embarrassed me. She was just another one of those poor people who could only sample and not purchase. Now that I could afford these types of products, I bought them for her to make up for all that lost time.

We drove around Jersey in our Oregon car with Neil Young blasting, the windows rolled down, the sun warming our skin. It had been a long dark, wet winter in Portland. All those trips I had taken, all that stress that I had endured. I rested my hand on my tight belly and stared out of the window, relishing the quiet comfort of having Drew at my side. He hadn't been back east with me since before we were in Amsterdam, before we knew that my mother was sick. I thought about the first time we had traveled to New York together. Drew and I had visited a good friend of mine who lived in the city.

When we were about to leave, she whispered in my ear, "That guy is handsome."

***

We checked into a hotel near the assisted living palace. I took a long hot shower. I put on a patterned cotton sundress resembling a long tailored shirt that was not too tight around the middle, something of a potato sack. I didn't want anyone at my mother's party to take notice that I was pregnant. After I had coaxed him out of his jeans and a tattered black T-shirt, my husband begrudgingly put on a pair of medium-brown pants and a cotton collared shirt from American Apparel that I had packed for him.

When we got to the assisted living palace, I was

hit with another tremendous wave of anxiety. A cold sweat washed over me, and I felt like I might pass out. I remembered feeling this way many times over the years before attending chaotic family parties. Both my father's and my mother's people are of the boisterous Italian American variety, so the loud voices, the crowded spaces made uncomfortably warm with bodies and breath, the too bright light—they have never sat well with me.

But it just takes time for me to settle in these environments. I am usually able to find a quiet corner where I sit with a plate of food on my lap and end up having an okay time.

I have definitely made the connection that this need for quiet within chaos is less about my family and more of a side effect of growing up around a stepmother who was prone to screaming, who had a sharp, loud voice that would radiate through the house, setting my nervous system on high alert. Now I sat in a chair in the lobby while Drew looked around the fancy palace.

"Damn, this place is posh," he said.

"I know," I said.

After I gave him a brief tour, I led him to the community room where the party would be held. We were greeted by my two boy cousins and their wives. They had driven down from Connecticut with my mother's sister, my aunt Joanie. Her husband, my uncle Sal, had passed away suddenly a few years before from heart failure, and Aunt Joanie was a bit lost without him. There were my two brothers and their wives and my oldest brother's four children and my sister and her two kids—all of my mother's grandchildren, all of them grown into awkward preteens or overconfident, full teens. They huddled together in a corner like I used to do with my own cousin cohort.

Everyone was standing around the large dining table, greeting one another, hugging and laughing. My mother was sitting in a chair near a large window in the center of the room, her walker perched by her legs. She had been doing well without the oxygen tank, so that was back in her apartment for the time being, until she felt the need. She was wearing something of a turban on her head because most of her hair had fallen out from the chemo. Earlier in the day, my sister had managed to get her into a celebratory skirt and blouse and helped her put on a face of makeup. Our mother hadn't been dressed like this in many months, since before she knew that she was sick. She looked lovely and bright, surrounded by all the people she cared about in life. The only person missing was her own mother, my grandmother Ana. But I could feel her presence, because I kept catching whiffs of my grandmother's perfume, something that I have experienced throughout the course of my life, since her death when I was a kid. For many years, it creeped me out, scared me. But that day, it made me feel good.

The room was getting loud and heating up. I held onto the side of a chair for support, riding waves of dizziness. As much as I was not stomach sick, the hormones were still coursing hard through my body, the baby growing into a bigger and bigger ball as the days continued. Every once in a while, I put my hand on my belly to make sure the dress was hiding my secret pouch. Drew wandered off to chat with a cousin while I took a seat in the corner and tried to relax into the familiar voices, the familiar smells.

We had procured large aluminum trays of eggplant Parmesan and baked ziti and chicken Marsala from an Italian restaurant, which were now hovering over small flames. There was a large cold antipasto platter with glistening meats and cheeses and olives surrounded by bowls of thick Italian bread. There was a big, drippy salad. At one end of the table, there were bottles of cheap wine and neat rows of brightly colored soda bottles, plus a plastic bowl filled with ice next to towers of short plastic cups. My sister and her kids had decorated the room earlier with lilac-colored balloons and streamers—my mother's favorite color.

As the party got going, I could tell that my mother felt proud of where she was living. I caught her telling family about all the amenities, the bingo multiple times per week, the beautiful meals in the dining room, how attentive that staff members were to her needs. She was a princess in a palace. How many times we had had these raucous family gatherings at my mother's apartment, the environment so unwelcoming and squalid. But it had been filled with the same people who were there now, and there had always been laughter, and there had always been joy in the love that we all had for one another. No matter the circumstances, no matter whether checking accounts are in the red, no matter whether bill collectors have been calling for weeks, no matter whether there won't be enough for groceries for the week, when there is love, you are fed. That was what it felt like that day. We were stuffed.

When my brother Mike brought out the large sheet cake topped with candles, when we all sang "Happy Birthday" to our mother, when you looked around the room and saw that everyone was smiling but also welling with emotion, you knew that this woman at the center of the fold held tremendous meaning for all of us there. She was a far from perfect mother. She hadn't taken very good care of herself for the past few decades. There were so many mistakes that she had made in her life. But none of us blamed her. We couldn't.

***

When the party wound down and our extended family left to head home, the rest of us, just her four children and our partners and a few of her grandchildren, went up to my mother's small apartment. We all crammed into this tiny studio apartment that we had made so nice for our mother.

"I have something to say," I said over loud voices

My husband, Drew, was standing next to me. We were basically hovering in the doorway. Drew had this big nervous grin on his face, and I could feel my insides quivering because I was so scared, so very scared, to share something so intimate. With friends, I had always been able to be myself, to share details of my life, but with my family, because there was this lack of trust from feeling so invisible as a child, I had a hard time. I had hidden myself back then, and I still tried to hide myself, but I wouldn't be able to hide much longer, because the evidence was growing.

"We are going to have a baby," I said.

There were a million questions at once, coming at me from all directions. The room got really loud and chaotic; residents in the other rooms were probably wondering what the hell was going on in there. And then there were so many hugs and kisses, and there was a big giant pile of happiness at the palace. We left our mother alone to rest. It had been a long day for her.

"I cannot believe it," my sister said to Drew and me when we all got down to the lobby. "This is so amazing."

Drew seemed contained but a bit frazzled. He was also not used to so much attention. He was also one to hide himself from the people who were supposed to be the closest in his life. When we got into the car, I thought about my mother being alone in that apartment going through the details of the day in her head. I wondered what she was thinking, what she was feeling right then.

We were back at our hotel a few miles away when my mother called.

"Ana, I had so much joy in this day," she told me. "I feel so full. I just cannot believe that you are going to be a mother."

***

I have read so many stories of people who have fought hard in The Cancer Wars. If they are lucky, there is this period when they start to feel better, when they get to catch their breath for a bit, when the people who surround them get to rest for a while. There is the initial grief and the madness, the existential questions after initial diagnosis. Then the chemical and radioactive treatment commences, and then the oftentimes violent, horrific side effects of those poisons surface. There are hospital visits. There is a lot of panic. You think it's over, but then it's not over. Your person gets a little better. They organize recipes and they put together photo albums; they might even bring up things that have been locked away in family vaults for years. This period at the assisted living palace was that time for my mother, even though nothing got swept out from under the carpet. She'd never been one for keeping house.

Back home in Oregon, the baby bulge was showing, just as the sun warmed our skin and revealed so many details of the past months. Now that my mother was stable, all of those layers of stress about her sickness were beginning to be shed. I thought about being in Amsterdam, the time before I knew that my mother was sick. I remembered sitting in a dark pub in what the Dutch call a brown bar, drinking cheap wine with a colleague not long after I learned about my mother's illness. It had been autumn, and the North Sea rains had been pissing on the cobblestones outside. We had just come from a long stressful day at the ad agency and were talking about the ridiculous deadlines, the outlandish budgets, the unbalanced egos. When I told my colleague I had just found out that my mother had lung cancer, he sat in silence, smoking a Nat Sherman and peering down into his watery pint.

"My grandmother had lung cancer," he said to me.

"But she was old," he said. "She was rather old."

I didn't feel comfortable sharing any details about my mother. She was pretty old. And she had been living in poverty for many years. Her health hadn't been good for a long time, as she was not taking care of herself, eating horribly, hardly moving around. She had no teeth left in her head, and she often wore filthy, tattered clothing.

"Yeah," I said. "My mother smoked for too long."

And then I plucked a Nat Sherman from his hard pack and ordered another glass of wine. I hadn't smoked a cigarette in years. For a while, I would smoke while drinking and had enjoyed the habit casually.

"My mother has lung cancer from smoking," I said. "And here I am smoking."

We laughed.

"I haven't told Drew yet," I said. "I'm not ready."

And then I lit another cigarette.

***

When I called Drew at work, he often talked to me like I was just another person in his life, not his wife, not the soon-to-be mother of his child. I knew it was because there were other people around. I knew that he was shy about intimacy.

"Hi," he said. "What's up?"

"What's up with you?" I said, mockingly.

"Nothing," he told me. "Just working."

"I want to go back to Amsterdam," I said. "Let's go this summer."

"Well, we need to—"

"We should take one of those babymoons," I interrupted.

"One of those what?" he asked.

"You know, take a big trip before we have a kid in tow. They call it a babymoon," I said.

"We can look into it," he told me. "Look at flights, I guess."

I set out to make travel plans right away. I decided to spend some time without Drew in Amsterdam. I decided to also take a short trip to Barcelona by myself and to then meet up with two girlfriends in San Sebastián, in the north of Spain. And then I would rendezvous with Drew back in Amsterdam, so we could spend some time there before renting a car and driving to Belgium together.

***

The days that I spent alone in Amsterdam at a friend's place were like a big gulp of healing medicine. She was away in France with her partner and their small child. I had the place to myself. It was a second-story canal house flat, so I spent hours by the large open window listening to the boats, to the ducks, to the people dinging their bells as they cycled past. I slept long and hard, cocooned in their child's small bed, surrounded by many colorful pillows and soft blankets. I bathed for hours in the deep tub, the warm waters covering my now prominent swollen belly.

When I walked the familiar cobblestone streets, attempting to make peace with the city that I had left in a panic months before, filled with fear about losing my mother, riddled with confusion about abandoning a thriving career—I felt a sense of wholeness. I did the right thing by leaving, I said to myself.

When I ran into a former colleague, a well-dressed, handsome Englishman, he took a look at my belly, and he said, "You're a yummy mummy!"

After a few days in Amsterdam, visiting with some friends and resting hard, I flew to Barcelona and took to bed in a stylish hotel room in a lively neighborhood not far from the Picasso museum. I sipped mineral water and ate crusty sandwiches wrapped in paper while making my way through a worn paperback copy of *The Stories of John Cheever*. A friend back in Portland emailed to see how my trip was going. I wrote and told her that I had hardly left my hotel room, that I had been spending the past few days reading in bed with the window open, listening to loud conversations in Catalan from the narrow streets below.

"Get out of there and go see some shit!" she wrote.

"But it's so hot," I wrote back. "And I'm pregnant."

Thanks to guilt and slight peer pressure, I walked down to the center courtyard with the Cheever book and sat on a bench for about an hour watching children play before returning back to my room for a nap. I took a train to another neighborhood and managed a steep walk up to Park Güell, the park and gardens designed by Antoni Gaudí in the early twentieth century. I sat and observed couples having romantic picnics and watched parents laughing and playing with their young children. I thought about Drew, how much he would like it there, how we would someday have a child to play with at a park. But I was blissed out to be alone in this dynamic city, to be able to take this time to be reflective, to observe people outside of myself. I often thought about Elizabeth Bishop's poem "Questions of Travel."

"Is it right to be watching strangers in a play in this strangest of theatres?" Bishop wrote.

It certainly feels right to me, I thought.

***

After three beautiful hot days of solo respite in Barcelona, I took a pleasant train ride to San Sebastián, a smaller city in the Basque region. At a rented flat, I met two American friends whom I had grown close with while living in Amsterdam. We shopped at the local markets, we cooked, and we ate tapas in the afternoons. We lay on the crowded beach for many hours, chatting and reading, and when we needed to cool our skin, we wandered into the womblike waters of the Bay of Biscay. I wore a two-piece bathing suit, and the sun tanned my expanding belly. The Spanish women who were also with child looked at me and smiled, like we are in a secret club together. I was five months pregnant.

The girls and I flew back to Amsterdam. Drew and I convened at our friend's flat.

We spent a few days wandering around, seeing art at the museums, and having elaborate dinners with good friends before driving to Belgium. We stayed in a country inn in the cinematic town of Bruges. On our first morning there, Drew spilled hot coffee on me, and I raised my voice at him before storming out of the breakfast room in tears. The grandmotherly Belgian woman who was setting out breakfast stared at my display. It felt like something was about to come undone.

When Drew came back to the room, I cried and we lay on the bed together without talking. These types of emotions, these intimacies, were too much for him; they made him uncomfortable, which made me feel neglected, like I had felt as a child. This feeling would turn to anger, and then I'd lash out, which would push him further and further away. This was the dance that we would engage in for many years. When I had released the remains of my emotion and once my nervous system had settled, we washed and dressed and left the inn. I breezed past the innkeeper who had seen my tantrum earlier. Luckily, she was helping another couple with checkout. Drew and I walked along the canals, through the picturesque town. The beauty was almost too much for me, and I teared up in silence, without Drew noticing. Drew took black-and-white photos with a vintage film camera.

When we left Bruges, we drove to Brussels and checked into a simple designer-style hotel with heated towel racks and breakfast on offer. We walked the city for many hours, stopping off to eat home-style food at the cozy brasseries and gushing over the Art Nouveau architecture. On our last morning in Brussels, I woke early and headed to the dining area for a hot tea. I sat on a couch sipping tea and reading quietly while my husband slept in our room downstairs. A few people were milling about, consulting maps, and discussing their travel itineraries. When I checked my email, I found a short note from my brother:

Ana,

Mom is back in the hospital. You should come here on your way home. It doesn't look good. Call me when you can.

Mike

As I sat in the hotel's common room, I could feel my body pulsing with fear hormones. But unlike in those months before I was pregnant, my body was able to protect me better now, because it had to protect my thriving baby. As hard as this reality was to face, being so far away from my family, I tried to remain calm and grounded. I sipped my hot tea, and I thought back to the day that the cancer doctor had told my brother and me that our mother had six months to live. Those six months actually coming to a concise and legitimate end had been such an abstract concept at that time. We have all heard stories of people being told they have one year to live, and then it's ten years later, and they are leading a normal life. We know that a prognosis is based on statistics and that human beings are organic in our makeup and that our cells are constantly evolving.

Maybe it's just her time, I thought to myself. I held on to my belly and sipped my milky warm tea. The couple that had been sitting at the dining table began to speak loudly to each other in German. The woman stormed off with a paper map in her hand, leaving the man to sit alone at the table. He put his head in his hands. I kept my own head down and did not make eye contact with him.

My mother had been fighting hard, first the radiation, then the chemotherapy. Her body had not been healthy to begin with, never mind the cancer tumor that was sitting in her lung. She had been in and out of the hospital many times, and then she had been moved from her room at my sister's, where she had lived in a chaotic household with two kids, into an assisted living apartment by herself. I knew she wanted to hang on long enough to hold her new grandchild, but I didn't know if that would be possible. She was a strong-willed woman, but her physical constitution was just so weak—so many years of trauma and no recovery.

There was something about our shared history, our relationship as mother-daughter, that told me that her dying right before I was to become a mother would be the tragic ending to our difficult story. It had never been easy for us. The only times that it had been easy between my mother and me were when she got paid and we would go out to dinner. There was a dark and cavernous Italian restaurant in our town that we had both loved. We would take a booth, and she would always order steak, and I would always order baked manicotti. When we were served our dinners, my mother would cut a small piece of her steak, and she would place it into the pool of red sauce that sat in my silver manicotti tray. This was how she could love me.

I went to my room to call my brother. Drew was still in bed, now half-asleep, tossing about, mumbling. My brother picked up right away.

"What's up with Ma?" I asked.

"The chemo is weakening her too much, Ana," he said. "It's really bad, but listen—I have go . . .."

"Okay," I said.

"And try to get here when you can," he said.

When I got off the phone with my brother, I argued with Drew. He wasn't being responsive, but I was not telling him what was going on even though he knew something had to be going on. He just lay there like a frozen animal, void of emotion, unable to access compassion. As I was about to call the airlines to get a flight back to New York, I felt a strong intuitive sense that we needed to finish out our trip as planned, that I needed to go back to Portland for a solid rest before going back to Jersey.

We returned to Amsterdam, where I continued to grapple with going to Jersey. But then I called my brother one afternoon, and he set me straight.

"She's getting a little better," he told me. "Don't worry about coming here right now, Ana."

"You sure?"

"Yeah, she might be released from the hospital in a few days," he said.

***

When I got home to Oregon, I was jetlagged, completely drained of energy, and fully tapped of emotion. I slept for what seemed like days. In between talking to my siblings about our mother's state of health and figuring out when I would have the strength to make it back to Jersey, I sat in cafés. I ate good food, and I took short walks with our dog. When I got word that my mother was about to be released from the hospital, when I knew that she would be returning to the assisted living palace, I crawled back onto the airplane.

My siblings and I were now on high alert. We were uncertain of what was to come next. The second round of chemo really did her in—it got her good, like a bullet in the head. "It's a birthday gift to myself," she had told me weeks before when I had asked if she was sure she was up for the treatment.

"You sure, Ma?" I had asked.

"Yes, honey, it's what I want," she had told me. "I feel good."

And I knew that she felt good, because I could hear it in her voice. She was happy with where she was living; she was making new friends at bingo and thriving for a while there. And I could tell that she wanted to keep fighting.

EIGHT

I arrived at the assisted living palace and could see for myself that my mother was not well. She was now unable to get out of bed without the help of an aide. She could not make it to the bathroom on her own. If my sister was not around to help her to the toilet, she called down for someone to assist her. I knew that it was time to come to terms with the fact that my mother might never get any better. She had passed the six-months-to-live mark by a few months, and it was clear that she was on borrowed time. At this point, she could no longer take her meals in the dining room, and so the staff brought trays of food up to her apartment. Her appetite had waned.

"Ma, you want me to get you something from the deli?" I asked her.

"No, no, honey, I'm fine," she told me.

When she didn't want liverwurst and potato chips from the deli, I knew something wasn't right. I called Mike and told him that we needed to find our mother a different level of care. I also knew that better care would cost a lot more money than we were already shelling out.

We had considered hospice care back when our mother had landed in the cancer ward, after those trips to the emergency room. When she had been unable to breathe on her own, when she had been barely hanging on. But she hadn't been ready to stop treatment, and now that she had done more treatment, she was just too weak to continue. She had no appetite, and again, she was in a lot of discomfort and pain. The idea of hospice care came as a relief to our family, yet we also knew that it was a one-way ticket toward death for our mother. She knew this too, but she also knew that the assisted living fairies could only do so much. They had been tending to her needs as best as they could; we had had to up the level of care, which was costing Mike a lot more, and it was still not enough. She had been leveled. She could no longer do anything for herself.

Our mother agreed to hospice as long as she could stay where she was, in her assisted living apartment, and she could. They did not have to move her—the hospice people would come to her.

Two days later, the local hospice brought in a special bed that moved up and down, so my mother could sit up in bed, so they could get her out of bed. They brought a wheelchair and a freestanding toilet called a commode that began to appear in my recurring nightmares. A nurse would come most days to take her vitals, to administer meds, to discuss changes in health status. They would send a social worker to talk to all of us about the different facets of end-of-life care, and they would send a volunteer over to spend some time with our mother.

I knew that my mother would be okay with most of this, as she had gotten used to medical professionals taking care of her needs, some of them the most personal. But I knew that she would not be okay with this volunteer person. My mother had never been one to brush shoulders with strangers. She had made a few friends down at the dining hall and at bingo at the assisted living palace, but that had taken some time. Her social life prior to moving there had been narrow as hell, solely limited to talking to her sister on the phone and, every once in a while, to an old coworker from the camera company. She had gone to bingo near my sister's place for a few years and definitely had a casual crew there, but she hadn't spent quality time in many years with anyone other than the bingo cohort and her kids, mostly my sister.

When she was with my father, they had had a thriving social life.

"Everyone loved Mom and Dad," my brother Mike has told me. "They went out with other couples all the time."

But after they divorced, my mother's social circle had deteriorated.

***

It was a blazing-hot summer afternoon, and my sister and I had come to the assisted living palace to spend time with our mother. We also needed to figure out what she needed—adult diapers, wipes, supplies for the apartment. I was especially anxious because I knew that the hospice social worker had scheduled a volunteer to visit with our mother.

When the woman appeared at the door of our mother's apartment, it was evident that she was a much different breed of woman from our mother. It was as if this woman had just hopped off of a page from an Ann Taylor catalog and into a Volvo Cross Country. She wore her medium-blond hair in a neat bob, and she was probably in her mid-sixties.

I got a sense straight away that she had lost someone close to her recently, maybe her husband, and was trying to work through her own grief by paying it forward as a hospice volunteer. As much as she seemed to be a kind, lovely, classy woman from in or around Princeton, it didn't seem that she would be able to fit into our ragtag posse of working-class, red-sauce-eating Italian Americans.

But my mother has always been polite, so she gave in and let the volunteer woman wheel her down to bingo. My sister and I headed out to the store with a list, both a bit nervous about our mother's little date but also relieved that she was being looked after for an hour or two.

***

My sister and I were unpacking our shopping bags, wiping the sweat from our brows, when the two women arrived back at the apartment. Right away we could tell that our mother was having a hard time. The blond bob was behind our mother, who was sitting in the doorway in her wheelchair with an oxygen tank trailing behind. Her face was white as a sheet and clammy with perspiration. It was a hot day outside, but inside the palace it was climate controlled, so we figured something was wrong. My mother had put on a face of makeup in preparation for the volunteer, and now her face was smeared with black mascara and pinkish rouge. She was a sickly, haggard clown. She began pulling at her blouse, blowing steam, obviously in some kind of physical discomfort.

The blond bob was oblivious to my mother's state. She told my sister and me that things had gone really well down at bingo, before turning to our mother and saying that she looked forward to visiting with her again. My mother refused to look at the blond bob. It seemed like she was willing the volunteer away with her witchy Sicilian vibes. Finally the woman excused herself, my sister and I thanked her for her time, and then we shut the door behind her.

Right away, our mother said, "I need to be cleaned up."

"I'm dirty," she told us.

"What happened, Ma?" my sister asked.

She told us that she had lost control of her bowels down at bingo, that she had thought it was just gas pains. I could tell that she was horrified, as anyone who shits themselves in public would be, and especially ashamed because it had happened while she was sharing company with that higher socioeconomically placed, proper woman. I knew this wasn't going to go well, I thought to myself. My sister attempted to help our mother out of her clothes while I walked down the halls to enlist some help from the assisted living fairies.

After my mother had landed back in the hospital and then gone back to the palace, we had to up the level of care. This bump in levels cost more money and Mike had to cover those expenses. There were nurse's aides on site who were supposed to help with hygiene and administering medication, and it had become evident that these aides were underpaid and overworked. Even though we paid for more of their time, it still took a while to get an aide to come up. My mother was sitting in her own shit, and my sister and I were trying to keep things calm, doing what we could to keep our mother comfortable. After the aide came in and cleaned her up, my mother lay down in bed.

I don't think she ever got up again.

***

My mother could not sleep at night because she had started sleeping most of the day. And the assisted living fairies had begun to dole out hospice-approved pills like they were jellybeans. I was alone with my mother one afternoon when she asked me to go downstairs to ask the head nurse for a Xanax.

"Go get me my anxiety pill," she said.

"Okay, Ma," I said, happy to have a task, to be helpful.

So the baby belly and I went bounding down the red-carpeted stairs like a pregnant princess. I walked through the marble-floored front desk area and toward a short hallway of private offices. Every time I went down there, I felt like peeling the wallpaper off the walls so I could see the true bullshit that was underneath.

Now I was hovering in an office doorway, waiting for the middle-aged nurse with long pretty brown hair and French-tipped nails to get off the phone so I could speak with her.

"Sorry to bother you," I said when she was off of the phone. "But my mother is asking for her anxiety pill."

She didn't look up at me. Instead, she pulled out a binder and looked at it without speaking. Then she went to a cabinet, unlocked it, and pulled a pill out of a large plastic bottle, like the ones you see the pharmacist dispense meds out of at the pharmacy. She put the sole pill in a small white cup, clunk. She wrote something in the binder and handed me the cup.

"Also, can I please see a list of my mother's current medications?" I asked.

When she didn't answer me, I said, "But no rush. I can come back later."

Ever since my mother had gone on hospice care, she had been taking drugs like Xanax and Ambien on a daily basis. This was my mother's choice, and I was not judging her at all. I was curious for my own reasons, and at the same time, I was concerned for my mother.

"It seems like you are unaware of your mother's current regimen," the nurse said.

"Listen, I'm sorry," I said. "But I live on the West Coast, and I am only here for a few days, so I just want to know what medications she is being prescribed."

The nurse opened the binder again and wrote some shit down and held out a scrap of paper with a list of meds.

"Thank you," I said and plucked the paper from her hand.

And then the baby belly and I and bounded back upstairs with Xanax in a small paper cup.

"Thank you, sweetheart," my mother said.

I gave her a cup of water and her pill. She settled into bed and slept for the rest of the day.

***

I took the train into Manhattan, where I planned to bury myself in movies and coffee and books. Then I would spend the night in Brooklyn with a friend.

"That woman is a total bitch," my brother Mike said when I told him about my experience with the head nurse.

"Totally," I said.

"But, we need her on our side," he told me. "So we have to treat her well."

I was sitting in Washington Square Park, where I had spent countless hours in my teens and early twenties, eavesdropping, smoking Camel Lights and sipping ginger ale.

"You're right," I said. "But I don't know if that place is as good as we thought."

"What do you mean, Ana?"

"I'm just not sure if they are really taking care of Ma," I told him. "That they have her best interest in mind."

"I get that, but we don't have any other choice right now," he said. "And hospice is doing a lot for her now."

"You're right," I said, even though I wasn't sure if he was.

When I got off the phone, I left Washington Square Park. It was the tail end of summer in New York City, and the sun was about to go down, so muted yellow-orange rays of light shone onto the sides of old tenement buildings, into narrow alleyways, onto the cracked sidewalks. There's so much history here, I thought. I felt warmth in my chest, right around my heart, that must have been love, the love not for a person but for a place, this place.

As I wandered down the streets, I thought about my family coming over here from Italy not so long ago, hoping for a new life, somewhere to raise a family, to eke out a decent living. There must have been hot summer evenings when they watched the sun go down; they must have seen the same yellow-orange glow on the buildings, on the sidewalks. I knew that their lives had not been easy. So many of them died too young, their bodies taxed with the stress and anxiety of making ends meet. I thought about my grandmother raising two young girls on her own, and I wonder if she had ever walked these streets and felt the same love. Or had it all just been too hard to bear?

I thought about my mother as a little girl in their tenement apartment. "When it got too hot inside, we slept on the fire escapes," she had told me. "Was it fun, Ma?" I had asked her. "Of course it was, honey," she had said.

I ducked into St. Mark's Bookshop and hid away in the familiar comfort of the stacks. I wished that I could just stay there forever.

***

The woman who managed the staff of nurse's aides, a kindhearted but overworked black woman in her mid-thirties, told my brother Mike that our mother had been calling down for help many times during the night. "She has been really hard on the aides who work the night shift," she told him. She told him about one night in particular a few weeks back, how my mother had gotten out of bed and attempted to heat up a hot pack in the microwave. She had caused quite a stir.

"There was a lot of smoke," the woman said.

She told my brother that families often hired overnight nurses when they found themselves in this predicament.

"I'll look into it," he told her.

She said that she would give him some names.

When my brother told me all of this, I impulsively considered renting a temporary apartment. I figured we could pull in all family members and huddle around my mother and take turns spending the night. This is what people do, isn't it? I asked myself. I've seen it in the movies, I told myself.

I was sitting at Small World Coffee in Princeton nursing a coffee and combing Craigslist for furnished apartments. My brother Mike and I could split the expenses, and then we could pull our sister, Dani, and our brother, Anthony, into the equation, maybe even some of the older grandkids. The apartments were very expensive. And who would want to rent to a dying woman on hospice? Fuck! I thought. None of this was making any sense. It all felt so impossible, so out of reach. Fuck, fuck, fuck, I thought and put my head in my hands.

It was hard to say where my mother truly wanted to spend the last months and weeks and days of her life. It was hard to say what she had meant by "home" back when she told me that she wanted to be home with family. I had assumed that her wish was to go back to live with my sister, but I felt in my heart that she just wanted to be safe and to be surrounded by her children.

For the moment I came to terms with the fact that my mother had to remain in the assisted living palace. She had the added layer of hospice care, and now my brother would look into a night nurse. The thing was, our mother had never said that she wanted to leave her apartment, had never said that she didn't want to be there, even though the days of classy meals in the dining room and unlimited bingo and quiet time in a simple, clean apartment had since faded into the fancy wallpaper.

"Go back to Portland, Ana," my brother Mike told me. "I'll get someone to spend the nights with Ma," he said.

"You think you'll find someone?"

"You look worn out," he told me. "And you need to go take care of yourself right now."

***

The day that I was due to fly back to Portland, I met with the hospice social worker. I had met her in passing the day before, while she was checking in with another patient who lived down the hall from my mother. She had quickly poked her head in to introduce herself, but of course my mother had no use for her, was not at all interested in delving into anything with a stranger. "Just call if you want to talk about anything, Tessa," the woman had said. "Okay, dear," my mother had responded.

When the social worker walked back into the hallway, I followed her. I told her that I was curious about the dying process. I told her that I was feeling confused and wanted to know what was to come.

"I understand," she said.

I let out a sigh.

"Let's sit down and talk," she told me. "I'll come back this time tomorrow."

The next day the social worker came to get me in my mother's apartment. Dani was sitting in a chair beside our mother's bed with the television going in the background, and the two of them were chatting. The social worker and I greeted each other.

"We're going to talk down the hall," I said.

"Okay, honey," my mother said.

I could tell that my mother was curious and also a bit annoyed about the two of us going off together like schoolgirls. She knew that we would talk about her. I felt good about putting my mother off a bit. I knew this might be one of my last chances to rebel against my mother.

We ended up in a small meeting-type room with a round table and simple padded gray chairs. The social worker was a fortysomething woman with medium-brown hair; a modest, wholesome look; and a kind but somewhat guarded temperament. I was visibly pregnant by then, and she had not yet mentioned my condition. I told her that my mother was having a hard time getting comfortable in bed, how she had been struggling to get into a restful position.

"I have been having the same problem being pregnant," I said.

She looked down at my stomach.

"Putting pillows between my knees helps a lot," I told her. "Maybe I should tell my mother to do that too."

I paused and waited for a response, but got nothing. She sat quietly with her hands folded.

"Sure, that could help," she told me after a long pause. "Talk to the nurses—they will be able to help her with that kind of thing."

And then she began her talk, walking me through the various stages of the dying process. Even though I sat there nodding my head, saying, uh-huh, uh-huh, right, right, I was only able to process sound bites of what she was saying. "She will not want to eat much, if at all. She will lose control of her bodily functions more and more. Her blood pressure will change. She may stop talking or will talk only intermittently. Her breathing will sound different."

"I understand," I said, when there was a break in conversation.

And then I blatantly asked how much time she thought my mother might have.

"It's hard to tell," she said. "Because your mother is not yet actively dying."

"Actively dying?" I asked, trying to make sense of that term.

"We will know when certain signs show," she told me. "The nurses who come every day will pick up on this, while they are checking her vitals."

"What I gather is that my mother is dying but she is not yet close to death," I said.

She sat silently again. And then she perked up and looked at me with a bright smile. Here is her kindness, I thought.

"You know," she said, "I worked with a family once where there was also a baby about to be born."

"Okay."

She told me that the person who was sick and dying held on until the baby was born. She told me that the patient didn't let go until a few days later, once she had held the baby, once she knew that everything was okay.

"That's pretty amazing," I said. "Do you think that my mother is holding on to wait for the baby?"

"I'm not sure," she said. "But the nurses will know when things begin to change, so they will let you know."

The social worker and I wrapped up our talk. We headed down the hallway. She peeked into a room with an open door and said hello to another resident. When we got to her apartment, my mother was lying in her hospice-issued bed tethered to oxygen. They had recently installed a guardrail, so she would not fall out of bed, which had made the room a lot more medicalized than it had been when we first moved her in there, when she was back up and running. The late summer afternoon sun was blaring through the windows, blinding me. My head was throbbing, my mind reeling as I began to unravel what the social worker had just told me.

As my mother lay in bed, in and out of sleep, my sister stood on one side of the doorway, and the social worker was on the other. I had an evening flight to catch, and my sister was about to drive me to Newark airport. I walked over to my mother's bedside and bent down. I gave her a kiss on the cheek. Her face was sunken in, and she was not completely lifeless, but she was close to lifeless, because she would usually have wanted to kiss me on the cheek. All my life, my mother had worn lipstick, and when she would kiss me, she would get lipstick all over me, and I would wipe if off in a huff. But there was no more lipstick.

"Bye, my baby," she said. "Be safe."

"I'll be back in a few weeks," I told her.

My mother waved her hand, gesturing, Oh, stop!

The sun shone in our eyes, and I could hardly see her.

"I love you, sweetheart," she told me.

"I love you, Ma," I said quietly.

I walked toward the doorway. My sister was now sobbing, the social working consoling her gently with a hand on my sister's shoulder.

I do not know if I had ever told my mother that I loved her before. I must have as a small child, but I have no recollection. We were certainly close when I was younger, and my mother has always told me that she loved me. She sat with me as I bathed. I brushed her hair affectionately. "You and your mother were very close," my father said to me once. "We were?" I asked. "Sure," he said.

But I didn't remember the true feeling of closeness that I had shared with my mother, the ability to feel safe and secure enough to tell her that I loved her. It must have fallen apart for me when she left my father. I must love her, I thought to myself. I have traveled here so many times over the past nine months, have been so concerned about her health and well-being, have advocated for her whenever I could, have paid her bills when necessary, have practically drained my own accounts. When I thought about my mother being gone—no longer being around to ask me what I was making for dinner, no longer being around to call me those endearing but annoying pet names, no longer being around to tell me that I need to set my clock back—I felt a white void, a giant space that could only be filled with the love that I must have had.

When my sister's emotions settled, we got into her car. She was a bundle of nervous energy as usual, her breath short and her driving erratic, so I kept the conversation to small talk: How were the kids doing? How was work? That kind of thing. As we made our way down the New Jersey Turnpike, toward the airport, I thought about the family that the social worker had told me about earlier, how the dying patient had hung on to wait for her grandchild to be born before passing on. I created a sweet narrative of sad but grounded loved ones huddled around the dying person in a big cozy house with a pot of soup cooking on the stove. They did not want to let go of their person, but they knew that they had to remain strong, stay positive, in order for the passing to be kind and compassionate.

This was what I had done as a kid. I had created scenarios that I didn't get to have, because my parents did not provide them for me—houses that I wanted to live in, present and attentive adults who saw me for who I was and not who they thought that I should be. I wished that my mother could spend her last days in a beautiful, warm environment surrounded by her children, could be home with family as she wanted. But this was not what was available to her. I hoped my mother would stay alive long enough to meet my child, that we could share motherhood together if even for a brief moment in time, but I was not sure that we would get that.

I decided not to tell my sister the story that the social worker had shared with me, concerned that she might not be able to emotionally handle it at that point. She was tapped of strength, about to cave. She had been the main local point person for our mother throughout these long, hard months, years really. When my mother needed something—a prescription filled, a pack of adult diapers, food to satisfy a craving—Dani had to drop everything and run out. After my sister pulled up at the curb, I grabbed my bags, we hugged good-bye, and she began crying again.

"Just go," she said and shooed me away.

I knew that there was nothing I could do to make this easier for her, so I went inside the airport and called my brother Mike. I told him about my meeting with the social worker, how she had told me about this sick woman who had hung on until her grandchild was born.

"And then once the baby was born, the lady dropped dead," I told him.

"Jesus, Ana!" he said.

And then we both laughed hysterically. With tears streaming down my face, I headed toward the security gates and grounded myself to head back home to Portland.

***

My mother continued to remain awake during the nights. She was fully alert in the darkness, only intermittently during the daylight hours. She constantly asked for pain pills and antianxiety pills and sleeping pills. She was on the full hospice plan now, and there were nurses and nurse's aides in and out of her apartment throughout the day. My sister, Dani, was there every day bringing things to make our mother feel good, mostly food she never managed to eat anymore. My brothers visited and they did what they could to make our mother comfortable because at this point, it was all about doing what could be done to make sure she remained as pain-free and comfortable as possible. This was the hospice credo. All of my mother's grandchildren came to visit. Her sister and her nephews came. Her friends from the assisted living palace checked in, including bingo buddies and off-duty nurse's aides.

When she could still speak on the phone, our father called to talk to our mother. They probably hadn't spoken on the phone in almost twenty years, since when I was still a kid and they had to talk about me being dropped off at one or the other's house. My sister answered the phone, but our mother refused to talk to him. "Dad wanted to talk to Mom," Dani told me later. "But she wouldn't talk to him," she said. "Ma put her hand in the air like she was shooing him away," Dani told me. "I had to tell Dad that she was sleeping," she said.

As my sister told me this, I tried to imagine how my parents' conversation would have gone. I knew that our mother did not have a lot of energy left in her, that she was on a shit ton of medication and was pretty comatose. Would they have told each other that there had been some good years together, back when we all still lived in Queens? Would they have said that they were proud of their kids and grandkids? Would they have apologized for anything? Of course my mother shooed him away, I thought to myself. She left him after twenty-five years of marriage for a reason. But I would imagine that if you had gone through everything that they had gone through together—having four children and mourning one stillbirth—there would be a love there that would just never die. But in the end, I could hardly even remember my parents being together, and so I could not make sense of what they would have said to each other.

"That is so weird," I said to my sister. "I can't believe that Dad actually called to talk to Mom."

"Oh, I know," she said, and we both giggled.

***

The assisted living palace was having a hard time accommodating my mother's needs, most especially through the nighttime hours. She lay awake and anxious. I thought back to the conversation that I had had with the social worker about the active dying process. I remembered her telling me that the patient might begin to get quite agitated; how they would not eat much food anymore, if any; how their vitals would change. Clearly my mother was becoming agitated when it was dark and quiet and lonely, but she was still taking food. I knew that she was on all kinds of psychopharmaceuticals, and I figured those meds were putting her out for most of the day, so she was up through the night. I was waiting for a call from hospice to alert me that my mother was in the active dying phase and that I better fly out soon.

I never got that call.

As I tried to make sense of the dying process, I also began to wrap my head around the idea of giving birth. I had never witnessed a birth other than in movies. Drew and I had started attending birthing classes at the local hospital, so we were learning how to recognize the signs of labor in addition to drafting up a birth plan. I did not want to have a medicated birth unless necessary. But this was all I knew right then, and so I went to the classes in a bit of a daze, not really investing in what the other couples had to say, not really listening to the instructor. At one point during the talk on active labor, I found myself thinking about the signs of active dying. "Things really shift," the birthing instructor, an earthy, middle-aged Oregonian, told us. This piqued my interest. "The woman's vital signs change, and she might not be able to communicate anymore," she told us. I could feel the fear rise in me. As I sat next to Drew in this sterile conference room at the end of a hall in the hospital, surrounded by wide-eyed soon-to-be parents, it truly hit me that my mother was having to face something so similar to what I was having to face. She was scared as shit to die, and I was scared shitless to give birth, and there was a fucked-up, witchy, magical energy to all of this.

My brother had hired a night nurse to look after

our mother—well, two night nurses, because they were sisters, and they tag teamed the overnight duties. Really these women just sat in my mother's comfortable chair in the studio apartment while my mother lay in bed thinking who the fuck knew what, feeling who the fuck knew what. But they were there, and after a few days, the agitation seemed to cease. She must have felt safe in their presence. The hospice team had now prescribed our mother morphine for pain, as she had been reporting a spike in pain levels. You would think that I should have known that for a dying person, the morphine drip symbolized the end of time and space and communication, and it also meant the end of who you were. But I didn't. I was just this pregnant fool waiting for someone to tell me my mother was actually dying and please, please come fast.

So as my mother fell on and off the morphine nod back in Jersey, as my siblings did their best to go to work and tend to their lives, I wandered around Portland in a hormone-fueled daze. I was in my final trimester of pregnancy, and I still had a bit of energy, but I was certainly slowing down, napping a lot, nesting. It was early autumn now, and the sun shone through the big evergreens in the nearby park where I walked my dog. They were the most glorious muted rays of light that you have ever seen.

As I looked up at the enormous trees, things felt so pure, so hopeful. I thought about how it had been only a year since I had wandered around the city of Amsterdam in a different kind of light-inspired daze. Even though it felt like over a decade ago.

It had been only a year since I had found myself astounded by the beauty not of the trees but of the centuries-old architecture and how the light would hit those crooked buildings with a magical glow. How the light would shine onto those canals with an otherworldly glisten. I thought about the person who I had been back when I was living in Amsterdam because I was not that person anymore. How I had drunk so much wine and smoked so much weed to cope with my stressful job. How I hadn't had any idea what was ahead of me in life. How I had been trying to figure out if I wanted to stay for longer than my original contract. How I had been meeting with department heads and trying to get a more respected job at the agency. How I had been talking to expat parents about what it was like to raise a child in Holland, about what the educational system was like, about how the health care system worked, how much maternity leave I would get. How I had been looking at flats to rent for the longer term. How I'd also had to consider my husband's career, how if we had a child, he could stay home while I went off to work.

And then I had come home one evening from the agency, and after I had parked my bike on the rack outside of our flat and after I had let myself inside and put down my things, I had sat on the edge of my bed in the clean beige room with the gabled roofline.

My mother had said to me, "You're not gonna like it."

"It's can-cer," she had said like it was two separate words.

"But they are going to get rid of it," she had told me.

And then all the prettiness of the place—the tidy flat on the charming street, the possibilities of a thriving career, the thought of raising an international kid—it all fell into the canals.

***

My brother and I were on the phone many times throughout each day, discussing the status of my mother's very recent decline into not speaking, into not eating, into a morphine-fueled nothingness. I made plans to head back to Jersey in a few days' time, as Drew and I had a birthing class that we needed to attend beforehand. I had reached out to the hospice social worker multiple times, but she had not called me back. At this point, my mother was hardly ever alone. Hospice people were in and out throughout the day, my was sister coming to sit and bring her foods that she might want to eat, my brothers were coming to visit, and then there were the night nurse sisters. The assisted living staff were also around to check in, although, most of my mother's care was now being handled by hospice.

As the days passed slow and long before I flew out again, I shopped for baby things. I went to a store that sold natural cloth diapers, organic cotton onesies, sustainable nursing supplies, a line of German diaper creams and soaps. I was comforted by the neutral tones and the welcoming smells. I wanted nothing to do with bright colors and scented baby things. I wanted everything clean and simple and pure, as my inner landscape was too cluttered with the fear and anxiety of too many unknowns.

The person closest to me who was a new mother was my good friend Michele, whom I had met while living in Amsterdam. She had a two-year-old girl, and we had been very close since the moment we'd met, she and her partner and the child living in the downstairs flat, me upstairs. There had been many long-discussed, well-planned communal meals, lots of evening hours spent sitting on the steps in front of our building sipping wine and talking smack while her little girl busied herself on the cobblestones. As Michele had been riding the waves of some relationship drama and had had to leave Holland to take temporary refuge at her mother's condo in Michigan, we had spent countless hours over the past weeks talking about the birth and babies. We had talked through the play by play of the nonmedicalized birth she'd experienced with patient midwives in a London hospital, the true base essentials of what I would need for the baby, the different types of carriers that I might want to experiment with, the initial struggles and the inevitable pain but then the ease and joy of nursing, what type of crib or bassinet we might consider, and of course, of course we had talked the hell out of the over-controversial topic of co-sleeping. We'd talked it all out. Both of us were well-informed, aware women with home bases in progressive cities, where shit tons of alternative health care options were available. We knew there were choices.

And yet, I still had no idea what it would be like to actually give birth to a baby, what it would be like to nurse, what it would feel like to no longer have just an emotionally unavailable husband but now a co-parent who I would need to lean on heavily. So really, really, I had no idea what it would be like to be a mother. I had thought about it many times before. I had known for a while that I wanted to have a child, that I wanted to be a mother, that I had waited long and hard for Drew to come around to the idea.

But in the truest, most honest depths of my inner being, I did not know what any of this would be like. I had never felt compelled to hold babies. I had not babysat as a kid, not even my own nieces and nephews, who were born when I was in my teens. I don't think that my siblings trusted me, as I was such a wayward adolescent. Sure, I had looked after Michele's daughter a few times so she could run out to the market, and I had hung around with plenty of friends who had kids. But that was as far as my résumé went. I had changed a diaper once because Michele had made me, and even though I had held babies, I had never felt that strong emotional charge that many people say they feel. I was not even sure what it meant to be a mother, because mine had just been so damn fucked up at times, and now she was dying.

NINE

The last person in our family to see our mother alive was my sister. She went to sit with my mother after work, as had been her routine for the past few months. My sister sat at our mother's bedside and fed her mashed potatoes with a spoon. Our mother held up her head and ate the food, seemed to really enjoy the taste, which my sister took as a good sign since our mother hadn't been eating very much if at all for the past few days.

"Mom was doing really well when I went to see her tonight," my sister told me when she got home.

"Oh, good," I said.

I was relieved because I had been extra worried since my mother was not taking in much food, since she was talking only in mumbles and whispers, and since she could no longer come to the phone. I knew that she was being heavily medicated now with the opiates, and I figured that she might come back around. The hospice social worker had still not called me back, so I sat back and waited to head back there in a few days.

By this point in my pregnancy, the seventh month, I was really slowing down. Ever since I had gotten back from that trip to Europe over the summer, after the last time my mother had been sent to the hospital and we had all gone on red alert again, I had been feeling super worn down and bone tired, as if all of the marrow had been sucked out of my bones. It was the last year really that had taken me down. It was all of the travel and the stress of

The Cancer Wars, being displaced from my home and husband. And then being pregnant through part of it, a massive energy suck in and of itself. But I also knew that I was privileged as shit, that I had had the time and resources to fund this fucked-up adventure to cancerland. I had been able to afford to fly across the country many, many times to be with my mother during the last year of her life. I had been able to contribute to the assisted living palace fund instead of her having live in some run-down, state-funded nursing home. I had been able to take reprieves with yoga and healthy food in my cozy home in Portland. I hadn't had to work through any of this.

And I had a partner who supported all of this too, who hadn't ever told me not to go back east, that I shouldn't stay in those hotels, that I should stop spending so much money. He wouldn't have done it that way himself, he would have gone much leaner, but he had never told me not to do it my way. I hadn't worked since I had left Amsterdam the previous winter, and now that I was fully pregnant and about to become the primary caregiver for a baby, who the fuck knew when I would be able to work again? Drew was the sole breadwinner and might be for a while. He did well as a graphic designer, but there were always unknowns when you worked for your own company. And as much as he was probably just sweeping a lot of this fiscal reality under our organic wool carpets, he still told me to do what I needed to do.

It was me who had a harder time of it, feeling as if I didn't deserve it, as if I wasn't the one who had worked my ass off to bank those euros. When I had gotten the call about taking that overseas contract, I had already given up on advertising. I had been more than done, had already enrolled in entry-level psych classes to begin pursuing my dream of becoming a therapist. But for some reason, I knew that I had to go, that it would be the last gig I would take. It would take me a while to realize that I had needed it, that my family had needed it, that I would never have been able to afford the year of fighting The Cancer Wars otherwise.

***

When my sister had said good night to our mother that evening, the sun had just set. My mother's apartment had turned a deep dark blue. The only source of light came from the lights in the parking lot outside her window. After my sister kissed our mother good night, as she began to walk toward the door, my mother whispered something.

"What it is, Ma?" she said. "I can't hear you."

My sister bent down near the bed, got closer to my mother so she could hear her.

"Daniela, can you turn down the lights?" she asked my sister. "It's too bright in here."

"Ma, there are no lights on in here," my sister said. "It's dark."

"Okay, honey," she said.

***

It was a beautiful early fall morning, and I was puttering around my house. Drew was on a client call in his studio upstairs. My brother and I had been talking constantly during the past few days regarding the state of our mother's health, her deep decline into morphineland. Now I picked up the phone.

"Mom is gone, Ana," my brother said immediately.

"Are you sure?" I asked.

"The head assisted living nurse just called me," he said. "After the night nurse left, they went to check on her, and she was gone."

I didn't know if I was still breathing.

"I have to go," he told me, weeping hard into the phone. "You have to call Dad."

"What?" I asked, weeping.

"Please just call Dad," he told me.

I got off the phone and screamed for my husband.

"My mom died!" I yelled.

And then I was no longer speaking to my brother on the phone. I was no longer in my house. I was no longer sitting on the floor in my hallway, my back leaning against the attic door. I left for a moment, and then I was back in the hallway. And then my body rose up toward the sky. It was me that passed away and not my mother, because part of me had died, the part that brought me here. And then I held on to the baby belly for support, and I slid up from the floor in my narrow hallway, my husband appearing at my side. He held me in a long embrace, a look of deep concern on his face.

We remained silent.

It was that early autumn light that came through the windowpanes in the attic door. That let me know that there was still so much love—that my mother was there with me even though she was gone. I was filled with a growing baby, and I was filled with this light, and I was filled with this pure but tragic love that my mother had given me. I had to call my father.

My stepmother, Diane, answered the phone.

"My mother died today," I told her right away.

She started crying and said, "I'll put your father on."

"Okay, thanks."

"It's Ana," I heard her say.

"What's up, kid?" my father asked.

"Mom died," I said, choking back tears.

"No," he said. "Oh no, I'm so sorry."

I know that he had lost someone dear to him too. He had lost the mother of his four children. "Your father is very sensitive," my mother had told me over the years. "You'd be surprised," she had said.

"I gotta go, Dad," I said.

"I'm so sorry, Ana," he said before hanging up.

It's hard to say how I passed the time before flying out the next morning. I do remember sitting in the passenger seat of my husband's pickup truck in downtown Portland while he went into a big glass building to pick something up from a client. How I leaned my head on the cool glass window and called my closest friends. How affected they were by my mother's loss, how supportive they were, how close I felt to them in those moments. I do remember having to pack, having to think about what clothes

I would wear to my mother's funeral, what dress clothes still fit me. Nothing fit me anymore, my belly just so big and taking up so much space. I found a big flowery skirt and a flowing cotton top that my friend Michele had given me when I was in Amsterdam over the summer, something that she had worn while pregnant. It'll have to do, I thought. I do remember not wanting to go anywhere, not wanting to get on a plane, wanting nothing more than to stay in bed for days, weeks, months.

The fatigue was deep, needy, pining.

***

When we landed in Jersey in the early evening, Drew and I headed straight to a hotel near my sister's place, not far from the assisted living palace. My brother Mike was going to pick us up himself, but he sent a car instead. I was disappointed that we didn't get to spend time with him and had to be driven by a stranger.

"I'm so tired, Ana," he told me on the phone as I was walking through Newark airport. "I got you a car service through work."

After we checked into the hotel, we settled into the large comfortable bed. We ordered room service. We watched a brainless comedy, and I tried to laugh, but it was hard. I talked to more people on the phone. I existed in a blur of only partial reality. It was as if I had taken some kind of psychedelic drug, because nothing seemed real. I felt calm but disconnected. It must be the hormones surging through my body, protecting the baby from emotional trauma, I thought. I wept quietly.

There was a free day between arriving in Jersey

and my mother's wake and then the funeral at the family plot in Queens. After a restless sleep and a half-assed attempt at breakfast, Mike picked us up from our hotel. We had plans to meet our sister and our brother at the assisted living palace because we needed to clear out our mother's things. None of us wanted to wait, and all felt the desire to get it done sooner rather than later. When we walked inside the palace and headed toward the front desk, the rental manager guy who initially had rented us the apartment offered his condolences and handed us a set of keys.

"Take your time," he told us. "Anything you want to donate, just leave and we will have people pick it up for you."

He had clearly been through this process many times before.

The woman who managed the caregiving staff, the person who had called my sister to say that our mother had passed, came up and embraced both my brother and me. She had had a soft spot for our mother, and she was genuinely sorry for our loss. I could also imagine how hard it must have been to make that call, that it probably didn't get any easier to play that role.

"She didn't want me to call anyone," she told us. "I went in to check on her early in the morning, and she seemed really out of it, so I asked her if I should call one of you, and she shook her head."

"Okay," my brother said.

"I knew the hospice nurse would be coming soon to check on her, but when I checked on her again, she was gone," she said.

***

In the days, weeks, and months that followed, when I truly began processing the narrative of my mother's last days, I would imagine this woman going to check on my mother that morning. And when I picture my mother so close to dying, no longer able to speak but for a few barely uttered words, I couldn't believe that this woman really went in that morning to check. I couldn't believe that she asked my mother if she should phone her children. I don't think she went in that first time.

Maybe I just don't want to believe her. Maybe I had hoped that our mother had wanted someone at her side, someone to hold her hand. "Sometimes people need to be alone when they die," a family friend had told me a few years earlier when she was telling me about her own mother's passing days. "They hang on when someone is with them, especially their children. They can't let go. But everyone is different," she told me. When I truly sit with it, I guess that I would have pegged my mother as someone who would want to be alone when she let herself go. I also can't help but remember that she had just started on morphine.

At the core of my being, I think it was the morphine that took her down in the end. There were no warning calls from hospice that she was declining. As a matter of fact, I would not get a return call from the social worker until the week after my mother had passed. The term "actively dying" was never discussed again. She was put on morphine by hospice, as she had been complaining of pain, and then a few days later, she was gone.

"It can hurt to die," the social worker told me. "So we do our best to make sure that the patient is as pain-free as possible."

And it had been our mother's choice to take the strong pain meds. She had signed off on it, yet I don't think that her already-compromised heart had been able to handle the opiates. But that is my personal narrative, and for a long, long time, I was angry that my mother was alone when she died. It saddened me, caused me tremendous grief, and I blamed hospice for not communicating well. I felt awful that she may have been scared in that studio apartment but not had the energy to call for help. At the root of it was my awareness that she had not been home with her family; the heart of my anger and grief was that I had not able to provide that for her, that I had been unable to be there for her.

"Nobody called me," I told the social worker.

I had been standing in front of a yoga studio in a busy commercial area in North Portland, about to head into a prenatal yoga class, when the woman finally called me back. She had already phoned my three siblings, and it seemed like she was following a script, the protocol after a patient passed, to make sure there weren't any loose ends.

"I'm so sorry about that, Ana," she said.

But she thought that I meant my siblings had not called me to tell me that our mother had died.

"That happens sometimes," she said.

By that point, I didn't trust her anymore, so I let it drop. I never said what I wanted to say to her. I never said, You told me that hospice would let us know when she was close! I never said, You promised me that you would call me and you never did, so I wasn't there with her at the end! Instead, I went into my yoga studio and cried silently through class on my mat.

***

My brother Michael and I were the first to walk into the apartment. My husband was outside making a phone call. Dani and Anthony had not arrived yet. The first thing we saw was our mother's bed, stripped of linens, void of the person who had spent so many long hours there during the past weeks. We both broke down sobbing. It was hard to comprehend that this was where our mother had actually died. Hard to make sense of the fact that she was no longer there; this was where that reality truly hit. And yet it felt like she was still there, about to walk out of the bathroom any minute.

Give me a minute, my sweethearts, I could almost hear her say, the toilet flushing in the background.

But she never walked out, because she was no longer there. I could feel the void. My sister walked in and saw us weeping.

"What's wrong?" Dani said.

And then she realized and broke into sobs.

When my brother Anthony arrived, we all went complete gangbusters and purged the shit out of that apartment in some type of cathartic fugue state. As we sorted and packed, we told stories about our mother and laughed hysterically. Sometimes we cried. Then we left anything that we didn't want to keep in a big heap in the middle of the room. The nurse's aides took a lot of it for their families, the rental manager guy had told us. We felt good about that—it was the least we could do to give back to the women who had taken care of our mother even though they had been spread so thin most of the time.

Because she hadn't been living there that long and had been doing so in a somewhat temporary way, most of her super personal things were still back at my sister's. There were a few special things, but not much, so it was like packing up a dorm room and not a long-lived-in home.

"Look, I got Mom's little owl!" I told my sister.

I held up a small marble statue of a gray owl that my mother had always had sitting at her bedside, one of her sacred talismans.

"Good, Ana," she said. "I'm happy that you have it."

***

My siblings had arranged a simple wake at a funeral parlor in a small historic town near where my sister lives, close to where my mother had spent the last years of her life. They had picked out a casket, brought clothing for my mother to wear, talked out the details with the owner of the funeral parlor.

"It was one of the hardest days of my life," my brother Mike told me when he got home from that meeting. "I am so emotionally exhausted."

When he told me this, I felt left out of the planning, and I was pining for control over something.

"Just make sure to tell people not to send

flowers," I told him. "Flowers are stupid."

"What do you mean?"

"Just tell them to donate to the American Cancer Society," I said.

"Okay, Ana," he said. "I will."

***

Drew and I got to the funeral parlor, and the room where my mother was laid out was ensconced with many giant ornate flower arrangements. I bristled for a moment at the fact that I had requested for people to donate instead of buying useless flowers. The scent was debilitating. At the front was a glimmering casket with our mother's made-up body inside of it. The casket was half-open, exposing only her head and a portion of her chest, which looked stuffed with filling. I looked in that direction many times throughout the day, but I did not go up there until the very end of the wake. I could tell from a distance that my mother looked shiny and fancy, no longer sick and cancer-ridden. I spent most of my mother's wake sitting in the back row of chairs, surrounded by my close friends, some whom I hadn't seen in years.

My childhood friend Elise came with her mother. They cried when they looked down and saw me pregnant.

"I didn't know that you were having a baby," Elise told me.

I felt pangs of guilt for not being in touch with her.

A couple of my close friends from high school flanked me on either side for most of the day like bodyguards. Friends from Uncle Joe's, girlfriends whom I had worked with in Manhattan, and my college roommate and her brother came.

I looked around the quaint antique-filled room in a centuries-old building and wanted nothing to do with my family, wanting only to be with my friends.. My brother Mike attempted to introduce me to work colleagues, and I snapped at him to leave me alone.

"You were so nasty to me today," he told me later.

"I wasn't in the mood to be social," I told him.

I even kept a distance from my aunt Joanie, my mother's younger sister, and my two boy cousins. Instead, I opted to giggle and make fun of relatives with my friend Donna.

Throughout most of the day, Dani came apart. She was inconsolable and crippled with intense emotion. We had all known this would happen when our mother passed away. They had been so close through the years, even if they hadn't always seen things the same way. But my sister had taken care of our mother in ways that the rest of us hadn't. They had lived together in close quarters.

"Dad, Dani is freaking out—you better go deal with her," I said to my father.

"I know," he told me. "I was just with her."

My dad was somber in spirit, but he also knew that he needed to be there for his kids and grandkids, so he held it together for us. And my brother Mike worked the room throughout the day. He gave a funny, heartfelt eulogy. He told a story of taking our mother to Atlantic City. How they blew through all of their money and didn't even have enough to buy a bottle of water, so they went into the bathroom and drank out of the taps. My brother Anthony recited a prayer, and his wife and kids giggled at him being serious.

After most of the guests left, it was just our immediate family in the musky old, wall-to-wall-carpeted, over-decorated room. This was when we were supposed to go up to the casket and say good-bye to our mother. I thought about the other funerals that I had been to, how I found this tradition to be torturous, painful, and at times counterintuitive.

I thought of the preserved bodies that had burned holes in my memory. This ritual was supposed to offer closure, but it had always given me bad, creepy feelings. The worst of them had been a friend and former roommate whom I had known when I was in my early twenties. She had died at twenty-three in a terrible accident, crushed by the rear of her own car, a heavy old Saab. She was standing behind it on an incline when it popped out of gear. She screamed and nobody responded. I didn't know what to make of losing her, was haunted by her screams for a long time. Our relationship had soured months prior to her death, as friendships do when you are young and immature and driven by emotion and impulse. When I saw her vibrant but soulless face at the wake, I became dizzy and practically fell into her poor mother's grieving arms.

"Oh, Ana!" her mother said to me before I walked away in silence.

And then there was a cousin who had also died too young, after suffering for many long years from an awful degenerative disease. My father would take me to sit by my cousin's bedside when I was a young kid, and it scared me to see her like that, as I remembered her as a thriving teenager. For many years, I had nightmares about my cousin sitting in a wheelchair and howling in pain. And then there was my grandmother Daniela, my father's mother, who had gotten weak with age and died of natural causes. We had never been that intimate, but she was my grandmother and had been a constant throughout my life and in my father's life, as they were quite close. When I sat next to her hospital bed, seeing her clawing and choking for words during the last days of her life, I could feel that she was trying to tell me something. It was awfully frustrating and sad.

Those are the images that are imprinted in my memory of these people who were crucial parts of my life. I can only see the exteriors that had been altered to look healthy again—fake, pickled. Before our mother's wake, I had gone to the funeral parlor to drop off a piece of jewelry that my sister had forgotten to give them. It was a gold bracelet that my brother had given our mother for her birthday only a few months earlier. When I walked inside the old house-cum-funeral-home, I was greeted by a well-dressed petite middle-aged woman with short reddish-brown hair. She seemed more like a successful realtor than a mortician.

"Can I help you?" she asked, looking down at my pregnant belly.

"We're having my mother's wake here, and I was wondering if she could wear this bracelet."

"Of course," she told me.

I handed her the jewelry.

"I am not doing the work myself, but I will give it to the woman who will be."

"The work?" I asked.

"Preparing the body," she told me.

When I left the funeral home, I couldn't stop thinking about some strange woman poking and prodding at my mother's dead body in the darkened bowels of that old building. And I kept thinking about how familiar the shape of my mother's body was to me, how I had always been so repulsed by its odors and how, in the last years of her life, she had let herself fall into such disrepair, like an unkempt house. I thought of her calloused feet and her long, thick talon-like toenails, how the woman doing the work would see all these parts of her. For the last time, I felt the shame that I had felt as a child. And I thought of the tumor that still sat in her lung, the site of the cancer that had brought her down in the end.

Now here was the shell of my mother all done up and fancy. Drew and I were standing side by side next to the casket holding hands.

"She looks amazing," I said to Drew.

He nodded.

"Peaceful," I said.

He put his arm around my shoulder. In my hand was the letter that I had written to my mother when she could no longer come to the phone, when

I could no longer tell her how my pregnancy was going, how I was feeling, what kinds of things I was buying to prepare for the arrival of the baby. The day prior, when we were clearing out our mother's apartment, I had gone to retrieve her mail. The card had still been in her box. It had arrived the day she passed away, and she had never gotten to read it. So now I tucked it inside her casket, between her right ear and the silken padding that lined the box. I left it near her ear, where for so much of my childhood she had cradled the phone. There was the eternal image of my mother sitting on the end of the couch in a housedress with her legs crossed, a cigarette dangling out of her mouth while she yacked on the phone with my aunt Joanie.

"Good-bye, Ma," I said, bending down to kiss her sunken, waxy cheek.

We walked away from my mother's body. Drew held me up by the waist so I wouldn't fall down.

***

We drove from Central Jersey out to a cemetery in Queens. It was my immediate family and all of our aunts and uncles and cousins there, in addition to my father and stepmother. I stood a few feet back from the gravesite, located in a family plot that had been purchased many years ago. Once, I had casually asked my mother where she wanted to be buried. She had been in the hospital at the time.

And in a groggy, rattled voice, she had said, "With my mother."

My mother's casket had been placed into the ground on top of her own mother, my grandmother Ana. Adjoining them were my grandmother's parents and her three siblings. It was the Manhattan skyline behind me that offered the only true solace on that sad, sad day. It was here where everyone in my family had been born, where we had all started our lives. My father had been born in Brooklyn, my mother had been born in the Bronx, and all of their kids had been born not far from where we were in Queens.

I said quietly, "Ma, is this where you meant when you told me you wanted be home—when you wanted to be with family?"

Feeling a strong sense of overwhelm, similar to how I often feel at family gatherings, I walked off alone as people talked in small clusters at my mother's grave. There I was, standing alone under a beautiful old elm tree in the cemetery on a gorgeous autumn day with my husband and the entirety of my family in the immediate distance. There was my father and my stepmother, Diane. There was my oldest brother, Anthony, and his wife, Susan, and their children. There was my sister, Dani, and her two kids. There was my brother Mike and his wife, Gina. There was the rest of our extended family, aunts, uncles, cousins.

I would have to learn how to be a mother, having just lost my own mother. I would have to go back to Portland and get ready to have a baby, to go through the birthing process and then ride the ups and downs of the postpartum time while grieving the loss of my mother. And there was that early autumn light shining through those old trees, so familiar from all those years when I had been a kid who wanted my life to be different, wanted a way out. There were those same warm rays of hopeful light that had always stopped me in my tracks, comforted me, made me feel not so alone in all of it.

HOME BIRTH

TEN

Drew and I had just arrived home from the last of our childbirth preparation classes. The instructor, a middle-aged woman with frizzy brown hair and the kind of warm, earthy disposition that can be quite common out here in Oregon, had escorted our class into the labor and delivery rooms of the local hospital for a tour. She had wanted us to become familiar with the birthing center. This way, when it was time to arrive at the hospital during labor, we wouldn't be thrust into unfamiliar territory. Labor at home for as long as you can—this had been her mantra all along.

And so it was evident to me that by the time you got to the hospital, you were in the throes of some serious shit. The more predictable the environment, the better for everyone involved, baby included.

There were eight of us in the birthing class—four expecting mothers heading toward the tail end of our pregnancies and looking like we were ready to burst, along with four support people, not everyone intimately coupled, three men and one woman. All of us had frightened looks on our faces as if we had no idea what we had gotten ourselves into. Wondering how we might get ourselves out of it.

Trailing our instructor, we wobbled and squeaked through the sterile, shiny hospital corridors that eventually led into the birthing-center rooms. It was like we were in the middle of some kind of strange science lab where babies were made. I was so rattled that I asked one of the other pregnant women if she had any other kids.

"Why would I be taking a birthing class if I already had a baby?"

"Good point," I said, ashamed.

I could see that the rooms where you hung out during labor and childbirth were nice enough, that there had been attempts to make the environment somewhat homey. Calming neutral colors, pullout couches for the support people, access to a big Jacuzzi-style tub down the hall to help with labor pains. But they also lacked a general sense of warmth. They felt more like your average chain hotel rooms, where you just slept and showered and then got the hell out in the morning.

And as much as they called it a birthing center and touted it as a homelike environment, it was nothing like a home. It was a hospital. And because I had spent a good portion of the last year of my life, the last year of my mother's life, sitting on the edges of uncomfortable hospital chairs, not knowing if my mother would make it out alive, a hospital was the last place that I wanted to be when it was time to meet my baby.

***

"I don't want to go back into a hospital," I said to Drew. "I'm not sick, and I want to try for a home birth." We were cozied up in bed, me with a body pillow under my large belly and in between my knees, Drew flat on his back next to me. It was a cool fall night, and we had our French doors open to the backyard, the air fresh and clean, with the northwest fragrance of fallen wet leaves.

"Really?" he asked.

"Yeah," I said. "I'd like to try to stay home."

"Okay."

"We could always go to the hospital if we need to," I said.

This was something I had thought about long before getting pregnant. A few people I knew around Portland and Amsterdam had given birth at home. I had noticed that there were these intense charges to their birth narratives. The women who had birthed at home seemed empowered and spoke as if their labors and childbirths had been entirely natural and beautiful, even though they'd had to endure tremendous physical pain without the aid of meds. They seemed to relish having been able to bond with their babies in their own homes. How cozy it was to sleep in one's own bed after a long birth marathon.

Even though she had focused a lot on breathing methods and how to recognize signs of labor, our instructor had also walked us through the different medical interventions that were often used at the hospital. There was Pitocin to speed up labor, there was an epidural to ease the pain, and then of course there was the dreaded and sometimes controversial but medically necessary C-section.

The other thing that I had realized was that the actual shift in environments—going from your warm, cozy house and into a car and then having to check into the hospital—could really slow things down during labor. And even though you might think that the game was on, you might not be in full labor. This was what had happened to my friend

Michele when she was trying to have her baby in London. She kept going to the hospital by taxi and then kept getting told to go back home, that she was not dilated enough. It took her a few days to get that baby out of her, maybe because all of those transitions kept slowing down the process.

So once we had actually toured the hospital—the site where these things could happen—I could see how a medicalized birth could possibly take a laboring woman's power away. I knew that having a baby at home was not for everyone; neither was going pain-med-free, and my slant was never judgmental. Many of my friends from Jersey hadn't given their epidurals a second thought. They had gone into labor, gotten put in a wheelchair while they checked into the hospital, and then they had put their arms out for the port. For some, birthing was just something that you did in the hospital, and you didn't ask any questions.

Drew and I had recently watched a documentary about birth being an industry. We had seen different sides of the equation, since the film had unpeeled and unpacked some major layers of perspective. Of course these tragically overworked health-care providers didn't want you howling away in a labor and delivery room for days on end, and for first-time mothers, sometimes labor can be pretty fucking long. These people have shit to do. And so after a while, they are somehow going to get that baby out of you, and that somehow is going to be labor-inducing medication or a C-section.

At the core of my being, I knew that I did not want to be medicated. I needed to be sober, because

I needed this birth to be a release, to help me break through the grief wall that I had been bumping up against for the past year. And I knew that if I walked into a hospital in any kind of pain, scared as shit, full of grief, and super-vulnerable, I would beg for drugs like a street junkie. So after wandering around through that hospital birthing center, it had hit me hard that I wanted to go for something totally different than I had thought initially.

"No more fucking hospitals!" I said. "I'm done with them!"

"But what about the midwives that you have been seeing?"

"I dunno yet."

***

When I had found out that I was pregnant and had had to decide on which health care path to take, my decision had fallen somewhere down the middle of the curve between hippie squat under a tree near a river and a standard hospital birth. I had chosen a group of certified nurse-midwives who were associated with my local hospital. I had been riding the ups and downs of my mother's illness during a majority of my pregnancy, and so this had seemed like a decent middle-way solution at the time. It felt as if I was getting the best of both worlds, the care of gentle female midwives and medical interventions if necessary.

"You really think you'd be up for just staying at home?" I asked Drew.

He was quiet for a minute, looking up at the ceiling.

"Sure, why not?" he said. "Fuck it."

He spoke in a tone that made it feel like we were planning on doing something bad, as if we were breaking rules. I mean, in a way we were breaking rules because we were editing a cultural script.

And I think that's where the fear and uncertainty could have easily come in, around going against some grain, but I also knew that I wouldn't let it overtake my desire to stay home. "You're strong," my mother had said to me one day when she was in the hospital. I thought about that for a moment and really connected to what my mother had meant. Even though I hadn't asked her, I knew that she'd meant that I was a resilient being—that I had endured some hard times through the years and that I had come out on the other side.

"I'm strong," I said to Drew.

"I know you are," he told me.

***

I arrived at my scheduled visit with one of the nurse-midwives, a warm, middle-aged woman with curly hair and a big glowing smile. She was definitely the midwife that I had felt the most kinship with out of the three that I had been seeing, so I felt like she would understand my plight. Right away, I mentioned this pull to give birth at home. We were crammed into a tiny, sterile examination room with no windows. I was in nothing but a thin gown, sitting on an uncomfortable table covered with paper. She looked up from her clipboard with wide eyes.

"Why not?" she said.

"You think it's okay?"

"You're super healthy and could transfer to the hospital if you need to," she told me. "All your records are here in the system, so it's an ideal setup."

I prattled on about just having lost my mother and not wanting to go back to a hospital.

"You don't have to make excuses for yourself, honey," she said. "You have a right to stay home if you want."

I was fully aware of the fact that many women with planned home births ended up transferring to a hospital. It had happened to one of our neighbors a few years back. I remembered walking into their house with a basket of fruit and tea. There had been a blow-up birth tub plopped in the middle of their living room, already drained and half-deflated. The new mother, a mid-twenties petite woman with a full sleeve of vibrant tattoos up and down one of her arms and long disheveled brown hair, was parked on the couch nursing her newborn baby. She was wrestling with one of those donut-shaped nursing pillows, obviously having a hard time getting into a comfortable position.

"It's the stitches," she told me. "They hurt super bad."

"That sucks," I said.

"I ended up at the hospital," she told me.

And then she gave me a brief but loaded narrative. After pushing at home for hours and hours, the midwives had taken her to the hospital, which had resulted in an emergency C-section. Standing in that living room, I could feel this woman's physical pain, but I could also tell by the tone of her voice that she was really sad, in a grief process. That something she had wanted had been taken away from her.

"It happens a lot," she told me.

"I'm sure," I said.

I knew that sometimes things did not go as smoothly as one would like. A birth plan was a plan, but it was not the end result. And it was not as if I was going to give birth in a one-room cabin a hundred miles from the nearest town. The hospital was a ten-minute drive from my home. The nurse-midwife sent me off with a recommendation for a group of home-birth midwives.

"You'll love these ladies," she told me. "But call them right away, because you don't have a lot of time."

"Thank you so much."

"Just know that we're here if you need us," she said.

"And let me know how it goes!" she yelled down the hall.

***

Within a matter of days, Drew and I had an appointment to meet with the home-birth midwives. They worked out of a well-kept Victorian house on a leafy street in Southeast Portland. The house also served as a fully functional and super-cozy birthing center, where women could give birth in the comfort of a home that was not their own home.

While we were checking in at the front desk, a very pregnant woman with a thick nest of curly light brown hair hobbled toward us. She was making her way down the hallway from an eat-in kitchen, and about halfway down the hall, she stopped to hold onto the shoulders of an older woman who looked like she was most likely her mother, as they had the same type of hair. The laboring woman let out a steady guttural howl. Everything quieted. The receptionist stopped what she was doing for a few moments. Drew and I stepped aside toward the doorway, as if we might just decide to run away.

A bearded man then appeared at the laboring woman's side, the older woman moved away, and the younger woman and the man held each other by the shoulders and leaned into each other. Once it seemed as if the wave of pain had passed, the laboring woman quieted, and the bearded man guided her up a wooden stairway. The older woman made a call on her cell phone in a large living room.

"Well, she's having the baby now," I overheard before she shut the double wooden doors for privacy.

I thought about how calm and present and supportive this woman had been with her daughter. I had never seen that kind of mother-daughter connection before, and neither had I ever witnessed a woman in the throes of labor. I was intrigued and also very freaked out.

The receptionist escorted Drew and me into one of the main-level birthing rooms, which closely resembled a room at a New England bed-and-breakfast. We sat on the edge of a bed that was topped with tons of pillows and a big fluffy comforter. The receptionist left and two women appeared. One was around my age, mid-thirties with medium-length blond hair and thick-rimmed glasses. She looked more like a hip librarian than a home-birth midwife. Celia introduced herself as an apprentice and explained that she was in the training phase of her midwifery program, that she would be assisting the other two certified home-birth midwives on duty. The second midwife, Anne, was fortysomething with dark features and a bit of a rugged, outdoorsy way. I assumed that she mountain biked and kayaked when not delivering babies.

"Melissa will be joining us later," Anne told me. "She's in the middle of a birth upstairs."

"Okay, cool," I said.

"You might have seen the laboring woman."

"Oh yeah," I said, smiling.

Anne asked me point-blank why I had decided on a home birth so late in my pregnancy. I was three weeks from my due date.

"My mother passed away a few weeks ago," I told them. "So I really want to be able to stay home if I can . . ."

The room quieted. I could feel Drew's energy shift.

"I am so sorry," Anne said, her eyes welling with tears.

I saw that both of these women were a bit skeptical of my mental state, possibly concerned that I was too deep in my grief process to be flipping the script at such a crucial point. Drew continued to sit quietly, more of an observer than a participant.

He smiled awkwardly while I held back tears. The room swirled with emotion. About halfway though our conversation, which mostly involved reviewing the medical records that the hospital midwives had sent over, a bigger-bodied woman with a giant beehive of blond dreadlocks and exuding a complete earth-mother air came swooping into the room.

"Hi, I'm Melissa," she said, a little out of breath, shaking our hands before sitting down next to the other two women at a small round table near the bed. "Sorry I'm late." Celia and Anne caught her up on our chat. Melissa read over the notes and then looked up at me with a sweet, warm look in her eyes.

"I am so sorry for your loss," she said. "I understand why you would want to stay home." The room quieted. Drew shuffled and coughed.

"The past year has been really hard," I said.

In that moment, I felt fully safe and secure in my decision to stay home. There were these two layers of both warmth and strength that I had never experienced before in a medical environment. After our appointment wrapped up, we left with a long list of things that we needed to gather in order to prepare to have a baby at home. I felt a sudden lightness wash over me.

"We're totally doing the right thing," I said to Drew as we walked to our car.

"Yeah, they are pretty awesome women," he said, smiling.

***

On the drive home, I held the list in my lap, knowing that it was what would keep me occupied for the next few weeks, when all I would want to do was lie in bed alone and weep. I knew that my mother was no longer in pain and that she was no longer suffering. But now I was not only suffering the loss of my mother as a living person but also feeling the loss of the joy she would have been able to experience had she at least been able to stay alive to meet my child.

My mother had been through so much pain—not only in her battle with cancer, but throughout her entire life. And it had become evident to me in the past weeks, after she had died, that she must have struggled with a serious and often-crippling depression. All those times she hadn't been able to get out of bed. How she had let herself go physically—the teeth, the body, the clothing. That she had been unable to support herself and had had to move in with her adult daughter. I wished she could have experienced this supersized dose of joy, but that just hadn't been in our plan.

***

I drove to a medical supply store not far from where I lived in Northeast Portland. I was there because I needed to purchase disposable pads that absorbed blood and urine and whatever rogue body fluids appeared during and after childbirth. I had been putting this off for days, instead focusing my energy on things like stocking the house with supplies that would give me strength while I was laboring. Miso soup packets, Recharge Energy Drink, saltine crackers. I had bought a plastic sheet for my bed, a bunch of thrift store linens that could be tossed after the messy birth, a small fishnet in case someone had to scoop shit from the portable birthing tub. I had purchased bras and tank tops with clasps for accessing breasts easily while nursing. I had bought comfy drawstring pants to wear postpartum and big cotton underwear to hold those large pads that you had to wear after you had a baby. I had even bought those large maxi-pads. And the second bedroom that had recently been an office now had a crib and a dresser filled with all kinds of baby things.

When I walked through the glass doors, right away I caught a glimpse of the oxygen tanks, the portable commodes, the canes, the walkers, the wheelchairs. I wanted to flee. It felt as if I had gone backward in time, as if I were moving toward sickness and death and not toward an impending birth. A gray-haired saleswoman saw my panic and approached me.

"Can I help you?" she asked in a flat, unemotional tone.

I told her what needed. Another one of those risky home births, she was probably thinking to herself. After she rang me up, I left the store and got into the relative safety of my car. I was overwhelmed with a sensation of having escaped out from under something. I had escaped out from under something. As I sat with my head resting on the steering wheel, it hit me that there was no longer that constant fear of getting another phone call saying that my mother could not breathe, that she was back in the hospital again, that I had to get on another plane, that this could be it.

"I pictured you and Drew having to drive from Oregon out to Jersey for Mom's funeral," my brother Mike had said to me a few days after our mother had passed.

"You did?"

"Yeah, because I knew that you wouldn't be able to fly too close to your due date," he had said. "I envisioned you laying in the back seat of your car."

"I can't even imagine."

"So in a way, I was relieved that it happened when it did," he had told me.

As I drove along the treelined streets of Northeast Portland, a deep sense of relief washed over me. It felt like the true end of my mother's suffering. I felt peaceful, calm. And now my home birth prep list was complete. I had all the basic baby essentials, diapers, blankets, organic cotton this and that. The house was fully stocked with food for me, for the midwives.

"Now I have to figure out how to get this baby out of me," I started telling people.

***

My son was born at home in a darkened room under nothing but flickering candlelight two days after my birthday. "He's going to be born on the same day as you," my mother had said to me a few months earlier. "That would be funny," I had said.

To say that I made the right choice to stay at home to give birth would be an understatement. I stood on my back deck in nothing but a sarong and a large blanket wrapped around my shoulders, the cold rain pouring down on me. I walked barefoot in the wet grass through my yard, felt the earth. This was between long, painful contractions. One of the midwives had told me to try to walk a bit, that standing upright could move things along a bit more. Being out there in nature was primal, beautiful, healing, even though I wanted nothing more than to be done with the pain.

"We wish we could share some of the pain with you," one of the midwives had said to me while the other two nodded.

I had just come back inside when along came yet another intense labor wave. The three women were curled up on my couch in the living room, sipping tea and chatting with one another. I felt so safe in their presence. And I felt comfortable in own my home, being able to have uninterrupted alone time with Drew as we journeyed through the various stages of labor together. As much as Drew is an emotional stoic and mostly avoids anything intimate and hard, he was a solid labor partner, constantly tending to my needs.

Every once in a while, one of the midwives would come around to check on me, to check the baby's heartbeat. I found solace in having them there, in hearing the midwives puttering about in my kitchen. But they were never invasive and gave Drew and me the space that we needed. They gave me the space that I needed to work through what I needed to work through, which was a lot more than giving birth.

At one point, midafternoon on the day after I had begun labor, I was feeling like I couldn't take the pain anymore. I had been laboring through the night and into the next afternoon. I was physically and emotionally exhausted, not to mention in a tremendous amount of pain. I was sitting on a chair in my dining room, near where the portable birthing tub had been placed, Drew at my side letting me squeeze his hand super hard. Melissa, the most earth-motherly of the midwives, saw me burst into tears and came right over. She held me in her arms.

"I know," she said softly. "I know," she repeated like a birth mantra.

And then I could feel my mother's presence. It was as if I was a small child again and she had just warmed up salt on the stove to put into a sock and place on my belly when it hurt. It's okay, my Ana; it will be over soon, I could almost hear my mother say.

And even though it still took quite a while longer, after a full twenty-four hours of labor, it was over. I got to eat chocolate cake and macaroni and cheese in my bed, snuggled up tight with my gentle husband and my sweet, healthy, beautiful baby.

Bringing my son into the world after what I had gone through during the past year, being able to take a long hot shower in my own bathroom and to use all my witchy essential oils and to then nap and nurse in candlelight for the days afterward, was a true catharsis. Even though so many layers of grief still needed to be unpeeled, even though so many wounds were yet to be healed, for the time being, I was blissed out.

"Are you having a moment in there?" Celia asked, cracking the bathroom door.

I was sitting on the toilet with my head down, running my hands over my deflated belly in complete disbelief that I had just had a baby.

"Yup," I said. "I'll be out in a minute."

***

Meeting my son for the first time was funny. I didn't weep with emotion like many women do, clinging to their partners in tears, the slimy baby still attached to the umbilical cord screaming and squirming on the mother's chest like an alien being. I was lying on my back in my bed when I finally pushed him out of me. I had been laboring a full twenty-four hours by that point. We had tried the birthing tub at various points, and I had certainly used it when I needed relief from the pain—the midwives actually called it liquid morphine. But I didn't want to be in there when I was in active labor and about to give birth. The tub was in the middle of our dining room, and it felt too exposed, surrounded by windows, and being immersed in water was not comfortable.

It had been storming like crazy throughout most of my labor, lots of fierce wind and hard rains. And so I felt drawn to my bed, to being in the pitch dark. While I was pushing the baby out, the midwives had to use flashlights to see what in the hell was going on down there.

When our son's head was out, I heard my husband yell, "Oh my God!"

And then there he was. A boy, like my mother had predicted.

"When did you know he was a boy?" I asked my husband later.

"When I saw the flashlight shine onto his balls," he told me, and we laughed.

Once that kid was fully out of my body, when I no longer had to push anymore—I had nothing left to offer. I was shattered. And I was not in a clearheaded mind state. Right after I finished pushing and knew that he was out, I looked down and saw that I was sitting in a pool of blood and almost passed out.

"Oh, no, no—the bleeding is totally normal," Celia said to me when she saw my face go white.

And then she quickly took the disposable pads out from under me and put fresh ones down. The midwives then put the baby up to my chest. I looked right at him, and it felt like I had known him for years. In a groggy voice and as if I were talking to an old friend, I spoke to him for the first time.

"Hey, Bug!" I said. "Mom just needs minute to get sorted out, okay?"

I felt dizzy and needed time to stabilize. The midwives did not seem at all concerned. They just swooped him up. I did overhear Anne tell Drew that sometimes it takes the mother a while to bond with the baby, which caused me to bristle a little even though I had zero energy to fight back.

My husband cut the umbilical cord with a giant scissor, and the midwives cleaned and swaddled the hell out the baby. He was a tight little sausage with a bright red face. My husband placed him in a cotton sling and carried him around the house while I pushed out the afterbirth. Anne also gave me a few stitches. I liked that part, because I knew that the worst was over and my body was still able to fight off the pain.

The midwives and I chatted and laughed like old friends, while Anne stitched me up. They gave me some Recharge Energy Drink, and I could not get enough. Celia came over to inspect the afterbirth. She worked it through her hands, looking for possible lesions.

"It looks really healthy," she told me.

I could not take my eyes off of that gorgeous, brightly colored mass.

"It must be all the kale that I ate while I was pregnant," I joked.

***

Once my body had settled back into itself and once I had regained some measure of physical strength, they gave the baby back to me. Drew and I were in our bed. The midwives had just made it up with clean, fresh sheets. I held my child in my arms and placed him to my breast and he suckled away. I looked down at him. I could not stop looking at him.

And then for the hours, days, and weeks afterward, it was all warm, cozy love. It was so much nuzzling and nursing and healing.

EPILOGUE

In the first two years after my son was born, I was physically and emotionally exhausted. I was the kind of tired when all you want is to be left alone to sleep in a big soft bed with crisp white sheets and a stark white duvet, and you want to bathe in a white porcelain tub, and you want to wash your body with creamy white French-milled soap, and you want to dry off on thick white cotton towels. I would dream of sleeping in this fictional bed, ensconced in bright warm sunlight coming through big, open floor-to-ceiling windows. In fact, I was never able to sleep restfully, my nights and naps consistently disturbed by the baby's needs, so my inner and outer worlds became these short spans of meaningless time.

I spent most of my days walking loops around my inner Northeast Portland neighborhood with the baby tucked into a sling; later, when he got a little bigger, I nestled him into a stroller. Even if it was pissing rain, I found solace in the trees, most especially the huge firs that stand like sentinels in the park near our home. As strange as it may sound, I looked to them for answers—they were how I communicated with my mother, as if she had somehow taken up residence in their bark. My neck and shoulders ached with leftover body pain from childbirth and then from awkward nursing positions, sharp spasms sometimes radiating into my head and down my spine. I got postnatal bodywork. I saw an acupuncturist regularly. I went for chiropractic adjustments.

A woman with long gray hair tucked into a bun and clad in a long skirt came to give my child craniosacral therapy. He had become colicky and would cry like a mad baby for many hours throughout the evening. They called it the witching hours. She gently massaged the bones in his skull, so they would go back into place. My mother had always told me that I was a colicky baby, and I had never known what she meant, had always thought it had to do with stomach pains, which I had suffered from throughout my life.

I was so utterly sleep deprived, my nerves so rattled and hot, that I felt as if I was hovering just above the ground, never fully connected to the earth. Long walks to the grocery store and stops at the café for too-strong coffee. There were so many sweet smiling faces who would admire my beautiful child. But I avoided intimate contact, my eyes so heavy with darkness and despair. I had fallen so desperately in love with my child, but I had also become riddled with a deep well of fear that something would happen to him. He was so fragile, and I was scared that he would break.

One night when he was still so teeny tiny, so newly born, I was about to get in the tub. I placed him on the bath mat and thought that I might accidentally step on him and crush his skull like an egg.

Drew went about his life like nothing had changed much, getting a good night's sleep, waking late, and then sipping coffee in the mornings while checking his emails. He would pack a lunch and cycle into his design studio five miles away and would return home around dinnertime, a hot dinner on the stove waiting for him.

"We fell into a dated 1950s marriage trap," I told a friend.

And a lot of the anger that had been borne out of the grief of losing my mother and had mixed with the baby-induced insomnia was propelled back at my husband, who became a somewhat innocent yet checked-the-fuck-out target.

For the first time in our relationship, I truly needed him. But I also hated him for having a living mother who got to hold our son. I hated him for being able to look the other way, and more than anything, I hated him because he got to sleep.

I couldn't resist thinking about what it would have been like had my mother lived to meet my son. What types of witchy Sicilian wisdom I could have gleaned from the woman who I had sometimes hated more than anyone I had known. There had been so many times I had wished my mother away. She was a force that could wreak tremendous emotional havoc on me in ways nobody else ever could. There were times it caused me to punch walls, to punch myself, to punch her in the fat part of her arm that I had used as a pillow when I was a little girl needing to be consoled, comforted.

I thought back to when she was dying.

When she had said to me, "You got so mad that you bit me once."

I thought back to when she was so sick with the cancer, half-awake in that hospital bed.

"You used to brush my hair," she had told me.

After my son was born, and after the bad sleep took hold and didn't relent for a long time, I grew angry.

"Just so you know—anger is a secondary emotion," a therapist would tell me years later. "Something else is buried underneath, and to heal properly, you need to uncover what is really there."

My child did not cause my anger. He was just a fat little baby who drank sweet, warm milk from my body. I couldn't get enough of his dark eyes, his perfect tiny feet, the smell of his hair. I could have kissed his sweet face for days and I did. And it wasn't my husband who caused me to be angry— even though there were times I hated him.

As I fell deeper into darkness and despair, Drew began to retreat further and further away from what was in front of him. He turned away from me. He adored and loved the shit out of his son, but he was not the child's caregiver. He did not respond to the baby as I did. He wasn't tuned into our son's needs—as if a certain biological switch never got flipped on inside of him. He would ignore the baby's cries, most especially during the night when it was dark and cold. I hated nothing more than to see Drew sleeping soundly, so I hated him. But I also knew that it was not about him, that it was about me, and that it also wasn't about me. I knew that the anger came from my mother. And it wasn't because she had never had enough money for bills, and it wasn't because she hadn't taken care of herself, and it wasn't because she had smoked too many cigarettes and gotten the cancer.

***

During an especially rainy autumn afternoon not long after my mother was gone and before my son came into the world, I was wandering around in my backyard. The ground was wet, and there were piles of freshly fallen leaves scattered about. We have a stone Buddha statue that sits peacefully in the middle of some native shrubs in our yard.

I had been turning back to Buddhist thought and meditation, something that had first piqued my interest when I was in high school. Even though I was raised Catholic, I had never related to church or the Bible and had taken more to Eastern philosophies. So when I tried to parse, to make sense of where the essence of my mother had gone after she passed on, I read about the Tibetan Buddhist practice of assisting your loved ones during the crucial transitional period after their passing. It is kind of like midwifing their souls to a better place, like holding a flashlight behind them in a dark room, showing them where to go.

So I sat in the wet grass near the statue, which had become a shrine to my mother, and I guided her. I placed flower and herb cuttings from my garden in the Buddha's lap and also lit a candle. I heard a message: It's her anger. It's not yours; it's hers. And then I felt a physical shift inside of me. My understanding of who I was became clear.

At the time, I didn't really know what the message meant, but I knew that it held deep meaning. It resonated. So by the time the initial sadness and the constant tears after my mother's death began to cool and were followed by anger — you could have called it a stage of grief, but I never subscribed to any of those ideas—I knew that it wasn't because my mother was gone, because she had abandoned me before I became a mother. It was because I was grieving the loss of what I had never gotten to have. It was because my mother had been so unwell all of her life, with the traumas, the neglect, the unmet needs, and so all of her grief had gotten passed on to me. I could feel it deep in my tissues. And so I had taken on all the anger that she had died with.

The thing about my mother is that she was a strange sick bird not only during the last bits of her life but also throughout the first thirty-four years of mine. She was so full of love for her children that she couldn't breathe sometimes because the love would almost choke her to death. She was sick to death with cancer and love. She smoked so much and she stared at the walls because all she had was love, nothing else.

You could tell that it was too painful to bear: the mountains and rolls and dips and valleys of flesh and bone and cells that went who the fuck knows where when she was near the end of her life, after the sick took hold for good. All the parts of my mother that I knew so well and hated so much got flushed down the toilet and into the sewer with all the other garbage.

My mother was scared of the affection she had for her children. I didn't really understand this until I had a child of my own, how hard it is to love your child, how heart wrenching and heartbreaking and painful it is to fully love. How scared you are to lose them. My mother lost that first Ana—a stillborn.

And it seems to me, she never recovered, never truly healed. She always knew that a child could be taken from her.

When I was getting to know my child, during those first few days, months, years, I became very anxious. I loved him so much that if I thought about something horrible happening to him, I would be overcome with a tremendous blanket of fear. He was so vulnerable, innocent, his skin so raw and fresh. And he needed my body for nourishment, my affection to thrive.

My child needed me so he wouldn't die, and so there was this level of responsibility that I had never known before. It scared the shit out of me.

"I feel like I am not old enough to have a baby," I told a friend.

"I know what you mean," she said.

I wasn't sure if I was capable of mothering, because I was still so buried in my own childhood pain. But I did. I loved the shit out of my child. And of course my mother had had to die right before I became a mother, because in all of the grief and the pain and the loss and the eventual joy, I finally started to become an actual person for the first time in my life.

Acknowledgments

This book would not have made it to print without community. I would like to first thank my dear friend and confidant Chloe Caldwell, who witnessed a majority of the struggles that it took to make this a book and who was always up for talking them out. I also had the honor of briefly working with master writers on some early drafts, which I am very grateful for: Dani Shapiro, Nick Flynn, and Lidia Yuknavitch. I am thankful for Meg Lemke at *Mutha Magazine*, who edited and published a handful of my personal essays—one of which inspired the writing of this book. Michelle Tea and Julie Buntin were true advocates—it takes more than a village for emerging writers, and I am truly appreciative of their efforts. Jennifer Hope Choi has been a solid friend and a wonderful writing colleague. Jess Funaro read a later draft and gave me the confidence to pull this book back out of the drawer. There were the sauna chats with Jess Kelso and the phone chats with Jess Steinke and the sips and nibbles (and epic family dinners) with Jess Donnell. I don't know what I would do without all these Jessicas. Sohi McCaw midwifed me into feeling like I can actually have a voice in the world—for that I will forever be grateful. Many, many thanks and appreciation to Summer and all of the other kind and generous behind-the-scenes folks at *Unsolicited Press* for investing their time and energy into this project. And thank you to Aimee Sisco for being a final reader and epic cleaner-upperer. My husband was my benefactor during the years that it took to develop my writing skills and to write this book without distraction, a privilege and a gift. And then there's my son, a true inspiration and the source of so much happiness and hopefulness. And more than anything, there's my family. Our parents are both gone, but my siblings continue to be the source of many stories and many laughs, and I feel so blessed that we have one another.

About the Author

Frances was raised in Queens, New York and Suburban New Jersey, but she now lives in Portland, Oregon with her husband and son. Her work can be found at *Mutha Magazine, Hip Mama, Longreads* and *Vol.1 Brooklyn. I Don't Blame You* is her debut novel. She is currently working on another book.

About the Press

Unsolicited Press is a small press in Portland, Oregon. The volunteer-based team produces fiction, nonfiction, and poetry, from award-winning authors.

Learn more at unsolicitedpress.com.

CPSIA information can be obtained
at www.ICGtesting.com
Printed in the USA
BVHW032134131021
618936BV00006B/141